"Libraries and readers … will welcome the intrigue, relationship developments, and bigger-picture questions *Nicholas Eternal* evolves. It crafts satisfying twists and turns, possibilities readers might not see coming, and confrontations that test the boundaries of good and evil intentions. The result is a story that is fresh, original, and thoroughly compelling in the process of transcending definitions of paranormal romance, urban fantasy, or anything in-between."

—D. Donovan, Senior Reviewer, *Midwest Book Review*

"A sacred tattoo … a painful existence and the nodes of fate … *Nicholas Eternal* is a mesmerizing, stay-up-all-night story of sacrifice, survival, and just how beautiful a broken heart can be. A must-read urban fantasy from author Kim Conrey!"

—McKinley Aspen, award-winning author of *Praesidium* (Shadows in the Wind Book One)

"This roller coaster ride of a story is beyond captivating. It's the most heartfelt tale I have ever read and absolutely brilliant."

—KJ Fieler, author of *Shadow Runner*

"A well written novel with characters that come to life with internal struggle, ancient powers, and a touch of noir."

—Ben Meeks, author of *The Keeper Chronicles*

The Wayward Saviors Series

Nicholas Eternal
(Soul Source Press 2023)

Noory and the Eternal Light
(Soul Source Press 2024)

The Ares Ascending Series

Stealing Ares
(Black Rose Writing 2022)

Losing Ares
(Black Rose Writing 2023)

Nonfiction

You're Not a Murderer: You Just Have Harm OCD
(A memoir about living with clinical OCD with intrusive thoughts)
(Soul Source Press 2023)

NOORY AND THE ETERNAL LIGHT

THE WAYWARD SAVIORS BOOK TWO

KIM CONREY

Author Photo courtesy of Cherie Lawley Photography
Cover Design by Marta Dec Art and Design
Interior Design by JW Manus

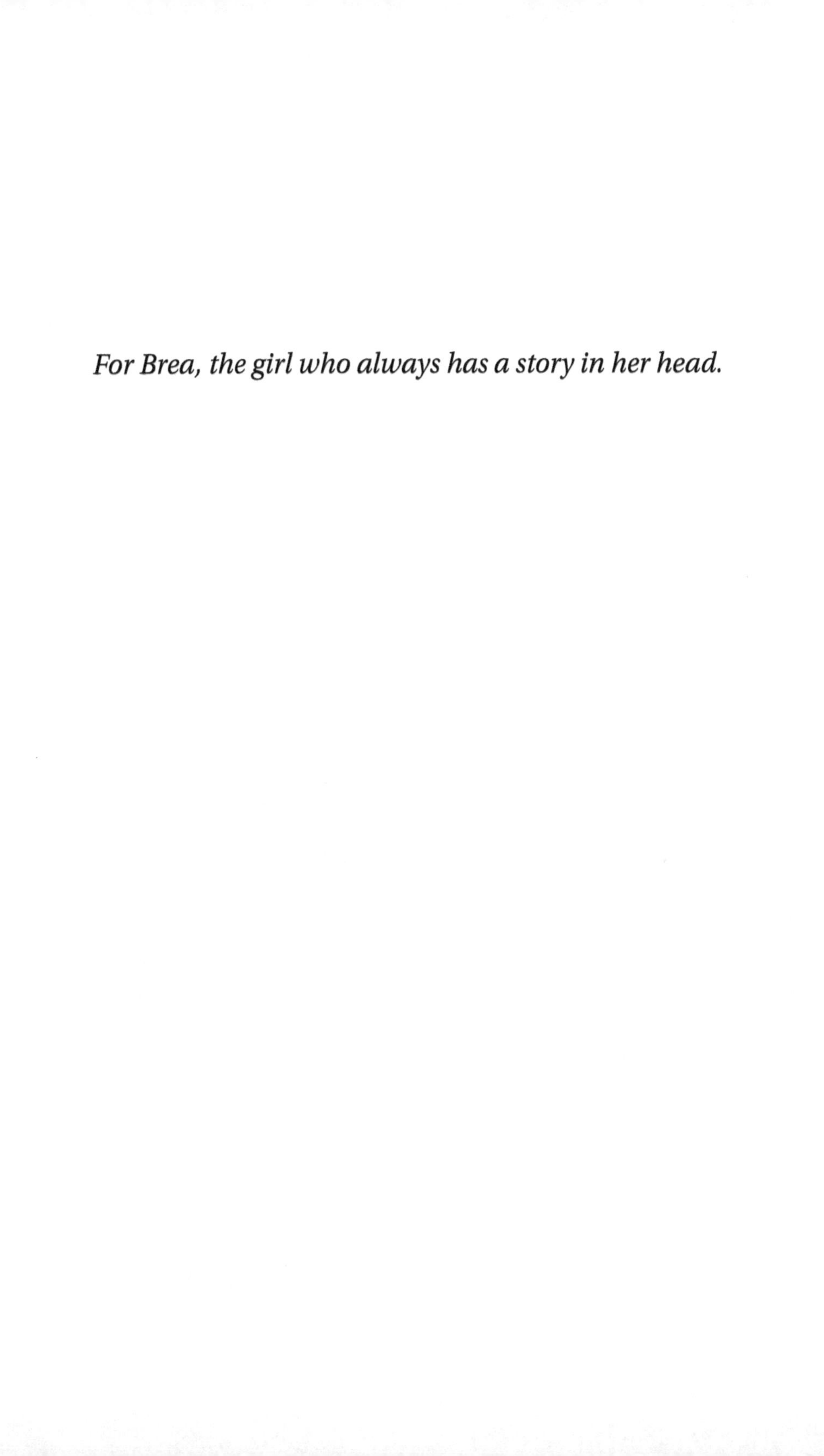

For Brea, the girl who always has a story in her head.

Acknowledgements

Though this is urban fantasy and with that comes a certain amount of darkness, this book is embedded with light: light within, light without. The name Noory literally means light and the big bad corporation in the book studies the role of photons within the microtubules in the brain— there is literally light inside us! What a beautiful and humbling thought. We also meet a magus in this book who is guided by light.

I find myself surrounded by light as well. Brea and Finn light my heart, and I am so proud they are mine. George Weinstein lights my world daily. The Atlanta Writers Club has brought me light in the form of friendships, critique partners, opportunities, and a chance to be of service, which continually lights my life. I want to thank Kathy Nichols, who has held a sword of light anytime I have been frustrated on my writing journey and is ready to swing said sword at my own big bad before I can finish whatever anguished writer's horror story I need to unload. Every writer needs a Kathy in their corner. They also need a Terra Weiss who will just "get them" no matter what.

Much light and love to Roger and Julie Johns for the lunches, support, and sincerity. Thank you to Makaylah Chambers for offering enthusiasm when I'm dragging and Cherie Lawley for the years of friendship and photographs. Thank you, Wild Women Who Write Podcast for the years of camaraderie and working together.

Most of all, loads of light and gratitude to the reader. You make it worth doing.

Chapter 1

Moonlight spilled across Noory's pale face as the demon shifted her in his arms. He glanced back at the shaman, who looked at him and grinned as firelight danced across his features before he headed back into his hut.

Another dead end, the demon thought. Now here they were in the middle of Machu Picchu. He could astral project, but that wouldn't get them *both* down the mountain and back to their hotel, not to mention that pesky little issue of having to leave his body behind for any old riffraff to find. Instead, he put some distance between himself and the shaman's hut. That bastard couldn't be trusted, which was saying something, coming from a demon.

He slipped into some ancient ruins on the mountainside. After laying Noory's shivering body down on the stone floor, he called forth fire before hypothermia settled into her deeply.

Once the fire was burning, he brushed her blonde hair from her face, hovered over her, and inhaled. Cassia, bergamot, vanilla. It was intoxicating. Power was always delicious. He leaned in, his mouth watering, but stopped himself. *You're not a damn vampire, for Hade's sake.* Besides, he liked her too much. Why? She couldn't do anything for him. She wasn't his—*Shit! Where did her heartbeat go?* She wasn't breathing anymore, either.

He tilted her head back, locked his mouth over hers, and pushed air into her lungs, then straddled her and began chest compressions, careful to keep his claws retracted. "Wake the hell up," he yelled. "That berserker Santa Claus of yours is going to knock my teeth out again." He knelt to breathe for her once more. "I knew you were going to get me into trouble." He sealed his mouth over hers again.

She woke with a start, forcing him to lean back and climb off her. "What the hell are you doing?"

"Don't look at me like that!" Damascus shot back. "You aren't my type. You don't even have the right equipment, honey."

"What happened?"

"What happened," Damascus said, bringing his claws out just long enough to make massive air quotes as she sat slowly up, "is that you got ripped off by another shaman in your ridiculous quest for immortality. And this time, it almost got you killed. Your heart stopped beating, Noory. *You stopped breathing*. If you'd come here on your own, you'd have died in that hut. Do you have any idea the dark magic he would have performed with your body? A body descended from the Holy Family?"

Noory shook her head as she trembled, clearly detoxing from the onslaught of the dark magic that would have killed an ordinary human.

"I can tell by that stupid look on your face you don't know. He'd have ground your bones to powder and sold it to corrupt practitioners to bind spirits, control humans, enslave. You'd be responsible for that shit. Even in death." He knew she worried about stuff like that, even if he didn't. "Stop living like the only thing that matters is an eternity with hot Santa. He's delicious, but not worth this!"

"You're one to talk. At least Nick respects me."

Damascus felt as if she'd slapped him. He couldn't look at her. He wanted to rip her throat out. He also wanted to cry in equal measure because she was right. Robert treated him like shit.

They both sat in silence. Damascus watched the fire dance and throw shadows across the stone walls.

Noory's soft, shaky voice barely reached him when she spoke. "I'm sorry. I shouldn't have said that. It was a cheap shot. I'm frustrated. Scared. I took it out on you. Thank you for saving my life."

"You're welcome. What else would I be doing? Robert doesn't want me around most of the time, unless he needs an errand boy." Or someone out of the way, he thought, but knew she didn't like hearing that stuff, "and it will be good for him to find that I'm not at his disposal for a while."

He watched her nod. Mercifully, she didn't comment further on the subject. though she could have. Robert had nearly killed her five months ago when she'd thwarted his attempts to load a mind control device onto a cell phone tower to impress the ancient powers at Second Sight. "It's really gross about the bone grinding and stuff." She wrinkled her nose. "He did originally say he'd take fingernail clippings or hair as payment."

"Sweet, dark Hades! Never give them your hair or fingernail clippings or a fucking used tissue for that matter! You should know better!"

"I do! I told him no. I'd heard people could do magic with shit like that. I just didn't know how serious the magic could be."

"Yeah! Real serious, Noory. This is why you shouldn't be messing with these people." He thought back to when she'd first approached him about immortality. She and Nick had only been together a few months before the itch to find a path to eternal life had kicked in. He'd wondered when it would. After all, she didn't just have Nick she'd be leaving but John as well when she succumbed to eventual human death. Double whammy. Taking up with immortals was always a problem.

She'd been doing research on her own and of course, had no clue what she was doing. He immediately threw out three quarters of it. It was either total bullshit to take her money or was going to lure her in and get her killed immediately. Only a few of the leads were promising at all. She was far too inexperienced to know that. John and Nick would have known how to help her with much of it, but of course, they wouldn't have allowed it, and her knowing she couldn't go to them was part of what got her into trouble. In that way, her dynamics with John and Nick had the markings of parents who kept their children from certain knowledge—"for their own good" of course—only to ensure the kids ran to it the first chance they got.

Now here he was, protecting a member of the Holy Family. This was one for *Demon's Quarterly*. It would go under the humor section for sure. He'd known her five months now. He'd known her odious lineage for more than two millennia, but bit by bit, he'd grown fond of her.

Noory looked like a newborn fawn as she stood on shaky legs, moved to a far corner of the enclosure, and vomited until she started dry heaving. Ayahuasca often did that to people. Combined with the other herbs being burned in that damn hut, she'd be sick the rest of the night. The shaman had said he thought Noory already had the mark of immortality upon her, whatever the hell that meant—she just needed to tap into it, but he said she'd know when she did. Clearly, she hadn't tapped into anything tonight but misery.

She held onto the wall as she slowly made her way back to her original spot and sat again. Damascus sighed out his frustration, retrieved a bottle of water from his pack, and joined her.

She drank half the bottle and handed it back to him. The shaking continued as she stared into the fire. "If Robert loved you—truly, truly loved you—wouldn't you want to find a way to keep you two together forever?"

Damascus stared at her, into those eyes that never really looked as frightened of him as they should . . . no matter, he liked the way she regarded him. "Yes, in that case, I'd likely try."

She stood. "I think I can walk now."

Damascus watched her sway and wondered how much more abuse by chemicals, unknown herbs, and magic her body could take before her search for immortality actually shortened her lifespan. He scoffed. "You can barely stand, much less walk, and tomorrow morning we have to go see some idiot who supposedly has magic powder to blow into your eyes." He extended a hand and sucked in the flame, which cast the ruins into darkness. He took the pack off his back, placed it on hers, turned away from her, leaned over, and said, "All right, climb on, I'll get you down the mountain." He heard her intake of breath, the beginnings of protest, but she was too weak. She clambered on, and they headed down the mountain together.

Nick would return from meeting with the Templars in a couple of days. What she didn't yet understand, and Damascus didn't bother telling her because he actually *wanted* her to get caught, was that there was no way hot Santa would miss the change in her aura, her energy field.

Even her eyes would have the subtle look of having been tampered with by rogue magic, and that sultry Saint Nick would lose his shit over it.

It wouldn't be pretty.

But he *hoped* it would save her life.

Chapter 2

Noory walked into Nick's penthouse, and his heart began a thunderous rhythm. The soft midnight blue sweater she wore hung off one shoulder just enough to reveal a black bra strap. He immediately began imagining slipping a finger beneath it and lowering it down her shoulder.

He'd gone so long without the touch of a woman in an effort to keep them from the danger of his world. Who was he kidding? It was keeping him from the danger of having to get close enough to lose someone to eventual death while he remained to grieve, and it had left him with a deficit that, once he began to relieve it, damned if it could be easily satiated.

Noory didn't seem to mind . . . at all. When she tossed her backpack on the couch, he knew she'd packed a few things, so she intended to stay the night. His jeans got a little tighter as images crashed through his hungry mind.

She gave him a roguish smile, as if reading his thoughts. "How was your trip?"

It took his brain a moment to catch up, his mind being elsewhere. At the moment, that elsewhere was on the curve of her breasts as they pressed against her sweater. He was preoccupied with wondering if the fabric was as soft against her skin as it looked. He could just reach out and . . . oh yeah, she had asked him something. "Oh, it was good. You know, just a bunch of Templars thinking about how to keep wandering evil from getting their hands on other stray relics."

"Missed you," she said as she wrapped her arms around him, and he ran his hands over her. Her hair smelled of peach-scented shampoo and beneath it, he searched for that unmistakable scent that was all Noory, his Noory. For one second, he found the hints of cassia, vanilla, and then . . . confusion laced with fear set off warning bells in his head.

Noory didn't practice magic, certainly not dark magic. Her very name meant light, but this was dark. Despite the shower she'd obviously just taken, the unmistakable scent of dark magic clung to her—earthy and deep, like burnt frankincense and cloves drifting in from the other side, acrid and wrong. She'd ingested something. *This is dangerous. Playing with fire. What is she thinking? Why is she doing this? And why would she shut me out of something so serious?*

She tried to pull back and look him in the eye. Instead, he kissed her deeply. He needed time to think before she read the hurt or anger in his eyes. Kissing her harder, he backed her against the wall, caged her with his arms, and pressed his hips against her. He felt her smile against his mouth. Only then did he pull back and search her eyes. She looked back at him, breathless, panting.

Say it, he urged with his mind. He wanted, needed to believe she wouldn't keep things from him. Of course, she was entitled to her private thoughts, but this, *this* felt like a betrayal. They'd dedicated their lives to battling dark forces, forfeited so much: he and her adoptive father, John, had given up their right to die, their right to live—on many levels, their sanity. She and John had chased *him* around the globe, telling him what a mistake he was making for using a device containing dark magic to ease some of the burden of his almost two-thousand-year commission. He knew now that his intentions were good, but the methods were wrong. It destroyed freewill. They were right. But they'd judged him for using dark magic.

Now here she was dripping with it. He even tasted it in her mouth, despite the minty toothpaste she'd clearly used. Dark magic lingered, clung. She was inexperienced and didn't understand. All the more reason she shouldn't keep this from him. Was she in trouble? Why didn't she come to him? He could help her. He wouldn't let anyone hurt her, blackmail her.

Her eyes didn't look quite right, either. He placed a hand behind her neck and a palm on her cheek, tilting her head up to look deeper into her eyes. She sighed with unmistakable desire as he studied their blue depths. They glinted in a way that was . . . beguiling. She was beguiling enough *on her own*. She didn't need magical residue giving her a predatory edge.

It didn't just make him mad and scared for her wellbeing.

It broke his heart.

He pulled her in close, held her to his chest, kissed the top of her head, then spoke. "You can tell me anything. You know that, right?" He felt her heart kick up to a gallop. She was nervous. *Guilty then. Damn.* No one had tricked her. She chose it.

"I know. I love you, too, Nick."

He felt a lump in his throat. She'd just allowed a critical moment to pass them by. A moment where she could have told him but chose not to. It made him feel . . . alone. He said nothing more but took her by the hand and walked her down the hallway to his bedroom, desperate to bond with her, despite the betrayal. She'd brought light into his life for the first time in seventeen hundred years. They'd fought so hard to be together. He refused to lose her to the darkness. He intended to remind her of every touch, every kiss, every reason they belonged together.

Then, afterwards, he'd move heaven and Earth to find out what the fuck was going on.

Chapter 3

After Noory's breath had evened out, and he knew she was asleep, he slipped from his bed, threw his clothes on, and materialized in the living room of John Abramson's farmhouse in North Georgia, a stark contrast to Nick's downtown Atlanta penthouse overlooking the city. It was just after midnight, but Nick knew he would still be awake. Years of working the night shift in the Atlanta P.D. had left Noory's adoptive father—and an ancient disciple of Christ known as John the Beloved—a night owl. John sat in his old recliner he, ironically, never reclined in. He leaned over an ottoman, which bore a stack of paperwork he leafed through by the light of a standing lamp while the muted TV cast alternating shadows in the dimly lit room.

"We need to talk."

"About what?" John asked, not at all surprised by Nick's sudden appearance. After nearly two millennia of knowing each other, they always felt when the other was en route.

"Noory."

John tilted his head and studied Nick for a second. "Whatever this is, you're sneaking around behind her back. Where is she right now?"

Nick froze. "In my bed," was not an answer he wished to give her father, but then John was even older than Nick. A second longer, and he would figure it out without Nick telling him.

John held up a hand. "Don't answer that."

"Wasn't planning on it. Look, I'm just worried about her. Before we left for Scotland to meet with the Templars, did you notice anything strange going on with her?"

"No, she seemed fine to me. You're awfully jumpy. Sit down."

Nick sat on John's couch.

John leaned forward. "Listen, Nicholas. You're used to constant tragedy and loss in your life. People like you and me can become so accustomed to it that when things are going fine, we almost don't know how to function. We start seeing problems where there are none. It can be hard to transition to something closer to normalcy."

"I understand, but—"

"Right. So, it isn't just the lack of turmoil, seventeen hundred years of trauma and heartache, it's also being clean for the first time in almost as long. It's a new normal, and it's got you rattled. It's hard to get used to the quiet. It can be deafening. Be careful you don't go looking for trouble where there isn't any. You could talk to your sponsor, Brother Thaddeus. I think the AA program covers this sort of thing, too, right?"

"Yes, it does, but—"

"You also can't go interfering in Noory's life, or she'll resent you. Believe me, I've gone that route before. You were there. She took the battery out of her phone and shut me out entirely."

"All that is absolutely true. Agreed. One hundred percent. Can't argue with you, but, John, when Noory walked in my door this evening, she reeked of dark magic."

John looked stricken for a second before he sprang into action. "I'll just grab my jacket, and then we'll get to the bottom of this. She's going to get herself into big trouble. That girl has no idea what she's messing with. She ought to—"

"Both of you sit back down this instant!" Father Roy called from the doorway of the kitchen as he looked at them with an incredulous stare. The priest had been rooming with John since accompanying Noory back from the purgatory. Roy had died over a decade prior, after getting shot in the Grady Hospital parking lot. Since he'd not been called back to the other side after helping them destroy a relic with the power to take away free will, he'd been helping Nick track missing children.

"Honestly, the two of you. I'll admit, this is cause for concern. No doubt. But Noory is a very smart young woman. How about you try honesty, Nick? *Tell her* exactly what you detect on her. *Tell her* you're concerned. Tell her you're scared. Tell her why. What are you doing here when you should be back at your place having an honest, actual conversation with the woman you love?"

"I'm here because she didn't confide anything to me."

"Did you ask? Did you speak to her about why you're worried before you popped over here to rat on her? Because that's exactly how she will perceive it."

Nick felt the irritation coming off John, mirroring his own, but he'd lived long enough to know that Roy was correct. This would only push her further away. "Damn it. He's right. I'll have a talk with her in the morning. Besides, I'm hearing a child," he said as the familiar energy traveled down his brainstem and then settled heavily on his chest.

"Would you like some company?" Father Roy asked.

"Sure. Let's go."

John looked at them both and spread his arms in frustration. "Well, I still want to do something about this. Damn it, Nick!"

Nick shrugged, placed his hand on Father Roy's shoulder, and the two of them dematerialized, leaving John and his annoyed face.

They reappeared in the dark behind an apartment building in Druid Hills, or the old Ninth Ward as some called it. "We go right," Nick said.

Nick heard muffled music coming from various apartment buildings. A baby cried, a couple fought behind one wall, in the distance a dog barked. Nick stood still and listened again as Father Roy waited patiently. "This way," Nick said. "He's over here. There he is. About to walk over to that car."

"The kid who looks about thirteen holding the freezer bag? So, he's the one selling the drugs? *His* spirit called?" Father Roy asked.

"Maybe he doesn't *really* want to be doing this," Nick said.

Without another word exchanged between them, Father Roy walked toward the young man and began speaking to him as if he'd known him his whole life. "What are you doing out here? You better get your butt back inside. You're on restriction for the rest of the month. No TV, no phone. No games."

The boy turned and looked at Roy with relief. Roy snatched the freezer bag from his hand. He ran up the stairs of the nearest apartment building and disappeared around the corner to the other side. Nick realized Roy could've passed for the kid's father.

Nick watched Roy lift a hand and pluck at the air. He was doing his trick he'd brought with him from purgatory where he read lines of energy radiating off people stretching from their past and into possible futures. As the man in the car began cussing Roy now that he couldn't score off the kid, Roy calmly told him things about his life he couldn't possibly know. Through the orange glow of the streetlight, Nick saw the man's eyes grow wide with fear. He licked his lips and looked around as if seeking escape from the madman in front of him. Once the man was properly terrified, Roy dropped a few cautionary bombs about where all his careless actions would lead him.

"You're one scary SOB," the man mumbled at Roy before he shifted the car into reverse by mistake, fumbled with the gear shift, got it into drive, and finally drove away.

Nick stood by laughing. "I thought *I* was scary."

"Nah. You're a teddy bear."

"Well, I'm wide awake," Nick said. "Wanna go get a bite?"

Roy nodded. "But what do we do with this thing? Burn it?"

Nick laughed. "Not unless you want to get half the neighborhood lit. I'll drop it by John's house."

A half hour later, the two were at a Waffle House near downtown having coffee and scattered, smothered, and covered hashbrowns—which meant potatoes with sauteed onions and cheese, a down south thing of beauty. Nick watched Roy reach into the air again and pluck at a line of energy after the bell rang above the door, signaling a new customer.

"You know this one. I thought the energy felt . . . close. Wow! She's about to get waaaaay more entwined with all your fates. Fascinating! Very special purpose."

"Huh?" Nick turned around and saw Grace walk through the door alone. The seventeen-year-old had a new confidence since Noory had brought her back from purgatory. He supposed being forced to ferry the souls of dead SS officers back into this dimension and managing to survive it might do that. However, the nose ring and just-this-side-of-goth attire was the same Grace he knew. Nick turned back around and spoke to Roy as he reached for his cup of coffee. "Yeah, that one gets continually pulled into mine and Noory's path."

"And it will always be so," Roy said with confidence. "Get used to it. She will eventually be your colleague."

"Pft. No." Nick shook his head.

"Yes," Roy said matter of factly.

Nick made eye contact with Grace, and she froze for a split second before regaining her composure. He guessed right about now she was assuming he wouldn't be able to just ignore the fact that she was out late at night downtown by herself, and she was right. "What are you doing out here?" he asked.

"Just hanging out with some friends," Grace said. "They headed home. I'm not tired."

"Mm-hmm. Well, you need to get to your aunt's home now."

"You aren't the . . ." she started to protest before she stopped suddenly and stared into his eyes as he thought of every horrible thing that could happen to her, as he did with every child he worried about. The fact that she didn't continue arguing with him was perhaps evidence of a newfound maturity. Then again, Noory had told him Grace had become something of a psychic after being used as a conduit between the mortal realm and purgatory in Jonah's unholy experiments to bring dark souls back across the divide. Maybe she could see that he was just scared to death for her.

"Yeah, I'll head home," she said softly.

Grace turned to go, but then stopped and looked at Nick. "Even a demon can be an instrument of peace. Leave a little room for surprise?" She looked up and to the side as if searching for the right word, ". . . or faith? I don't know. I hear this stuff as if I'm dreaming suddenly. Half the time I don't know what the hell it means, but people tend to show up later, telling me it was spot on. Like when Noory told me she took that 'leap of faith' I predicted. I didn't know it meant she'd be jumping off a fuckin' cell phone tower."

Nick smiled and suppressed a laugh at Grace's wording, chased by a shudder as he remembered watching Noory turn to leap off the tower with the mind control device he'd fought so hard for, knowing it was his fault. "I'll bear that in mind," Nick said and meant it. "Grace? It's too late to take MARTA. How will you get to your aunt's house?" he asked.

"Walk, I guess."

Nick shook his head. "I remember where it is from when Noory and I drove you home a couple of weeks ago." Nick threw some money on the table to pay for their food and waved to the waitress.

A few minutes later, Nick, Grace, and Father Roy found a place where they wouldn't be spotted slipping into the in-between realm. They reappeared in the dark street outside Grace's aunt's house. He felt better knowing she was home safe. She waved goodnight, then walked inside, and shut the door.

Nick stopped back at John's house to drop off Father Roy. After that, he lay in bed again next to Noory, tossing and turning. He looked at the clock. It was 3:45 in the morning. Noory had gotten used to him having to leave in the middle of the night now and then when a child was in peril, so she didn't wake anymore. He smelled the dark magic on her with every exhalation, reminding him of the danger she carried, making him wonder endlessly what she had gotten herself into. It was too much. He knew what Father Roy had said. But what if someone was after her? What if he was respecting her boundaries when she desperately needed him to help? A quick peek into her apartment, just to make sure no entities had been poking around in there couldn't hurt. It was for her own safety. Shouldn't he do all he could to protect her?

He didn't even get out of bed but simply materialized from his bed to hers. He got up and walked around her apartment, searching for anything that might be out of place. Sensing no other presences there, he followed his nose to her laundry basket, where he smelled her clothes. The herbs assaulted his nasal passages, burning, as he took in the residue of magic, deep dark magic, and . . . ayahuasca? So, she was altering her perception? Why? Who would help her do that?

The idea of herbs led him to her kitchen. Maybe he'd find a clue there. He looked around and opened a few cabinets. Then, as he leaned over to close a cabinet, he noticed a piece of paper underneath her kitchen table. Because it seemed out of place, he picked it up. "I'll be damned," he said to the empty room. The entire page was written in a jagged demonic script that he couldn't read and knew Noory had no chance of reading. So, she was being used by a demon or a demon was helping her with something.

Noory only knew one demon well enough to help her out with anything and whether said demon was using her or helping her, he was about to get his teeth knocked out . . . again.

CHAPTER 4

Nick tried to materialize inside Damascus' home but ended up on the front porch. He tried several more times but kept getting "bounced" back to the porch. "Tricky bastard," Nicholas whispered. Damascus had his home spelled up tight as a drum.

Nick thought for a minute about how to get in there. He'd already scared the demon too badly to simply ask to come in. That was the disadvantage to being so damn good at what he did. You hurt people enough, they tend to avoid you after that. But he couldn't let it go. His need to protect Noory, especially now that she had demonic script in her home, was reaching obsession-level and wouldn't be satiated until he got his answers.

A moment later, he stood over Robert Billings' sleeping body. His wife lay three feet away from him, mouth hanging open and snoring like a freight train. He clamped a hand over Robert's mouth with one hand, shoved his body firmly into the bed with his forearm, and whispered into his ear, "We're taking a trip to your study. I won't hurt you. I just need you to do something for me right quick."

Even in the darkness, he could tell Robert was searching his eyes, looking for evidence that Amaros might still lurk somewhere inside. Nick knew Damascus would have informed him he'd gotten rid of the entity. Still, the man was traumatized, and that was good. It would keep the bullshit to a minimum.

Nick had let the entity in when it was holding Noory captive and moments from breaking through her defenses, possessing her, and taking the souls of four others that Noory had been sheltering inside her body to protect them from the evil being. He'd held it at bay for weeks but eventually it started influencing him, and he had to be locked away in the basement of the monastery where Atlanta kept its supernatural criminals while the monks searched for a cure.

Thank God he'd finally gotten free of the dark influence. Noory's bio father had taken the entity as a final act of redemption, and Brother Thaddeus, the veteran monk who wore a pistol alongside a rosary at his hip, had taken out the man and the vile spirit with one shot.

Robert held no demon within himself. He was just a "shitty human being," as John would say.

They materialized in Robert's study. "What the hell do you want?" Robert said. Nick recognized the attempt at bravado, and good for him, but his voice shook all the same.

"I need to get into Damascus' house. I just need to ask him a few questions. I'm not going to hurt him."

"Pft!" Robert waved a dismissive hand.

Once again, the care between Damascus and Robert proved to go just one way, and Nick would feel pity if he weren't so sure Damascus was getting Noory into trouble and, oh, yeah, he'd attempted to kill Grace for Robert last fall.

"I'm not obliged to do anything for you after you betrayed me and fucked up all my chances with Second Sight. I don't owe you anything."

Nick was a blur as he grabbed Robert by the throat and slammed him against his desk. "Oh, you owe me plenty. I didn't kill you for taking a shot at my girlfriend on that tower. I can still arrange that. Keep pushing me, you slimy son of a bitch."

Grudgingly, Robert called Damascus and arranged for him to lower the spell on his home. He told him a story about coming over with another demon that he needed him to meet. To Nick, he said, "He'll lower it long enough for you to slip through."

"Thank you," Nick said, hoping it would be the very last time he ever saw Robert. The man made his skin crawl. He was one of the most opportunistic, shallow, cold, and calculating individuals he'd ever met. If he weren't worried about Noory's opinion of him, he'd go ahead and kill this prick before he hurt someone else. He could feel it. He would.

He'd lived long enough to know. Instead, he left without another word or glance at the man.

In the next heartbeat, Nick stood in Damascus' living room. Thinking it possible he might have been blipped into a trap, he willed his holy daggers into his palms. They'd been with him since his immortality began 1,700 years ago. They glowed a soft blue against his palms, oddly comforting despite the violence they'd done.

Sconces illuminated the room, casting a soft light against the walls and ceiling. Nick took everything in as he waited for the demon to appear. His taste in artwork was fascinating. He had several Kahlil Gibran pieces: The Outstretched Hand, The Great Longing, the portrait of Ameen Rihani. Nick had met Gibran in the 1920s and actually enjoyed the man's company; he understood some profound truths about sorrow and loneliness. He would've enjoyed talking with Damascus about Gibran if the demon didn't make him so damn mad.

He turned to find Damascus standing there with disheveled black hair, those disconcerting orange eyes, and extremely high cut cheekbones. He wore black, satin-looking sleep pants and no shirt, displaying ridiculously ripped abs beneath fair skin. Nick had a fleeting flash of yet another reason Noory shouldn't be around Damascus, besides the fact that he was a killer.

Nick could see the desire to pounce when Damascus realized he'd been tricked, but the fight went out of him quickly. He retracted his claws. It had to hurt knowing Robert had sold him out so readily; the man he loved wouldn't suffer for him.

"All right. Let's talk." Damascus waved a hand, and the lights came on behind him. He then gestured to his ornate dining room table.

Nick and Damascus sat at opposite ends of a rather long, formal table, designed to seat ten.

Nick got straight to the point. "Why the hell does Noory absolutely reek of dark magic? Are you using her?"

"No, she's using *me*."

Nick narrowed his eyes at the demon. "You're full of shit! I don't know what's going on here, if you're blackmailing her or threatening one of her kids or whatever, but I will get to the bottom of it. You think you can't be killed? I'll separate your head from your fuckin' body if you hurt her. No way she's using *you*," he said pointing one of the glowing blue daggers at Damascus for emphasis.

Damascus hung his head and ran a finger along the table. "You were able to get past my spell and into my house, and I'm a remarkably powerful demon." He looked up at Nick, making eye contact. "Why is that, Nick? Because I'm plenty capable of being used."

Nick couldn't deny that point, but he refused to feel sorry for him either. "You're going to get her killed. Look, Noory may be more street smart than the average person, but she isn't cautious enough around people like you. For whatever reason, she has a soft spot, blind spot, when it comes to you, but I do not. Tell me what's going on, or I'll end you."

Damascus fixed him with his disconcerting orange glare. "I'm the only reason she's alive right now. You're so used to your sixth sense figuring shit out for you that your powers of deduction on interpersonal relationships have dulled. That's something you'll need to watch out for. You know that, right?"

He didn't appreciate getting relationship tips in the best of times, not even from John or Roy, and he loved them, much less from this murderer. "Fuck . . ." Nick exhaled. He couldn't muscle his way through everything. He willed his knives away with a twitch of his wrists. He recalled conversations over coffee with his sponsor, Brother Thaddeus, who'd said something similar. Just because he was sitting in front of a demon didn't mean everything the bastard said was wrong. "I'm listening." Nick hid his hands in his lap so that Damascus couldn't see that he was clinching them into fists. Yeah, he'd love to punch his way through.

"I don't enjoy betraying her trust. I don't want her to get killed, either. I'll tell you everything, but in addition to you telling her you threatened my life, let's also tell her you smacked me around a bit, shall we? Make it good. Believable."

Nick narrowed his eyes. "I may yet."

"Do try and contain yourself, please."

Nick nodded.

"First of all, I left the page of demonic script under her kitchen table, knowing it would lead you to me."

"She shouldn't have demonic script in her house. Just speaking some of that shit can dissolve your bones."

Damascus rolled his eyes and laughed. "Only if a sheet called 'Dirty Jokes for Deadly Demons' is powerful. I swear, you people. Write a few archaic-looking lines on something and you automatically think it's hexed and out to get you." He shook his head and leaned back. "I also didn't warn her that no shower would remove the scent of dark magic from someone like you or John being able to detect it. I wanted her to get caught."

"Then why the hell make it so damn hard for me to get into your house?"

"I'm in popular demand, sweetie. I've lived long enough to piss off more people than *you*." Damascus waved a hand, and a tumbler of what looked to be bourbon on the rocks appeared in front of Damascus. He took a sip and continued. "Speaking of people that reek, you don't smell like ouzo anymore. Are you bothered by me drinking on front of you?" Damascus smiled and took a big gulp before holding it up to Nick in salute.

"Fuck off," Nick said to the teasing demon. Truth was, all the worry for Noory made him want to damn near break the demon's wrist to get the drink from him. Focus, Nick thought, as his mouth watered, and he caught himself chewing on the inside of his cheek.

Damascus laughed before turning serious again. "She's thrilled you're staying sober, by the way. Anyway, she's searching for a way to become immortal. She came to me with a list of shamans, witches, druids, wizards, and whatnot. Every fucking quack around the globe was on that list. And thank Hades she did, too. Several beings on there would've killed her the minute she walked through their door and cashed in on the standing scion bounty. Please tell me you know about that. Almost every dark organization out there has a reward out for her and most of them don't want her brought in alive. She's too much trouble conscious."

"I do, but John asked me not to tell her."

Damascus slammed his hand down on the table. "This is exactly the kind of shit you all need your asses kicked for, and *I'm* the one with the problem! I need another drink." He waved his hand, and the glass filled again.

"For the record, I told John we needed to tell her about that."

"She's your girlfriend now, Nick, and that stubborn Jesus Jockey ain't your daddy. Anyway, I threw away three quarters of her research because it would have definitely gotten her killed, and I agreed to accompany her on the few leads that *might* be legit. Not that I think the practitioners left on the list have the key to immortality, but I didn't think they would try to kill her either. I threaten them all to a degree you would consider unethical before they begin. However, she's desperate, and she's a grown up. You can't stop her. I can't stop her. At least she let me go with her."

"Well, this ends right now. No more."

"What are you going to do? Lock her in her room? You start bossing her around, and you'll ruin your relationship."

"Then stop helping her!"

"I didn't want her to do it either, but if I hadn't been there, she'd be dead right now."

"Why?" Nick felt suspicion rising.

"She had a bad reaction when we were in Peru. The ayahuasca, mixed with whatever the shaman was burning in that hut, caused her heart to stop beating. I did CPR on her, and she came back."

Nick teleported from his chair and appeared beside the demon. With a lightning-fast jab to his face, Nick knocked the hell out of him. Rage shook him as Damascus rolled to the side and quickly out of his reach.

The demon's claws came out in warning, and he pointed a talon at him. "You're just mad because she didn't come to you! Don't take it out on me."

Out of the blue, Grace's words from a few hours ago came back to him unbidden. "Even a demon can be an instrument of peace. Leave a little room for surprise . . . or faith."

Nick took a deep breath and checked in with how he was feeling, like the gun-toting prison guard of lawbreaking supernatural beings, monk and sponsor Brother Thaddeus, had talked about. *Allow the world to slow for a moment. Be present. Assess.* "You're right," Nick said. He paused a moment. Sober truth was *so* much harder. "Would you like a shot at me?" he asked Damascus.

Damascus shook the alcohol from his arm where his drink had spilled and then rubbed his puffy eye with the other. "What?"

"You saved Noory's life. I should be thanking you, not attacking you." Nick stood and spread his arms. "Take a shot."

Damascus stood and approached Nick. "Sobriety has done a number on you." Nick felt the demon's eyes slide over his body, before he spoke again in a seductive murmur, "Well, it's a damn shame to damage a body like that." Then he punched Nick's stubbled chin so hard his ears rang.

"Fuck me!" Nick exclaimed as he realigned his jaw. "You've got a mean right hook!"

"Don't dare me," Damascus said with a laugh. He shook his hand and let out the claws on his right hand and then retracted them as if trying to make sure they didn't get damaged. "Now, get your ass home and talk to your woman. Like, seriously *talk to her.*"

"Yeah, I'm getting that advice a lot lately."

"Pft! I doubt it's from John."

"Nah. Father Roy."

Damascus' features turned grim. "You're watching out for him, right? He scarred more than one demon the night he destroyed that mind control crazy box, and for some reason, their wounds won't heal. They're out for blood, entrails, his head. I mean, this is serious shit with that dude."

"Yeah. Well, luckily, he has some built-in defense mechanisms."

"The likes of which no one has seen in a millennium. Second Sight will either want to kill him or study him. Both, probably. Letting him alone won't remain an option."

Nick looked toward the window as the first rays of light touched the trees in Damascus' back yard. He had a sudden burning question as he rubbed his throbbing jaw. "Why do you care about Noory at all?"

"She . . ." Damascus began, but then seemed to think better of it. "One day, when you see me as something more than a killer, I might tell you. Although . . . you referred to me as "people" earlier. That was nice." He looked at the floor, then back up. "Noory has my cell phone number. Just call me next time you need to talk. And by the way, you need to remember the most important thing about all of this shit with Noory."

"Yeah?"

"Stupid fucker. I can't believe I have to tell you this. The most amazing thing of all is that she not only pictured herself getting old and dying with you but is actually looking for a way to spend an *eternity* with your sorry ass. I'm lucky if Robert wants to spend ten minutes with me."

Nick nodded and gave him a grateful smile, something he never thought he'd do, then re-materialized in the bed beside Noory. He'd spent all night running, chasing, fighting, threatening. He'd rather do any of those things than have one honest conversation with her about why she kept this from him. Apparently, she would too.

She'd literally died, at least for a few moments, and chose not to tell him.

This was bad.

CHAPTER 5

Noory rolled over to find Nick watching her. "Good morning. You feeling okay?" he asked.

"Of course. Why wouldn't I be?" He knew something. He was looking at her weird. She hopped up and went to the bathroom and had to work hard to keep from running. *Shit. I do not want to talk about this.* She had a feeling she would be talking about it whether she wanted to or not. She used the toilet, washed her face, brushed her teeth, and looked around for some other way to stall. *Can't hide out in the bathroom all day.* She took a deep breath and went back into the bedroom to deal with it.

She sat down on the bed. Nick placed a hand on her forehead as if he were taking her temperature. "What are you doing? I told you I feel fine."

He looked her in the eye. "Noory, some of the things you've been doing, ingesting, can make you physically ill, as well as susceptible to lower-level entities. Your lineage can't protect you from everything."

Damn it! Damascus ratted me out.

"I've known it since you walked in the door yesterday. I smell it on you. I taste it in your mouth and everywhere else. It's all over you. You can't wash it off. Had you talked to me, I could have explained all of this to you. If you run into a malevolent entity at least for another week or so, they will know you've been dabbling in dark magic, and they will try to use that to their advantage, possibly even launch an attack on you while you're still somewhat vulnerable. Certain herbs and spells weaken your aura and turn you into a conduit. You've opened yourself to the darkness. It makes it a little easier for them to infiltrate."

"Damascus told me that." She took a deep breath, wondering just how much she should tell him, but she hated how keeping secrets felt, like an oily sheen clinging to her, as bad as the dark magic. "He fought off a couple entities outside our hotel while we were in Peru using a counter spell to create a barrier around me until my aura got stronger. It was . . . bad. I was afraid he wasn't going to make it." She didn't want to talk about it anymore. They'd been trying to get in. It reminded her way too much of the time the entity had her pinned to the wall in purgatory while she was protecting Grace and the souls of the other teens she harbored inside her, and Nick had to take in the entity to save her.

"God, Noory." Nick ran his hands through his hair. "He didn't tell me that. I wasn't being all that . . . cordial with him."

"John will know too if I go see him. Shit, he'll know if he simply runs into me. He'll lose it."

Nick sighed, started to talk, and seemed to think better of it. It made her mad. It felt as if a parent were trying to scold her. *I'm a grown damn woman.*

He began again, "Well, that's not the point. The point is your safety. And full disclosure, I panicked last night when the remnants of dark magic were pouring off you like that. I thought maybe you'd been used or hurt, and I went to see John. I'm sorry. I know that makes you mad. I didn't know what else to do."

"You could have just asked me about it instead of running to tell my dad on me."

"You're right. And you could have told me about this instead of heading off to God-knows-where to ingest dark magic. I suspected Damascus helped you. For the record, I'm glad you didn't go alone. Even though it's possible he cares about you, I still don't trust him. I made him tell me why you went."

Noory huffed and started to get up. Nick grabbed her wrist, pulled her down, and held her in place with his body. "We have to talk about this stuff. You and I have a problem, Noory. We say we trust each other, but there's certain things we hide from each other, too, and we've only been together a few months. We can't keep doing this or we're doomed. We have to talk."

"Let me up."

"Why?" he asked with a wolfish grin. "You've never had a problem being pinned beneath me before." He pressed his hips against her pelvis.

He wasn't playing fair. She could already feel her back starting to arch, her core responding to the heat radiating off him. *Damn it! You sick, beautiful bastard.* "Well, see, now instead of actually talking to me, you're using sex to try and get me to talk to you. If you keep doing this, we won't be talking at all. We'll just be having sex again."

"If I move, you'll get up," Nick countered.

"I won't. I promise."

"You also promised me you wouldn't talk to Damascus unless I was with you. I didn't say that to be a controlling asshole. He's a murderer."

"I had a good reason for breaking that promise. But I did feel bad about it. I don't want us to have secrets."

He rolled off her. She put a pillow against the headboard and sat back against it.

She began, "Sometimes I'd catch you looking at me as if I were already moments from death. Like, you were grieving me in advance. I don't think you understand how often you were doing it. And I thought about how bad I would feel when I crossed that threshold where I finally looked older than you and you had to walk out in public with me and people assumed you were with your mother and then, later, your grandmother. I thought about how embarrassing that would be for both of us. The more you looked at me like that, the more I knew I had to do something."

Nick buried his face in his hands. "I'm sorry."

"No. I get it. It's scary."

"I can handle whatever comes our way. I'm willing to deal with it as long as we can be together for however long that is, even when you're old. It's okay that you won't always look like this."

"And that's lovely, but if there's a way for us to stay together, why not find it?"

"Because your heart stopped beating, Noory. That's why. I didn't even know that when I went to see your dad."

"Well, good God! Don't tell him!"

"I wasn't planning on it. I'm just saying, if you insist on doing this, I can't stop you. You stubborn pain in the ass," he said with a tight grin. "At least let me help make sure you do it safely. Maybe you also need to leave a space somewhere in your head for the idea that you might not be meant to be immortal."

"Easy for you to say!"

"Yeah, I get how you would feel that way, but do you know how many times I've wished for the ability to be able to move on, to be done with this life?"

"Yeah, I know." She remembered the sorrow she'd been through with him since they'd been together. She couldn't fathom the depths of it. Century after century of saving children—and sometimes failing to save them—from the worst humanity had to offer. How he had managed to hold on was beyond her, yet he had, and he was just beginning to crawl out of it, just beginning to walk into the light, find his sobriety and some semblance of peace.

He shoved her playfully. She knew he'd read the memories of the past few months in her eyes and didn't want to go there. He murmured, "What if you get tired of me? I'm a brooding pain in the ass as well as a stubborn one."

"And *I'll* always have a meddling father."

"True. Very true."

"I'm not going to stop trying. Don't ask me to."

"I wasn't going to. I know better than that."

She laughed.

"What are you going to tell John?" he asked.

She groaned. "Well, now that you've tattled on me, I don't know."

"Truth always works."

"Always?"

"In the long run, yes."

"For those of us who live long enough to see it."

She watched Nick look down and trace his finger along the seam of the pillow he held. "Yeah," he said.

She mentally scolded herself. She couldn't keep holding it against him that he had the eternal life she was out risking her health for. "Sorry, I shouldn't . . . take shots like that. You didn't ask for the life you have."

"No, I get it. Come here." He took her hand and pulled her to him, laid her head against his chest as she aligned her body with his like puzzle pieces meant to fit together.

He sighed, and she felt his body relax. A hot tear slid down her face. He'd never been able to relax before, unless he was completely drunk. Now, she noticed him being able to do it more and more when she was with him. She didn't want to live forever for her. It was for him. Always him. When she was gone, he'd be right where he was before, when she'd seen him in that alley, mourning over a girl he couldn't save and reeking of ouzo, and she couldn't bear the thought of it.

CHAPTER 6

Nick tore open the little packet of sugar and poured the third one into his coffee. He'd marveled at Noory's caffeine addiction, and John wasn't much better, but since Nick had stopped drinking, coffee had become a way of life. He turned up the little silver container of fresh cream and watched it swirl around and create a cloud inside the depths of his new, dark, liquid obsession.

Thaddeus sat across from him in the monastery kitchen with his own cup of coffee slowly cooling in front of him. He took a scoop of coconut oil in his coffee. Why not? That sounded about right for the combat Marine, turned officer in the Atlanta Police Department, turned monk-guardian of supernatural criminals in the monastery's basement.

"How are things in the basement?" Nick asked.

"Well, you know, never a dull moment. Last Thursday, Chance morphed his face to look like Edvard's, and I ended up serving him two lunches before I figured out, I'd been duped. At least it was a harmless trick. Then again, feeding a changeling too much makes them even prankier."

"Oh, right. He's the one that killed that one man, brought his doppelgänger through from another dimension, plopped him down in the middle of his other self's life, and the poor SOB went crazy."

"That's him."

"Good, Lord! That's heinous." Nick took a drink of his coffee and experienced his newfound bliss.

"So, things are going that good, then?"

Nick laughed. "It's a good cup of coffee."

"It's your new addiction."

"A little."

"How are things, really?"

Nick exhaled and ran a hand through his hair.

"That bad, huh?

"Eeeeh . . . I don't know that it's bad. I just . . ."

"More." Thaddeus motioned with his hand.

The man never let him get away with anything. It was annoying and probably exactly what he needed.

Nick told Thadeus all about Noory's quest for immortality and "a friend" bringing her back from the brink when she'd ingested ayahuasca and God knew what other plants the shaman burned that night. He knew better than to tell Thaddeus that Noory was friends with a demon. The man had dedicated his life to protecting the world from them. He might not be able to let it go, and the last thing Nick wanted was for Thaddeus to get John involved, and he likely would.

After his time in the Marines, when Thaddeus had served on the APD for a while, that's where he met John and ended up running the monastery prison. Those two were a lot alike. That wasn't a bad thing until you ran into a gray area. Neither could tolerate it.

"You're scared of losing her?"

"Yes. Of course."

"How deep does it go?"

What the hell kind of question is that? What does he want from me? How deep does it go? She's the love of my life. "Pretty damn deep."

"What I mean is, there's everyday fear—we always have the knowledge that we could lose someone we love, but we accept this as part of life—then there's the kind of fear that makes us want control and we can't control everything. That's why we turn ourselves over to our higher power."

Even as he spoke, Nick could feel his blood pressure rising. He could never accept Noory's demise. Hell, he had even used the word "demise" because he didn't want to associate the word "death" with her. "Look, I know where you're coming from. I'm not going to start drinking in order to relieve my worry. I've fought too hard for my sobriety."

Thaddeus nodded. "Have you given more thought to what we talked about last week?"

They talked a lot about old patterns and the Einstein quote, "The definition of insanity is doing the same thing over and over again and expecting different results." He'd thought quite a bit about his commission and how it wore him down. He often felt that he was beneath the boot-heel of it, continually. "I think I may be ready to meet some of them, the kids, get to know them. I was always afraid to before. I could rescue them, track down their killers, if it came to that, but I couldn't really get to know them. Touring the shelter felt impossible back then, but I think I might be ready now."

"It might also open the door to more pain, should one of them not make it later."

"Yes. That's why I've avoided it for so long." He thought back to Elliott, the child he'd fostered who'd later gotten into trouble and ended up in juvenile detention and blamed Nick for having to leave on calls to rescue other children. "I'm on a different path now. It's a new day. I'm strong enough." Nick took a drink of his coffee and felt the truth of his words.

Thaddeus nodded. "Call me if you need to talk about it."

"I will. Call me if you need me to help you wrestle a demon."

Thaddeus raised his cup. "Here's to the good life."

Nick raised his cup. "Indeed."

CHAPTER 7

Noory walked into the Holy Innocents shelter with Nick and picked up her messages. Her assistant, Ava, smiled at her, then smiled even bigger when she saw Nick. Noory was used to it. Nick had that effect on women—and many men too.

Noory saw Nick looking around, assessing the shelter's needs. He always did that. It was generous, sweet, and annoying as hell. She decided to derail it quickly by introducing him to someone. "Nick, come meet Evan." A dark-haired boy with soulful grey eyes was walking out of the kitchen. He stopped beside Noory. "Evan, this is Nick."

"Hey," Evan said. She almost laughed out loud as she watched Evan's demeanor change. He was small for a fourteen-year-old, but he was working to make up for it by lowering his voice and standing up straight.

"Evan, pleased to meet you." Nick shook the boy's hand, but Evan's focus was on Nick's shoes.

"Italian leather?" Evan asked.

"Yes."

"Cool. Cool," Evan replied in what he probably hoped was casual nonchalance, but he wasn't fooling anyone.

"Good eye," Nick said.

Evan inclined his head and briefly closed his eyes with the demeanor of a 60-year-old butler, not a 14-year-old boy.

As Evan strutted away, Noory leaned over to Nick and whispered, "We had an investment banker come in on career day. He's been enamored with the finer things ever since."

Nick smiled.

Grace breezed in holding a box with clothing overflowing its borders. "Hey, Nick!"

"Hey!"

Noory rushed over to take the box. "This is great. Thank you."

"My aunt said she threw out anything with holes or stains."

"That'll work. Please tell her the women will appreciate it."

"Will do."

"Hey, Grace." Evan sauntered out of the boy's half of the center wearing a blazer he hadn't had on a few moments ago. Noory turned her head to hide her smile. She was sure he'd run to put on the blazer to impress Nick but was likely glad to be wearing it when he spotted Grace. He'd been hopelessly in love with her since he'd arrived at the shelter with his mother three months ago. "How you been?" he said as he leaned on the counter by reception.

"Been good. How are you?"

"I'm well," Evan said as he straightened the cuff of his blazer that was far too long on him.

Noory stole a look at Nick who wore a huge grin as he looked back and forth between Evan and Grace. Noory liked that Grace was always patient and kind to the kid, even though the unwanted attention had to bug her now and then. "Nice blazer," Grace said as she patted Evan on the shoulder and headed to the kitchen. "I'll start prepping lunch."

Noory noticed Evan placed his hand on the shoulder Grace had just touched. *Dear Lord, that blazer's never coming off now.* She looked up to find Nick silently laughing, the effort to contain it creating tears in his eyes.

She'd never seen him so happy. She knew she'd do whatever she had to keep him that way.

CHAPTER 8

Catherine sat in the Second Sight boardroom at the head of the large oak table. She kept her back straight, face unreadable, and resolve firmly in place. She'd done many distasteful things over the years, but they had all been worth it to keep her daughter safe. After meeting with John a few months back, she felt some of the tension dissipate over what he would think of her if he knew she wasn't the same person anymore. She'd told him she had changed, and he didn't seem to care. He wanted her. Her body flooded with warmth when she thought of his mouth taking hers with such ferocity and gentleness, somehow all in the same kiss. It was both, just like him. God, how she missed that man. Her desire for him had not dimmed over the last two decades. If anything, it had become an inferno. She spent night after night thinking of what it would be like to be in his bed again.

She snapped out of her reverie and stood as the board members of Second Sight filed into the room. Locus, a demon, walked in first. His skin gave off a slight silver hue. Bright blue eyes, silver hair, and now, a scar across his face and neck that refused to heal despite having seen the best supernatural healers that money could buy. He demanded Father Roy Henderson's assassination. He'd never had an injury in all his three thousand years that didn't heal quickly and thoroughly. When he'd reached for the relic made by his people that Father Roy had been destroying that night in the in-between realm, the priest capable of walking in both worlds had burned him, on their turf.

Catherine knew the hatred for the priest would never be quenched. Father Roy was feared now and would therefore be hunted forever.

Locus had even known the auspicious date when the relic would be in play. He was able to pinpoint places in the future that would have special significance and make sure Second Sight was there for such events, to capitalize on them both monetarily and to gain power and prestige from them. When the tide turned politically, it turned financially and vice versa. Father Roy had turned the tide—and the tables—on Locus and his colleagues. Catherine knew it was more than just the scar Locus was furious about, it was the loss of *control*. He couldn't predict Father Roy or see past him when he used his demonic sight to view what turning points the man would bring forth. The priest created a blind spot. One that could not be tolerated.

Behind him came Janus, a demon capable of giving someone a whole new beginning but usually not one they'd asked for. She could see backward and forward, thus the eyes on the back of her head. She could cast a glamour that would make anyone look completely different without actually altering their appearance. This came in handy when one of their clients needed to disappear or were in need of punishment . . . She could hide their past and future as well.

Try as Janus might, she couldn't give herself a new beginning after she'd reached for the relic and Father Roy had burned her. A massive chunk of her hair still hadn't grown back, a huge problem for someone that used their thick, beautiful hair to cover a second face on the back of her head. Though the face on the back never spoke, it only looked. The past was done.

The other board members were human but in Catherine's experience every bit as dangerous and evil as their hell-spawned counterparts. In fact, she trusted them even less. At least the demons had an ancient code they lived by rather than an "everyone for themselves" philosophy.

Catherine called the meeting to order. They connected online with the Second Sight owner, Malachi—audio only. In the two decades she'd been there, she'd never heard his last name, nor seen him in person. She wasn't sure she wanted to either. The energy coming off his voice didn't feel right. It wasn't just that he was the leader of an evil corporation that had stolen the last twenty years of her life—everyone there was foul. There was something else about Malachi, something ancient and disturbing.

They went over numbers on their holdings, reports on new leads to fulfill their ultimate agenda of a more equitable society, which Catherine knew to be code for controlling everyone, and then Malachi gave Catherine an assignment.

"So, from time to time all of my employees are given a test of loyalty," Malachi said from the black speaker in the middle of the table.

Catherine's blood boiled. They kept her from family for two decades under the threat of harm coming to Noory. She'd had to assassinate rival business owners who didn't bend to their demands. Thus far, they'd been almost as shady as Malachi, but there had to be people out there who loved those she killed, and that kept her up at night. She hated her existence, but if she died, they'd go after Noory. It wasn't just the assassinations they kept her around for, either. They took her blood, often. As a descendant of the Holy Family, they considered her something of a revered relic too. In the beginning she'd objected, but they simply replied with, "We can go get it from your daughter if you'd like," and she quickly complied.

Even though she'd known it was coming, she still felt sick as he gave his orders. "Our faithful board members have been harmed beyond repair. They've been loyal to our company, our cause, and deserve retribution. Catherine, please take Roy Henderson off the map. I'd like it done within the week."

"Sir, this is a man who can collapse his mortal form. He cannot be punched, stabbed, shot, anything."

"Oh, come on. You're a bright woman. A Faraday cage will take care of that little problem. You know our technicians have the Faraday nets in the lab. Once you get the net around him, it will keep him from shifting into his spirit form. Then you can just destroy him."

She hesitated, as panic raced through her. Father Roy was no jackass running around stabbing people in the back to make his stock go up a quarter of a point. This man lived with John. She'd seen him out patrolling with Nicholas and Noory. She saw Noory laughing with him. He was her friend. Sweat rolled down her back. She hesitated just a split second too long. By the time she spoke, it was too late. Malachi had already detected her hesitancy, and the whole thing became a test of honor. Now, any lie delaying the order would become suspect. Any move to give Roy a way out . . . *Fuck!*

"Unless this is a problem for you?" Malachi poked.

"No, of course not."

"Great!"

Catherine looked down the table at Locus, and he smiled at her, revealing a gleaming white, feral smile. He'd been friends with that son of a bitch she'd thrown off her balcony a few months ago when he'd tried to bed her in exchange for not telling Malachi about her meeting with John. Had he told Malachi before she killed him? Did this evil bastard smiling at her right now already know about it, and they were all testing her? She resisted the urge to fidget beneath his gaze.

Catherine crept out of the tree line and made her way through the fields of John Abramson's farm in the cool of the nearly moonless spring night. She was dressed all in black and stepped softly. Years in the service of Second Sight had taught her stealth. She simply wished to do a little recon this evening. She had it on good authority that John was out with a rookie cop he'd been mentoring, giving him tips about handling the night beat.

A war waged in Catherine's spirit. She couldn't do this. Could she? Then again, if Roy was a holy man, he'd understand that she had to protect her daughter. *What the hell are you thinking? You can't make excuses for this!*

She had almost reached the house when she felt a presence beside her. "Are you looking for me, Catherine Abramson?"

"Jesus Christ!" she jumped as her heart thundered.

"Not even close," Father Roy said. "But I'm flattered. I was wondering when they were going to send someone after me."

It had been years since someone had rattled her when she was out on a job. She was no rookie. Taking down targets almost twice her size was a claim to fame. Now this priest with a voice like warm chocolate had managed to actually sneak up on *her*? Catherine started to speak but looked around first.

Roy closed his eyes and tilted his head as if listening. "Don't worry. You aren't being surveilled. You may speak freely."

"Why wasn't I followed? I thought I would be," she said as she controlled her breathing to get her heart rate down.

"Providence," he said with an assurance that half made her want to laugh, half cry.

"I used to believe in such things. It's been so long." An ache bloomed in her chest. She tried her best to ignore it. "Aren't you afraid? I came here to kill you."

He stepped forward, wrapped his arms around her, and spoke softly into her ear. "No, you didn't. I see you, Catherine. You came here to try and find a way to save me."

Two entire decades had gone by since anyone had wrapped their arms around her for a simple, platonic hug. Terror rolled through her body. Not because she thought he'd hurt her—she thought she might shatter. She'd worked so hard to stay strong. Now here this man was, making her feel a gentleness her resolve could not afford.

He continued speaking to her. "You may eventually decide to trap me, to kill me, and if you do, please know that I forgive you." Power radiated off him in waves as he spoke. Power unlike she'd ever experienced in John or Noory. She doubted even Nicholas possessed it.

She pushed him away, suddenly angry. "Why don't you burn Second Sight to the ground?"

As she looked into his eyes in what little light there was by the dim moonlight, she knew he was aware of his power, too. It usually burned a being to ash. Yet here he stood, thoroughly uncorrupted. "It isn't my path. I'm told that I am a catalyst."

"What the fuck does that mean? You see me, and I believe it. Then you must also see that I'm trapped, and here you stand with the power to help, and you do nothing. You and your God!"

He nodded as a tear rolled down his cheek. "I'm sorry. I wish, with all my heart, that I knew His plan."

She wanted to hit him so much her palms itched with the desire. But as she stood there watching him cry, she couldn't do it. Instead, she thought about how far away the other homes were from John's house, and she let loose a scream into the night and fell to her knees.

Roy knelt beside her and wrapped his arms around her once more. She sobbed for a while, then rose on shaking legs, and disappeared into the woods again, this time not bothering to keep quiet.

CHAPTER 9

Roy, Nick, and Noory jumped from building to building through the cool of late spring in the Atlanta night doing what they always did. A young girl had tagged an old beater car with gang signs, not even her gang, stupid as hell, and now she might well die for it. Turns out, the owner didn't see his car as a "beater" or find it adorable or badass.

Now it was going on 2:00 a.m., and they were down in an alley, where the trail had run cold. Roy looked over at Noory and noticed that she was fading fast. He knew she had gotten up at 6:00 a.m. to head into the shelter she managed and would have to go to work early again tomorrow.

Roy elbowed Nick, who followed his line of sight and caught Noory yawning. "I'm taking you home. You're exhausted, Light."

"No, I'm fine. I love being out with you and Father Roy."

"I know, but you don't exactly have the same . . . attributes."

Roy cringed inside. Poor Nick was trying his best to tiptoe around the subject. Noory was more sensitive than ever about her mortal status and pointing out that she tired faster than them wouldn't help. Though she was stronger than the average human, she still needed at least a few hours' sleep each night.

"I'll take Noory home and be right back," Nick said.

"See you in a bit. Take your time. I'll just keep an ear out for the kid."

Nick thanked him, took Noory by the hand, and blinked out of sight.

Roy closed his eyes and concentrated on where they might look for the girl when Nick returned. No sooner had he done so than he felt presences pop into the alley. Before he could shift into spirit form, a net fell onto him.

Not a man, Roy decided. An entity with a scar on the side of his silvery skin that seemed to glow in the streetlight and looked manically pleased to have him trapped. He punched Roy so hard, his jaw cracked and splintered. Pain. That's what this sensation was. Lightning racing over his skull. Anguish. Torment. His eyes watered. He felt as if he might pass out for a moment. Being human. That's what this was. It had been decades since he'd experienced such a thing. Not since the bullet had torn through his chest as he'd stood outside Grady Hospital after he'd been mugged. He'd given up his wallet, thinking that would be the end of it. It wasn't. Would this kill him, too? No. It just felt like it.

"Locus," a woman's voice came from the shadows. "Don't kill him. We decided to take him back to the lab first. You know that."

"Maybe I don't kill him but cause him the same anguish he caused me."

Suddenly a male voice whispered into Roy's ear, "I've disabled the net. Shift onto the roof of the Westin. I'll meet you there."

Roy felt a little queasy as he looked over the edge of the hotel roof. He no longer feared death. Thus, he realized this fear of heights was simply some lingering primal memory. He shifted his jaw and found that it had already healed. He'd wondered what would happen if he were to get injured now that he wasn't quite alive or dead anymore. Now he knew. He'd already taken on an incorruptible form. Having been so close to ascension and being sent back had made him something else entirely.

The city was beautiful from up here. He closed his eyes and let the cool night air wash over him. The sounds of ambulances in the distance, the hum of traffic, a car horn carried faintly on the wind. Something about it all made him want to cry. Below was a city full of people experiencing life. They were happy, sad; many were trying their best for those they loved, to make their highest vision of themselves come true. It was damn brave. How could a supreme being not want to create and observe with absolute *awe*? He wondered if this was at least some small glimpse of how the Creator felt about his creation. People often thought of God with awe while the Creator looked down on them with wonder.

"You've created a fucking shitstorm for yourself, Father," came a most irreverent voice from behind him.

Father Roy laughed at the juxtaposition, opened his eyes, and turned around to find an orange-eyed demon with impeccable taste in his shimmering midnight blue shirt, tailored black pants, and expensive-looking leather shoes. "I've heard a lot about you, Damascus."

"At your service." Damascus bowed with one arm across his chest and the other out to the side, claws extended.

Roy thought it added nicely to the overall effect. He was sure Damascus knew it did, too.

Damascus said, "Those were the demons you scarred, and they will never let it go."

Roy smiled.

"An incorruptible scarred them." Damascus pointed at Roy with a long claw. "Now they're marred for eternity. This will not rest. It would be best for you to find a way to finish ascending. They've got nothing to do for an infinity but hunt you, obsessively. Once they catch you, they will torture you . . . slowly."

"Whatever will happen will happen, but it didn't happen tonight. Why not?"

"I've got my reasons."

"Care to share them?"

"Losing you would hurt Noory. Noory is my . . . friend, I suppose."

"You don't suppose. You know. It's okay to admit it."

"Well, while we're forcing people to bare their souls, how about you admit that you're a little more attached to this life than *you* care to admit? You love those relics you hang out with: John and Nick."

"I do."

"Second Sight might pick them off to get to you."

"We can't have that now, can we?" Roy felt his power surge, and his eyes open wider as if his body were preparing to strike. It was a little unsettling.

Damascus smiled and winked. "There's the scary motherfucker I knew was in there."

Roy looked down at the city, then back at Damascus. "Even Jesus had a temper."

"True enough. He scared the hell out of me. I kept my distance."

Roy slowly approached as Damascus backed up a little. "I mean you no harm," Roy said.

"You're more powerful than me, and that's saying something. Your fri—our mutual friends—don't know this, do they?"

"Not fully, no. I only want to read your energy lines. May I? I won't if you refuse."

"Oh, hell." Damascus rolled his eyes. "You're interested in knowing if I really encountered *The Rabbi*. Damn fanboys." Damascus spread his arms in invitation. "I'll never wash these claws again," he said in a sing-song voice like a tween who had just fist-bumped their favorite pop star.

Roy approached and plucked at a line of energy. "Christ!"

"Told you!"

Roy did see a memory, a glimpse of Christ from a distance through Damascus' frightened eyes, but that wasn't why he exclaimed. Though he knew to still be cautious of the demon, the humanity inside Damascus is what had surprised him. He looked up at him and smiled.

Damascus took another step back and looked away.

"Thank you for coming to my aid," Roy said.

"You're welcome, Father. But look, I can't constantly follow your ass around this city. You need to ascend before they catch you."

Roy shook his head. "My friends need me too much."

Damascus threw his hands into the air and got in Roy's face. "If they fuck you up and then throw your bloody corpse on John's or Noory's doorstep, you'll wish you had listened to me."

"I appreciate your concern."

"I can't fucking reason with you, not until they start using someone you love against you. Then it will be too late. Believe me."

Roy looked down.

"They already have?"

"If they find out my boyfriend still lives. That's why I can never see him. That and . . . well, I wouldn't throw his life into upheaval like that. It's a cruel trick to come back from the dead."

"Your Messiah did it."

"Hmm. Yeah. Noory's mother is also being used against me."

"The woman is basically a captive there," Damascus murmured.

"If I let them catch me, maybe she can be free."

Damascus rolled his eyes. "God save me from the martyrs of this world. She wasn't free before you came on scene."

"You already knew they had Noory's mother?"

"Yes."

"You haven't told Noory?" Roy asked.

"No."

Roy whistled through his teeth.

"You haven't either! Fucking hypocrite. Look, I didn't tell her because she would go over there with guns a-blazin' trying to save her mom, and next thing you know, Noory would be in their grasp. I can't have that."

"How long have you known?"

"Since last November. I smelled the battle adrenaline of a woman who kicked the shit out of my boyf—a guy named Robert—for failing Second Sight. A couple days later, I talked with Noory and realized their scent was too similar not to share blood. Battle adrenaline shares many things in common, a sharp spike. Unmistakable. I never forget a scent profile. I knew it was her mother."

"Why does no one do anything?"

"I'm an ancient, powerful demon with the power to kill with the flick of my wrist, but this organization has been around even longer than me. They have reach in every country and have beings on their payroll who could kill me in a blink. No one has figured out how to take them down, and believe me, lots of people have tried and died for it."

Damascus and Roy turned when a shadow blocked the ambient lighting coming off the building and its tower. Nick stood a few feet away.

"You hear?" Damascus asked.

"I already knew. John told me about Catherine a couple months ago. What are you two doing up here?"

"Saved Roy from Locus and Janus, the demons he burned," Damascus said. "But back up just a damn minute. Is this something else no one has bothered to tell Noory?"

Nick gave an exasperated sigh. "She's young, okay? She'd go over there thinking she could just barge in and demand her mother back, and we know it doesn't work that way."

Roy nodded. "You *did* just finish telling me that," he said to Damascus. The warrior-priest placed his hand on his chest. "I recall being called a hypocrite a few minutes ago for the same infraction." He looked out at the twinkling city below them. "All the collective power we have between us, and we haven't figured out how to help Catherine. I offered her my life when she came to kill me. She wouldn't take it."

Nick shook his head. "Damn, Roy. Well, right now, we *can* save someone. That vandalizing girl is still about to get her ass killed." Nick looked to Damascus. "Care to join us?"

"Yeah, but not because I've gone soft. If we catch a bad guy, I get kill him, right?"

"No!" Roy said.

"Maybe," Nick said simultaneously before placing his hands on both their shoulders, and the three of them disappeared into the city below.

Chapter 10

Noory and Nick walked down West Peachtree Street. The cool morning would soon give way to a hot day. For now, everything felt right because Nick was beside her. She had her favorite coffee in hand, strong with heavy cream, a little sugar, and a sprinkle of cinnamon. She was headed in to do work that felt meaningful. Some days, she remembered to put her quest for eternity aside and appreciate the present. Nick had been coming to the shelter with her more and more often. She knew he was holding back when he looked at their financials. He had a head for money and thus never lacked it. Since he'd been visiting, many sentences started with, "Why don't I just . . . ?" followed by "get more sheets, food, computers," you name it.

And why not let him? He had the means—though no one would know it today as he was dressed down in jeans and a fitted t-shirt that hugged his muscled chest and abs in all the right ways. But his gift giving made her feel . . . what did it make her feel?

"Good morning, Ava," Noory said as she and Nick stepped through the door.

Nick nodded at Ava and smiled. Ava blushed even though wasn't after him. She was engaged to a wonderful man who she was crazy about. Ducking her head, she focused on her paperwork. Seeing how another woman reacted to Nick made her want to take him into the storage closet and . . . *okay, focus.*

Evan walked into the center wearing an old pair of jeans and a sweatshirt. He surveyed Nick's clothing and relief washed over his face. It occurred to Noory he didn't want to look like a pauper in front of his new mentor, and he relaxed once he realized Nick was dressed casually.

"You're up early," Nick said to him.

Noory watched Evan's face freeze as he tried to figure out how to answer Nick. He clearly yearned for his approval. His mother had shared with her that Evan had never known his father. She decided to rescue him with something Nick would love. "Evan walks his mother to the bus stop every morning. Isn't that the most responsible, mature thing you've *ever* heard?"

"It certainly is. She's very lucky to have such a wonderful son."

"Thank you," he said beaming. He shot a glance out the window.

Noory said, "Grace will be in around three today."

"Oh, hmm. Whatever." He blushed and then turned to go back into the boys' side of the center.

God love him, Noory thought. She picked up her coffee cup and took a drink. "Ack. This is getting cold. I'll go pop it in the microwave."

Ava looked up. "You can't. Remember? It's broken."

Nick said, "Look. Why don't I just—"

Noory turned and glared at him.

"What? Damn it, Noory. What good is having the means to help if it just sits there?" He lowered his voice. "You're being stubborn."

She blinked and looked at Ava as she stifled a laugh and pretended to concentrate even harder on her paperwork. Noory didn't buy it for a second. "Fine," Noory said. "Go ahead."

Nick walked into the kitchen. She followed, knowing he would order them a microwave plus a few additional things. Anytime she opened the door to let him help with one item, he snuck in three others. He sprinted through any opening he could. It was actually sweet. So why did it bother her so much?

"Just the microwave," she said.

He looked up at her. Busted. "Stop me, then."

"Excuse me?"

"You heard me." He stood up straighter and crossed his arms over his chest. "What are you going to do when the items show up? You gonna say, 'No. Sorry kids. You can't have nice things in this shelter because my pride is on the line.'? Is that where you're at?"

"My pride?"

Nick nodded.

They stared at each other. "You arrogant ass," she said, not knowing what else to say.

He was unfazed. He'd lived too damn long for most of what she said to bother him. It was hard to have a decent argument with someone like that, especially now that he was sober and clear-headed.

He said, "Look, I know you like the challenge of making all this work on your own. I get it, but you told me about stacks and stacks of paperwork and countless hours spent applying for grants to keep this place running, sleepless night wondering if you would have to close your doors, and now I'm here with money to burn, and you turn it down? Besides, do you have any idea how good it feels to be able to make a difference when it doesn't include violence, death, or the kind of destruction that scours my soul like steel wool? Come on. Try and see it from my perspective. Please."

She suddenly felt a little selfish. "Okay. I get it. Have at it."

"Thank you," he said softly and leaned in to kiss her forehead. "More than that, thank you for letting me be part of your world."

She leaned into him and savored the warmth coming off his body. She'd given some ground in her world. Now he would have to give some in his. She laid her head on his shoulder and spoke into his ear. She'd been waiting for the right time to bring it up, afraid he'd try and talk her out of it. "I got that appointment with Madam Boudreaux."

She felt his muscles stiffen. To his credit he took a deep breath, exhaled, and spoke. "Okay. I'm with you. Have you told John yet?"

"No. Promise me you won't. He'll try to stop me."

"I won't, but he loves you so much. He just wants to protect you. We all do."

"I know," she said with a smile. "And I appreciate it, but there is one thing none of you can protect me from and you know it: time. That's why I'm going to see her. You said she was legit." Noory knew she was saying it out loud to soothe her own nerves as much as his. She wouldn't say it to him, but her excursions into immortality with Damascus had rattled her.

"I truly think she is, but that still doesn't mean she can deliver. It just means I don't think she's a danger and she might have a genuine gift."

"Then I'll take it." She tried to sound confident, but she wasn't sure he was buying it.

She barely did.

Chapter 11

They waited on the front porch of the old house as minutes ticked by. Sitting in weathered rocking chairs, they watched as the Spanish moss swayed in the tree branches that overhung the veranda. It was mid-March, and New Orleans hadn't reached the stifling, sticky, dog days it would by June. For now, it was a pleasant 70 degrees with a slight breeze, but it all seemed lost on Noory. Nick watched her knee bump up and down. "It's okay. No matter what, we still have each other."

She nodded and smiled at him, but he knew it wasn't really enough for her. Not anymore. She wanted it all.

A tingle raced up his brain stem. *Not. Now.* He tried ignoring it as the tension built. He palmed the back of his neck then quickly put his hand down when Noory looked at him.

She said, "You're being called. Go. I can handle this. You know exactly where I am. It's not like I'm far away or you don't know the address, right?"

"Yeah, but still. Things can go south quickly depending on what she has you do in there. She might have toxic chemicals or spells that render you motionless."

"We researched Madam Boudreaux. She has an impeccable reputation. Remember?"

"Yeah. How about you just don't go in without me? Tell her you'll pay however much she'd like to wait until I get back. Blame it on your overprotective boyfriend."

She smiled. "I will, and I love you."

He put his arms around her and kissed her. "I'll be back just as soon as I can."

He looked around and saw no witnesses or cameras as he faded out of sight with the image of Noory on the porch fixed in his mind, a weight on his chest.

He materialized behind a building in the French Quarter. His sudden appearance scared off three rats and one cat in the alley but the pimp smacking the young prostitute barely seemed to notice. Nick beat him unconscious within a matter of seconds and tossed him in the bin with the trash before the woman moved from where she'd stood frozen.

"You need help," he said.

Blood poured from her nose as she nodded. She looked dazed. Stoned. He was never happy about such a thing but thought in this instance, it might actually work to his advantage. If she remembered traveling through the between realms with him later, she'd likely have no choice but to chalk it up to being high. He placed a hand on her shoulder, and they materialized behind the Family Services building in seconds. The girl promptly vomited.

Nick jumped back to avoid the spatter. "Feel better?"

"Yes," she said through the wreck her face had become.

He pulled a handkerchief from his pocket and handed it to her, walked her into the building, told the receptionist at the front desk what had happened, and left while the woman was busy calling an ambulance and a social worker, and tsking and fussing over the girl's pitiable state.

Once outside, Nick called the authorities to let them know who was lying unconscious in what particular dumpster and exactly why. No sooner had he disconnected than his phone rang. The number on the screen was Grace.

She didn't even say hello before she shouted, "Noory's in danger! Hurry!"

Adrenaline raced through Nick as he materialized inside the home of the voodoo practitioner. Papers and feathers from broken charms fluttered to the floor. He had missed them by mere seconds. He heard a screen door slam in a back room. Madam Boudreaux raced down the steps of her back porch. Nick traveled quickly into the other realm and popped out in front of her. He leaned to the side so their skulls wouldn't crack, and his body would take the brunt of it. She crashed into him. Hard.

"Oof!" she grunted before hitting the ground. She landed flat on her back in the patchy new spring grass and stared up at him with wild eyes. She began speaking in her thick Cajun accent. "Forgive me, Saint Nicholas. My magic is strong. The strongest there is. But theirs is stronger. They took her."

"You didn't have to do this! God! Who took her? Did you recognize them?"

"I did not."

Nick looked at the tree line as if Noory's captors might have disappeared into it.

As if reading his mind, she continued. "You won't find them that way. They appeared and disappeared just as you did. They've been holding my grandson for days behind wards I cannot penetrate." She broke eye contact with him and looked away.

Pity rose in his chest, and he reached out a hand to help her up. She took it and spoke as she stood. "I tried everything before selling out the scion." She reached into the neckline of her dress and pulled out a Miraculous medal, a medal of the Virgin Mary. "I revere the Holy Family and fear for my soul now that I've done this horrible thing." She sobbed.

A little boy stepped out onto the porch, looking confused.

"Vansant!" she cried and raced onto the porch to embrace him.

She asked Vansant one question after another, but his memory had been wiped clean. Nick didn't feel like badgering the boy anyway. He was so little. Couldn't have been more than seven.

Nick wrestled with his anger toward Boudreaux. She was just protecting her family, and he sensed no deception in her words. He followed her onto the porch. "At least help me figure out who took her, and I'll leave you be."

She nodded.

They sat at her kitchen table, Vansant by her side, and Nick asked, "How do you know who I am?"

"All the legitimate practitioners know who you are, and your woman, and John the Disciple. We hear rumors about a Lazarus priest, but we haven't quite figured that one out yet. Don't worry, we guard your truths just like your Templar brothers do. Serious practitioners don't run their mouths to civilians." She looked at him intently, not as if she expected to coax him to reveal his secrets, but as if by looking at him long enough, she wouldn't have to.

Nick ran his hands over his face. "Phone records?"

"You're welcome to look at my phone." She took it from her dress pocket and handed it to him. "But every time they called, it would wipe clean the moment they hung up, as if there had never been a call at all. I'm an open book. Any question. Anything I can tell you, I will." She showed him the days they had called, and that there were no remaining records.

"There's someone I'd like to invite here to see if he can get a read on whatever energy residue might be left," Nick said. "He can trace smells, that kind of thing. With your permission." It galled Nick to ask her. She didn't ask him and Noory before setting them up, but it wasn't her fault, and he was about to invite Damascus into her home.

"A demon?"

"Yes."

"Normally, I would never allow it, but I owe you after what happened. I don't want my grandson around him though. Will you transport him to his mother first?"

"People tend to get sick the first time they transport."

"They just transported him here somehow and he seems fine. I didn't hear a car pull up and drop him off. Did you?"

"No." Nick tilted his head to the side. "Whoever was holding him has someone like me then."

"Seems so." She nodded.

After taking Vansant home and making a call to Atlanta, Nick arrived back in Madam Boudreaux's kitchen with Damascus.

"Madam," Damascus said with an elegant bow.

"Humpf." Clearly the woman didn't care for having a demon in her home, which made Damascus' smile even broader.

Nick whispered. "The claws stay in. Don't get cute."

"Hadn't planned on it. We don't have time. Our girl's missing."

"What is it with you and—"

"Well, fuck me sideways!" Damascus exclaimed as he inhaled deeply, and his eyes went wide.

"Language, demon!" Madam Boudreaux slammed her hand down on her dining room table.

Damascus waved a dismissive hand at the woman. He walked from the kitchen into the living room. "They were standing here. Right here." He closed his eyes, waved his hands toward his face as if bringing the scent to him, and inhaled.

"Can you see them?" she asked.

"Almost," Damascus said. "Their scent leaves such an imprint. It always amazes me that humans barely smell it. How you people function is beyond me."

"Do you know who it is?" Nick asked.

"Oh, yes." Damascus grinned broadly and looked at Nick with a maniacal gleam in his eye. "*And we're going to burn these fuckers to the ground.*"

CHAPTER 12

Damascus and Nick stood in Madam Boudreaux's living room as she spoke a blessing over them. Despite the genuineness of her prayer, Nick couldn't help but notice the woman's sly smile as Damascus squirmed while she invoked the Father, Son, and Holy Spirit. She really didn't like the cussing demon in her home and was determined to show him who was in control. Nick placed a hand on Damascus' shoulder to leave but decided to ask Madam Boudreaux some more questions. They couldn't go storming the castle to save Noory without a plan. Nick looked at Damascus and gestured to Boudreaux's couch. He was beginning to realize the two liked pushing each other's buttons and wanted a conversation uninterrupted by it.

"May I ask you a couple of questions?" Nick asked. He doubted she would turn him down given how bad she felt about being part of Noory's disappearance, but she could also clam up if he didn't remain respectful.

"Of course," she said.

"If a magical practitioner could grant eternal life, wouldn't they do it for themselves, or do it for just a few people, charge a king's ransom, and then retire?"

Her answer surprised him. "Do you know why I'm renowned for having powerful magic?" she asked.

"I assume it's because your spells actually work."

"That's true, but I've never cast one that I didn't *foresee* working."

"You're a psychic?"

"Somewhat. If I can't see a fate either way, I don't take the client. If I don't see the outcome the client asks for, I don't cast."

"So, there is no magic in you. You simply see the future?"

"No, son. There's magic." Her eyes took on a dangerous glint as the hairs on the back of Nick's neck stood on edge. She reached into her pocket, grabbed a little pouch with dried herbs, and sprinkled some on the table. Speaking a few words in a language he was unfamiliar with—and he knew most of them by this point—she moved her hand in a circle, and a small tornado formed from the herbs. She continued swirling and chanting as it traversed the room, ruffling curtains and shaking the dishes in the China cabinet, until it came back to settle on the table as a pile of herbs again. "I believe I work in connection with the will of God. I pray before I go searching for the future."

Damascus had been sitting on her couch, picking lint off his nice suit, obviously pretending not to listen. "Pft!" he scoffed.

"Ridicule all you want, demon, but you are also a tool in the hands of God. Like it or not, doesn't matter." Madam Boudreaux held Damascus' eyes as if they were communicating wordlessly. Nick would've loved to have known what was passing between them. Judging by Damascus' countenance, he'd lost his bravado and sobered dramatically. Whatever he'd seen in Boudreaux's gaze was powerful enough that he didn't look away or mock again. After a beat or two, the woman turned to face Nick once more.

"So, if you were going to cast for Noory, then she has a future as an eternal?" Nick asked.

"A very likely one. Yes. But there are several futures. I think that one is *most* likely. It would be wise if you kept that information to yourselves. It's *her* journey."

"So, were you going to pretend to cast something?"

"Oh, there is indeed a casting for long life that I believe would have set the correct energy field around her to make her journey toward that future easier. None of the paths I see on the way to this destiny are smooth. Not by a long shot, but she will take them. That one was not born for the easy road."

"Was she always destined for this path?"

"Yes and no. It's an irritating answer, I'll grant you that, but if it were anything other, there would be no free will. She could change her mind tomorrow, and the tree of life would sprout new branches with different destinies."

"I'm familiar with this philosophy."

She nodded.

"Thank you, ma'am," Nick said. "We better go."

Madam Boudreaux spoke again, "I was going to tell Noory about a young, powerful psychic in your circle, but I think you may know her as well. If she ever needs help, you tell her to come see me. She is . . . an unexpected turning point, functioning outside of anything that was supposed to be."

Nick was curious. "You wouldn't have been able to predict her if you'd looked for her future before she . . . changed?"

"I'm not so sure I would have. No. I don't care to admit to that," she conceded, "but no."

"Is she okay? Did you notice her because she's in danger?"

"Oh, she's much better off than she was! I see that. It's just that, as I was focusing on your Noory, she was like a spot of grace burning bright, off to the side, that I couldn't ignore. So, I shifted my gaze a little, just to take a look."

Nick smiled despite his grief over Noory. The woman had guessed Grace's name whether she knew it or not. "I'll tell Grace she has a mentor in New Orleans."

Madam Boudreaux bowed her head. "You may do *exactly* that."

A moment later, Damascus and Nick disappeared and stood in Nick's living room.

Nick's expression was stone cold and ready wreak havoc as he turned to Damascus. "Who has Noory?"

"Those fuckers at Second Sight," Damascus said as his long claws slipped free.

CHAPTER 13

The moment Noory came to, she leaped to her feet, felt lightheaded, and stumbled to the wall before sliding down to the floor. She looked around her and saw that she was in a room with a familiar wire mesh lining the walls. *Fucking Faraday cage.*

She knew she shouldn't be feeling lightheaded either unless someone had messed with her big time. She recovered from injuries much quicker than the average person. So, what had happened to her? She turned her attention inward. What was amiss in her body? The insides of her elbows ached. She looked down at them. Someone had drawn her blood. Lots of it apparently.

A door-size panel in the wall opened, and a man stepped inside who looked to be in his early twenties, in human years anyway, though she doubted he was human. He was giving off a vibe that made the hairs on the back of her neck stand up. His eyes were brown in a way that leaned toward bronze, which they shouldn't. His auburn hair seemed to have strands of spun gold here and there. His skin had an ever-so-subtle glow, as if energy radiated off it. He wore a lab coat and carried a bottle of electrolyte-infused water. He sat it on the floor. "I'm Lorien."

She didn't respond, didn't owe him anything.

"You need to drink this. You've lost a lot of blood."

"Lost? Don't you mean it was stolen? You didn't get my permission to take it." She lifted a weak arm and flipped him off, leaving the insulting salute in the air for maximum effect until her arm began to tremble.

"So, it's okay for you to keep something for yourself that has the ability to help others? And you consider yourself the 'good guys'?"

The fucker was making air quotes at her. She wanted to break his fingers. Only one person was allowed to make air quotes for her, and he had long claws that made the gesture both funny and scary, and he wasn't technically a person either.

"So, draining me like a vampire is permissible?"

"Don't speak about my kind like you know us," he said in a low, clipped tone between gritted teeth.

This one has anger issues. Noory just watched him, knowing now wasn't the time to engage, weak as she was.

"I've never bitten you, and I've watched you from the shadows on more than one occasion." He lifted one side of his lip to reveal a subtly pointed tooth. He rolled the bottle of water across the pristine floor to her.

"I won't drink that. I'm sure it's drugged."

"The cap is sealed. Check it."

"You could definitely get drugs into a sealed bottle."

"You're dehydrated. *Noory*, it isn't drugged. You need the water. Please, I'm not lying to you."

He was right about one thing: if she didn't drink something, she'd never make it out of there. She was seeing stars as they spoke. They'd drained her hard.

"I'll come back to check on you in a little while. Drink the water. Get some rest."

She opened the bottle and drank it all, then looked around her. There was a couch, pillow, lamp, and a folding screen. She got up slowly and walked behind it to find there was a toilet and sink on the other side. The only mirror was polished stainless steel. They weren't taking chances with glass. Smart. She absolutely would've broken it to make a shiv.

She looked into the mirror and even in the dim reflection, she could see the dark circles beneath her eyes in the pale face staring back at her. The realization set in that the situation at Madam Boudreaux's had likely been a trap right from the start.

After splashing some water on her face, she went to lie down on the couch. She knew Nick, John, and Father Roy would be looking for her. In the meantime, she was at Second Sight. She was sure of it. This would at least be a chance to find out what they were up to. An organization that big, which had ties to the crazy box they'd destroyed last year, *and* also had employed her biological father . . . she couldn't help but wonder if they might know what happened to her mother. Oh, yeah. They had to know something about what happened to her. Why she never made it to purgatory. Why the entity that had inhabited her father had been looking for Catherine before it was banished, and he died.

Noory woke when a buzzer sounded, and a tray of food appeared through a slot in the door. According to the clock by her lamp, she'd dozed for nearly an hour. She hadn't meant to fall asleep at all. She was sure they'd drugged her. She had a memory of fighting them outside Boudreaux's house, but not much else until she'd woken in that room. She drank a glass of orange juice, ate a few bites of an apple, and downed some vegetable soup, waiting between every bite and sip, and repeated the process until she was convinced nothing was drugged.

Not long after she finished eating, Lorien walked in and asked her to follow. She was thinking of a hundred ways to hurt him but did as he asked. If she were to get free, she couldn't stubbornly refuse and stay in the room forever. She was also still too weak to fight. He led her down a series of hallways as she tried to remember every turn, every door, and the distance between them.

Finally, they made their way into a lab. There were rows of cupboards, computers, refrigerators, and filing cabinets, and in the center of the room stood roughly six and a half feet and hundreds of pounds of pure muscle. His dark hair was cropped short. His eyes were gray, like storm clouds, under heavy brows. "Sit," he ordered.

"No," she said.

"You don't make the rules around here, Princess."

"I'm not a princess, and I don't follow orders."

"Look, you're here. You aren't leaving. You may as well get that through your head right now. You could spend months or even years fighting us, and it will only lead to frustration."

Noory laughed. "You're precious."

"Your mother isn't allowed to leave. You won't either. We know where everyone you've ever loved is."

"My mother? My mother is dead." She felt her adrenaline spike. *Breathe. Damn it. He's fucking with you.*

"The fairy tales they let kids believe these days."

Noory saw red. She'd missed out on the love of a mother her whole life. Watched other children spend time with their moms and went home and cried, hiding it from John, protecting him, while no one was there to comfort her. She felt the energy in the room shift, crackle, coalesce and come to do her bidding. She'd not felt such power since the night on the rooftop when Blake had bought Grace last year. She unleased three quick punches to his face before he could register that he'd even been hit. Blood poured from his nose and flung from her fists after the last strike. For a moment she saw inside his mind, an occurrence that had only happened a few times in her life. He was stunned. He hadn't believed she had the power to hurt him. She realized as angry as she thought she'd been about the way her mother was taken from her; she had only scratched the surface.

The vampire was on her a second later, dragging her across the room. "Enough, Scion. It's only a test. Means nothing," he said softly.

"Means nothing?" she seethed.

She shifted in his arms and saw his irises had gone black at the sight of the blood on her fists, but he glanced away.

"No! It's not okay to take my mother from me. My entire life. How dare you. How fucking dare, you!"

The enormous man wiped the blood with his sleeve as Noory struggled in the vice-like grip of the vampire.

"Come at me! Let's go!" she screamed at the giant.

The door to the lab opened, and a woman with dark hair and blue eyes stepped inside. She was dressed all in black and wore a pair of combat boots similar to Noory's. There was something regal in her bearing, yet Noory detected a flicker of raw emotion that was just as quickly concealed like the falling of a heavy theater curtain upon a stage.

Recognition poured over Noory as her brain raced to catch up and deny all at once. *This can't be.* She remembered the few pictures she'd seen of her mother, sometimes blurred as she looked at them through tears. *Dear God, she's alive.* Noory recalled the information Nick had brought back from his visit to purgatory when he had consulted with his friend Willow on the other side. Willow had said her mother had never passed through purgatory, which had made no sense to Noory.

The woman pointed at the beast of a man with blood pouring down his chin. "Jericho, leave us." The man yanked a towel from the counter, held it to his nose, and glared at the woman on the way out. Why had he not counterattacked, and why did he take orders from her *mother*?

"Noory don't allow yourself to be baited like that. Be above it."

Noory's heart slammed against her chest, her blood roared in her ears, she sagged in Lorien's arms, and felt as if she were about to hit the floor. She couldn't breathe, couldn't move.

Her mother stood in front of her. Just staring into her face.

CHAPTER 14

Catherine looked at Noory. It felt so surreal to finally be sitting in the same room with her daughter. They sat together, unaccompanied, in the large breakroom at Second Sight, drinking tea. The orange and hibiscus drifted from her cup and gave her something to do with her hands as she held onto the little tab and string attached to the bag and slowly dunked it into the water. She couldn't take her eyes off her. She was beautiful.

The pictures from all the years of hacking Noory's phone hadn't done her justice. Even spying on her from a distance from time to time hadn't been anything like seeing her up close, and like most things in life, it wasn't the way she'd envisioned it all these years. She'd always thought a reunion with her daughter would be when she was free, reunited with her family, and there would be hugs and joy. Certainly, John would be there. Always. After all, he was eternal.

Even though it wasn't her fault, would Noory blame her anyway? She'd learned to hide her feelings in this place, from the jackals that sought to exploit her love for her family, from those who would see it as a weakness, from the empaths who reported back to Malachi, their leader. But Noory deserved to know how she felt. "I spent every moment trying to find a way to get back to you, but I could only ensure your safety by agreeing to stay here. I've thought about you every single day. You're my first thought when my eyes open every morning and the last thought before I go to sleep." Catherine paused, swallowed hard and continued. "I'm sorry I failed you. I got weak last year after I heard about the cell tower incident. I was afraid they'd lied to me about you surviving that fall. So, I came to check on you, and this is what happened."

Noory shook her head. "I didn't see you. I—"

"No. I couldn't let you see me. If you knew I was alive, if John knew, this would happen." She gestured to Noory. "I got weak."

"But you're so strong. Even the muscle here fears you. Couldn't you have gone to John earlier? He would have helped you. He's eternal. They couldn't kill him. You wouldn't have to worry about his safety."

Anguish poured through Catherine. This was the conversation she feared. "I've seen them kill an immortal. It *can* be done." She shivered as the screams of the nymph echoed through her mind.

"But maybe with Nick and John together . . . he knows so many powerful people."

"Trust me, Noory. I've gone through every scenario, every way . . . I was desperate to get back to you. They always knew where you were, showing me how easy it would be to bring you here and keep you. You'd have had no childhood, no chance at a normal headspace if you'd had to grow up behind these walls."

"Why bring me in now?"

"I'm in breach of the terms of my contract with Second Sight. They leave you alone as long as I offer my services and stay away from you, but when I came to check on you, I failed. They caught me."

She could tell Noory was afraid to ask what kind of services. She feared Noory already knew. "They use my blood, in part, to help keep some of their clients alive, much longer than they should be."

"They have the secret to making immortals?"

Shit, Catherine thought when she noted the hopefulness on Noory's face. "I know that look. Loving an immortal has made you susceptible. Avoid it if you can. The serum is very addictive." Even as she said it, she already knew; Noory was in love and would take it to be with Nick. Everyone kept a close eye on her relationship with Nicholas. If Noory knew just how much, she'd be mortified. The implications were fascinating, especially what kind of offspring the two might make if they were even able to procreate. Would their DNA allow it? If there was one good thing about being held there, it was that she had taken their immortality serum and now had more time to find a way back to John. She had no doubt Noory would try to do the same with Nick.

"They will also send you into the field now and then when they need someone taken out. They love their tests of loyalty. The good news is it normally isn't anyone you'd mind killing. They're all as terrible as the people holding us here."

"Assassin?" Noory asked. Her daughter didn't look too taken aback by what she heard.

Catherine didn't know whether to be happy or sad about that. She decided a healthy dose of both was in order. "Yes." She kept waiting for Noory to call her a monster. "I may not be able to get you out of here, but I can teach you to survive this place."

Noory nodded with a grim smile. "I could stand to burn off some aggression."

Catherine was standing across from Noory in the big gym. "I've seen you fight," Catherine said. She tapped the laptop sitting on a table to their left and pointed. They saw an overhead view of her fight last year. It was shortly after she'd met Nick and he'd followed Grace's call of distress when Grace had sold herself to the highest bidder. They watched from the angle of a camera that must have been mounted to the building and pointed toward the huge terrace. Her hair lifted off her shoulders, and outdoor furniture slid toward her as energy swirled about her. The lightbulbs above her head broke and rained down a fine spray of glass like snow over her hair. They watched as she broke the wrist of the man who'd tried to strangle her and buy Grace.

"Did you see inside his mind?" Catherine asked.

"Yes, but Nick and I had it out on the roof that night when I told him I hated seeing inside the minds of the people I fought and didn't want to do it anymore. I didn't fight unless they were very bad news, which meant there was something inside their heads that I did not want to see."

Catherine nodded and spoke softly. "If you're anything like me, it's almost too much to bear."

"Yes," Noory answered.

"You're marked now. You must embrace all your power. There is no

halfway anymore. You *will* look into their eyes and turn into the aveng-
ing scion war hammer you were put on this Earth to be. You will see
things that will disturb you, but in equal measure, you will see things you
can use against them. You will grab hold of that, and then you will shove
it up their ass will the heat of a thousand suns. Do you understand me?"

"Yes." Her ascent was quiet but clear.

"There is no other way now. Not here." Noory still hadn't called her a
monster. The fact that she understood made this easier.

Catherine went over the footage of her fight, correcting her form, giving her suggestions, and streamlining everything from the moment she
appeared on scene. "If you allow yourself to see into their mind, you'll
be predicting their next move. You're so worried about seeing the evil
in their heads that you're forgetting about the advantage. You'll know
where every punch is coming from, every kick, where every knife and
gun is hidden on their body. Do not miss the opportunity to get every
ounce of information from these sick sons of bitches that you can. *Use
them* like they used the people you are defending and *take them out.*"

Catherine paused and then yelled, "Jericho!" A door opened, and
the behemoth from the lab walked into the gym with a bruised face from
the battering Noory had given him earlier. "He hates you now, and he's
ready for revenge. Get in there." Catherine tapped the side of her head,
looked at Jericho and pointed him toward Noory.

"What the fuck, Mom?" she said as he ran at her with a wild snarl.

Noory crouched, looked into his eyes, and the lights in the room
began to flicker.

CHAPTER 15

Noory saw images of Jericho strangling the life from her. He reveled in it. So, he'd go for her throat if given the chance. She ducked a heartbeat before reaching him and pivoted her right foot around him and drove an elbow into his ribs as she went. He grunted and grabbed her arm to pull her to him and tried to twist her arm around her back. She felt joy surge through him at the idea of causing her pain. Before he could, she landed a solid kick to his knee, and he screamed. She backed away, hoping it would end now that he had to have known she was reading him, but it was just that pause that cost her. He slammed his fist into her gut and knocked the breath from her body.

"No hesitation," Catherine yelled from the sidelines.

Now anger welled in her for her newfound mother too. They'd barely had a chance to reunite before she threw her at this man who was twice her size. What had happened to her to make her so . . . so . . . what? Hard? Unfeeling? A smack across the face made her ears ring, and the joy he experienced made her angrier than her mother's training session possibly could. He'd not hit her with a closed fist like a man who at least respected his opponent. No. He'd slapped her, open-palmed, like an errant girlfriend or wife who'd taken up with an abusive psycho.

Sparing a glance at the chair she'd vacated moments before, she willed it to her. She'd never been able to use her energy quite like this. Telekinesis wasn't something she could just manipulate, but whatever was happening now was something else entirely. Maybe her mother was on to something when she told her to open her mind to her enemies' thoughts, maybe it opened her mind to the energy of the entire room and everything in it. Before it had only happened as a byproduct of battle, like on the rooftop last year, but if it could happen at will . . .

The back of the chair hit her palm, she swung it and heard an audible crack as it hit the side of Jericho's head. He stumbled and shook his head as if disoriented but wouldn't go down. The behemoth stuck out a foot to brace himself and shouted, "I'll fucking kill you. You arrogant little bitch!" He began stomping toward her.

"Jericho. Stop!" Catherine said. He completely froze. His chest heaved in and out. Blood ran from the side of his face and down his neck. Still, he didn't move. "Jericho, go to medical," Catherine said.

Jericho turned and walked out of the room as if in a trance.

"What the hell?" Noory breathed. "Did you hypnotize him or something?"

"No. He has an implant that responds to my voice."

"Well, that makes no sense. Why can't they just put one of those in your brain to ensure your loyalty. They could make you do anything." Horror flooded Noory. They could make her do *anything* with a device like that.

"It doesn't work on us. They've already tried." Catherine lifted her hair and turned so that Noory could see a scar at the base of her skull. "Our brains reject it. Even some human brains reject it. Not his."

"That explains the perpetual anger. That would piss me off too." Her mother using this man to challenge her pissed her off as well. And as nasty as he was, she didn't like her using a human in general to force him to fight her. It went against free will.

As if reading her mind, Catherine said, "Noory, he was an abusive psycho before. The chip didn't do that. He is what he is, and I can't change it."

Noory thought she'd seen so much in her life while taking care of the kids at the shelter, but this place was endlessly frustrating with its blurring lines of right and wrong and things she couldn't change . . . wasn't sure she *should* change. Jericho didn't need to be out on the streets unchecked, but this didn't feel right either.

If—no, *when*—she finally made her way out of Second Sight and fought to take this place down, was she simply fighting to cut someone like him loose?

She stood there aching all over, but for all the futility she felt, the biggest ache of all was in her heart.

Chapter 16

Sweat poured down Nick's face as he chanted and moved the heavy dragon skull in a counterclockwise motion for the hundredth time while Damascus sat beneath the skull, gazing into the polished cauldron filled with water.

"Anything yet?" Nick asked.

"Nothing, dammit." Damascus sat back and rubbed his eyes. "I've never had this much trouble with a locator spell. I think they may have both her and their headquarters cloaked. In which case, we would have to break both spells. I haven't bumped up against magic this powerful before. If we could just get close enough, we could use an 'unwinding spell' to get in, but we don't have a clue where Second Sight does business in Atlanta."

Nick sat the massive skull down on the floor of Damascus' spelling room in the basement. Relieved to be free of the weight, he shook his arms out. "Robert hasn't given you any clue where the building is?"

"No, just that they have an office in Atlanta, but the one time he had to report to the CEO, he had to go to the Manhattan office. When he came back from the Atlanta office, he couldn't remember exactly where it was. His mind had fuckery upon it. If you go there, you aren't allowed to remember."

Nick's phone vibrated in his pocket. He cringed. He'd been avoiding John. He would pay for it later. He intuited that he should answer it. "It's Grace," he said to Damascus, even before checking the screen.

As soon as he answered, she started speaking. "Something's wrong with Noory."

Nick exhaled. There was no use lying, and maybe she could even help. "Yeah. She's missing."

"When I think about Noory, I get a sick feeling in the pit of my stomach, I see myself when I was a little girl sitting on the steps of the Atlanta Medical Center downtown after my parents died. It was a very foggy night. When I looked up, I saw this dark building with squares like massive steps on the roof leading up to the pinnacle. There were lights coming off every square and hitting the fog. Noory is in that building. I just know it."

"Thank you!" Nick held the phone away and spoke to Damascus. "The office is in Truist Plaza. Grace figured it out."

"Glad I didn't kill her then."

Nick glared at Damascus, feeling thankful for the reminder that the demon in front of him was indeed a demon. He needed the reminders now and then. Lately, he'd come to enjoy his company.

"She was taken, wasn't she?" Grace said. "That's what this feels like. I'm coming with you."

"No, you aren't."

"She's my best friend. You'll need my help."

"She wouldn't want you in danger. End of discussion." Nick dropped the call.

"When are you going to tell John?"

"He'll just slow us down."

"And blame you again."

"Yes."

"I'd say y'all need to have a 'come to Jesus moment,' but that might prove a bit too ironic."

Nick thought for a moment. "We'll tell him just before we go in. That way, if shit goes south, we'll have someone on the outside who knows what's going on but not so soon that he can interfere."

Damascus looked at Nick with admiration and winked. "Calculating bastard. I like it."

Nick texted Grace: *Which floor?*

She replied: *Maybe all the way up. I feel dizzy when I think about it. Screw you for hanging up on me, BTW.*

Nick texted a quick "sorry" back before shoving his phone back in his pocket. "Sounds like it's all the way up top. In the mood for a little recon?"

"Absolutely," Damascus replied with a dangerous glint in his eye. "Gonna go tell John?"

"Well, it's just recon right now."

"Uh, huh."

They looked up some basic security for the building in general and to find out what might be listed on the topmost floors but of course, nothing even resembling an enterprise like Second Sight was listed. Damascus and Nick teleported as high as they could within the building proper without ending up in the utility spaces on the topmost stories and then walked past a series of unmarked doors, one office suite looking much like the next, never seeing anything out of the ordinary.

"It's all cloaked," Damascus said before he began chanting under his breath and moving his index fingers, one over the other, as if there was thread spooling up around them. Finally, he said a little louder, "Unwind."

The entire floor rearranged itself. No longer did they see the bland hallway with furnishings typical of the rest of the tower, but an ornate foyer with double doors containing inlaid wood patterns that looked runic but more archaic than Nick was familiar with and that gave off a soft glow. Damascus pointed at them with a glossy, black, manicured nail and shuddered, "That's some powerful old-school shit, even before my time. We're looking for a back way in."

"How? And won't they have already spotted us?"

Damascus laughed. "You're pretty but not always smart. Can't believe you're just now thinking of that. We've been cloaked since we materialized here. C'mon."

"Yeah, well. At this stage, I just want something to smash so I can get Noory back. I'll leave the finer points to you."

After a few minutes, they found a side door. "I don't sense anyone behind it." Damascus placed his hand over the locking mechanism, and it gave a soft click. They opened the door, stepped inside, and shut the door behind them softly.

Nick shook his head and squeezed his eyes as a wave of . . . something washed over him. He felt . . . heavier somehow. He looked at Damascus, wondering if he felt it as well. Damascus had a questioning look on his face but kept alert.

From the end of the hallway, a tower of muscle rounded the corner and spotted them. He tapped a radio on his shoulder, called for backup, and pulled a pistol from his hip. Nick watched as Damascus spread his hands with intent, but nothing happened. "Shit! My powers are disabled in here."

Nick opened a door on the other side of the hall, and they went inside. As the man got closer, Nick slammed the door into his face. He grabbed the arm with the pistol, Damascus took it, and Nick pummeled the man so fast and hard he didn't make a sound before he slid to the floor unconscious.

"Why didn't you bring a gun yourself?" Damascus asked.

"I like my daggers, and I enjoy a good pummeling. Pretty face aside," he said with a big grin at Damascus. Nick shook his hands out. He didn't remember his joints hurting that badly afterwards. He rubbed his knuckles.

Damascus held the pistol out in front of him, and the two ventured farther down the hallway. They'd only gotten ten feet before they heard footsteps racing their way and saw a corridor before them with no clue which way to go. Now, more footsteps coming from either direction with no way to tell which. Nick felt helpless and longed for a drink. He scrubbed a hand across his face as Damascus turned to look at him, orange irises flaring.

"Fuck," Nick whispered.

"Fuck is right." Damascus looked at him with awe "Your hair is turning gray."

"What?"

"I mean, it's rather distinguished on you." Damascus nodded.

"Hey, geniuses. Over here!" A woman's voice whispered from the left of the corridor.

"Grace! What the hell are you—"

"You wanna scold me or save your ass?" Her eyes were huge as she spared a quick look at Nick before turning to guide them.

They followed her, and the three of them took off running down the corridor.

"How did you even get in here?" Nick asked.

"I started toward this building as soon as I got off the phone with you, and it was like I was being pulled here. I mean, right to this very floor and walked right in. It's as if they, or it, want me here. I know where she is. C'mon."

They continued down the passage, took a left, and entered a door on the right. "Nick!" Noory cried. "What are you doing here? You're going to get in trouble. Please. Take Grace and leave. This place is far too dangerous. Somebody is going to get killed."

"I'm not leaving without you." He wrapped his arms around her and buried his face in her hair. The need for her felt like a visceral thing that threatened to consume him now that he could touch her, hold her.

"I saw my mother," she whispered into his ear in a voice that sounded more vulnerable than anything he'd ever heard from her.

She pulled back and looked at him. "You're not surprised that she's alive?"

Shit. "John asked me not to say anything. I only *just* found out, Noory. I swear. He was afraid you'd come snooping around this place and get yourself caught. It happened anyway. I'm so sorry. Let's get you out of here." She was looking at his hair and reached up and touched a spot next to his eye.

Nick motioned for Damascus and Grace to come over.

"You can't use the Santa travel. It won't work," Damascus said. "If I'm shut down. You are, too, and you've got bigger problems. You're aging fast." Damascus gestured to his face.

"I have to try." He wrapped his arms around all of them and prepared to shift, but Damascus was right. They were stuck. *I should have brought more weapons.*

The panic on Noory's face told him it was bad. "Get him out of here, Damascus." Noory held Nick's hand as a tear dripped off her jaw. Nick looked down. He didn't recognize his own hand. It was wrinkled and had age spots on it. "You weren't born with it. It's just supernatural. A blocking ward with the blackest magic can—"

Pounding began on the door. Now wasn't the time to feel sorry for himself. "Where do those doors lead?" Nick pointed to doors at the back of the room.

"One is a bathroom. The other is a storage closet," Noory said.

The pounding on the door was relentless. Finally, a demon with silvery skin and a scar running down the side of his otherwise handsome face simply materialized through the door.

"Well, this is no fucking fair," Damascus said.

Behind him, Nick heard keys jangle, and a man walked in with the alluring look of a vampire. He hadn't seen one in decades. It was always a little jarring.

The vamp nodded at Damascus. He nodded back in a decidedly neutral way.

"This little show has been interesting," the silver-skinned demon with the scar said. "It broke the monotony of all my paperwork, but I can't monitor this situation all day." Nick remembered where he'd seen the demon. Just before World War Two. He was there when all the munitions' factories were being built. The demon had stoked the war so that investors could line their pockets. It didn't matter those millions died. He was Locus. Spotting opportunities and exploiting them. Otherwise, the maniacal ideas might die before causing too much damage. Not with this sick bastard around. He snaked his way over to Grace.

"She can stay," Locus said as he ran a finger down Grace's cheek. "I sense a kinship. We see what others do not." She smacked his hand away, and the demon pulled his hand back as if he were going to slap her. Before the blow landed and before Nick could make it halfway there, a blur shot across the room and grabbed the demon's arm in mid swing. The vamp apparently had a problem with this opportunistic beast.

Nick watched the vampire-versus-demon standoff. He doubted the vamp knew Grace. At the moment, she appeared to be trying to get a read on him. Locus was certainly bigger than the vamp, so it was a curious thing that the demon didn't engage.

"Don't test me, Lorien," the demon said to him as he dropped his arm and backed away, but the threat lacked any real power, and Lorien *didn't* back away. *Interesting.*

Lorien waved his arm and a whooshing noise sounded behind Nick and Damascus.

"You two need to be going now," Lorien said. "Don't worry, I'll look out for Noory and Grace."

Nick felt his body begin to slide backward despite planting his feet. It was like trying to walk in a hurricane. In his mind, he heard Lorien whisper, *no harm will come to them.* It didn't matter. Promises from a vampire working for an evil corporation holding hostage the woman you loved and a child you'd vowed to protect meant very little.

"Nick!" Noory screamed.

He felt his body being pulled toward the tunnel, and he and Damascus tumbled into the abyss.

<h1 style="text-align:center">Chapter 17</h1>

The beaker Noory threw slammed against the wall, and glass exploded onto the tables and floor. "Where did you send them?" she demanded.

Lorien said, "They're fine. They were just bounced out of the building. They'll wake up in the basement of another building. I saved Nick's life. Another few minutes here, and he would have turned to dust. He's right back to his anti-aging, supernatural self now that he's left our offices. Now calm yourself."

"Don't tell me to calm myself, vampire. I'm being held against my will, you've kidnapped her—" she pointed to Grace "—and you've sent my boyfriend and a friend of mine to God knows where. I don't even know if they're alive. And this jackass needs to keep his hands off Grace before I fucking kill him."

"He won't touch her." Lorien's eyes flashed golden bronze, and he looked at Locus.

"At least send Grace home."

"No!" Grace said.

"Yes. You shouldn't be mixed up in this shit," Noory said.

"I'm where I'm supposed to be."

"You're not making sense."

"She knows where she's supposed to be and when." Locus spoke with his head tilted toward the floor but with his eyes looking at Grace though he spoke to Noory. "You don't see what our kind can."

Noory didn't care for the way the demon looked at Grace or the way Grace responded to him, as if she were interested in what he had to say. Her anger rose to a crescendo. Between being trapped there, being so close to Nick, then having him ripped away, and all the conflicting feelings inside over her mother, she was a powder keg and Locus was lighting the fuse. She turned without a second thought and punched him in the gut. The second he doubled over; she grabbed his head and rammed it onto her raised knee.

In a flash, Lorien was dragging her out of the room as Locus screamed in a language she couldn't decipher. It sounded ancient. "Dammit," Lorien whispered into her ear. "Please don't make me have to drug you."

"Fuck off!" Noory spat as he dragged her down the hallway and into her room. She'd never been in the clutches of someone infected with vampirism before. He was shockingly strong. Grace followed them through the entrance.

He looked at Noory as Grace stood by. "Hate me all you want, but I'm the only friend you've got here." He walked out, closing the door with a thump.

Noory stormed over to the small fridge and retrieved a bottle of water with shaking hands, hoping the mundane task would soothe her frayed nerves and help her think. Muscling her way out of this situation wasn't an option. She drank from it and sat on the bed, staring at the floor. When she spoke again, her tone was admittedly soft, almost defeated. She was too tired to mask it. "Dammit, Grace. What are you doing here?"

Grace sat down on the small rug on the floor beside the bed and started picking at the shag carpet. "Locus was right. I am supposed to be here. It's just something that I know. I can't explain how."

"He's evil. Nothing he says is right."

"Just because he's evil doesn't mean he's always wrong. There are just things I know sometimes."

The list of things Noory had to deal with just kept getting longer. Not only was she stuck here, but the rescue attempt had failed, and she'd had the unsettling experience of watching Nick age rapidly before her eyes. It was terrifying to think he could be gone in minutes. Now she had to worry about Grace, too. And their only ally appeared to be a vampire they couldn't trust. She needed to know more about Lorien and why he said he was their friend.

Chapter 18

Nick walked up the steps to John's house in the late afternoon, his vigor restored and his looks back to their perpetual just-turned-thirty youth but still feeling as if he were ascending the gallows for his own execution. Forced to leave Second Sight without Noory, he'd kept all this from John, allowing more time to pass. This might get ugly.

Dread curled in Nick's gut, making him wish for a drink. He could almost feel the comforting weight of the flask full of ouzo that he'd kept in his pocket for centuries. Now it was gone, and he had to deal with this kind of shit stone cold sober. God, how it sucked.

John seemed to be expecting him, opening the door before Nick knocked. John said nothing but turned and headed to the kitchen. Nick followed.

"Coffee?" John asked.

"Yeah." *At least it will give me something to do with my hands.*

John walked over to the coffee pot, grabbed a cup from the cabinet and poured for Nick. "Something's happened." John said as he set the cup in front of him.

"Yeah." They had repaired their relationship in the past several months. It felt so good to have his friend back. He knew he was about to ruin it, but he had no choice. Nick looked toward the sun-splashed windowsill, enjoying the last few moments of light, of friendship, before he destroyed their relationship again. He inhaled and looked at John. "Noory is at Second Sight."

"Excuse me?" His tone had taken a deadly turn, as had his aura. Dark, hazy red streaked with black poured off him.

"I told her I would go with her on her quest for immortality, since she refused to stop searching. We went to this practitioner down in New Orleans, Madam Boudreaux."

John's eyes went wide. Didn't take much for John to put together the locale and moniker. "Voodoo?"

"She's Haitian, but like many Haitians, she's Catholic with a little Voodoo on the side. Yes."

John exhaled a breath as if he were barely tolerating the conversation. John's demeanor, normally cool under almost any pressure, had gone tight, coiled. Nick would rather be anywhere else.

"Anyway, when we arrived, we were waiting on the porch for her to finish with another client when I got the call of a child in distress. When I returned, Noory was gone, there appeared to have been a scuffle, and on the back lawn lay Madam Boudreaux. She was a wreck. Second Sight was holding her grandson for ransom. Unless she delivered Noory, they would kill him. She's not a bad woman. She felt sick about it, told me everything she knew, and Damascus and I got into Second Sight. We found Noory and unfortunately, they have Grace too."

"My God! You got in? I take it you were not able to get them out?"

"No. I failed. I saw her. She's fine. Well, not fine. She's captive, but not harmed. They opened some sort of vortex or portal, and we were thrown out and ended up in a storage room in the bottom of an entirely different building in moments. Damascus couldn't even remember what building we'd been in. Somehow, I was able to retain it. The magic they employ is unlike anything I've ever encountered. John, you can't go in there. I started aging the moment I stepped through the door." Nick shuddered as he remembered the joint pain, the withered hands, the fatigue that got more wearying by the moment. Worst of all was the way Noory looked at him. She was so scared. "Another few minutes in that place, and I would have turned to dust. They've got it warded in layers. I've never had anything, in all my existence, do such a thing to me. I didn't even think it was possible."

The silence settled in around them, oppressive. This was John's daughter. Nick had sworn to him that he would protect her. That was their understanding. Instead, she'd been taken by the same evil that had taken Catherine from him. All John's worst nightmares were coming true. Right now.

"Just to make sure I've got this straight: Noory's been dabbling in black magic. She's stuck at Second Sight now. You're working with a demon instead of coming to *me* for help, and you just walk in here and tell me my daughter has been devoured by the same damn beast that took my wife?"

Nick had no idea what to say to the man. He felt he deserved whatever John threw at him. Hopefully, he'd even throw a fist. At this point, that might make him feel better. He murmured, "Yes. I'm so sorry."

"You're sorry? You should have come straight to me. What in God's name made you think it was okay for you to keep this from me? This is my daughter. My life. How dare you."

John's words sliced through him like a razor.

"I'm sorry. I failed everyone."

"Please. You keep all of this from me," John leaned forward, his brows furrowed and an arm outstretched to tap his index finger on the old farm table as he spoke, "then it takes Roy days to tell me that Catherine, *my wife*, came here to scout out how to assassinate him. Why does everyone hide things from me?"

Nick didn't know why, maybe he was just angry that he'd failed or too emotionally exhausted for a rant from John, but he told him the truth, or at least the truth on the tip of his tongue. "If you don't want people hiding things from you, then stop making us feel like we need to."

Nick got up and walked out the door without another word.

Chapter 19

Damascus walked out of the club and into the cool spring night with a beautiful human on his arm. The young man smelled of amber, cloves, masculine musk, and dried sweat tinged with alcohol from an evening of dancing beneath the flashing lights of the club. Damascus thought about Robert less and less these days, and this beautiful man could help with that. Though he couldn't deny he still loved Robert, something inside him had shifted. Robert no longer controlled his every waking thought.

"Tell your friend to head home," a deep, commanding voice said from the shadows of the alley to his right.

He knew *that* voice. Damascus forced the several inches of claws back into his fingers; they'd instinctively come out at the threat. He wasn't looking to scare off his date before he had a chance to find out if he was worth sharing any of this with him. He turned to find John dressed for work and standing in the entrance to the alley just past the club he'd exited with his friend. A beautiful friend. One he didn't want a scowling storm cloud in an APD uniform scaring off.

"Justin, honey, I'll meet you at your loft in a little bit."

His companion spared a worried glance for him, gave John an evil eye—cute, he had no clue who he was dealing with—before heading off into the night. *Bold. That one might be a keeper.*

"What can I do for you, John?"

"It's pretty simple. Stay away from my family."

"I mean them no harm." He wondered just how much the man knew about Noory and whether Nick had told him everything. These people had serious communication issues. So, he said as little as possible. May as well let John tell him what he knew.

"No harm, huh? You went after one of Noory's kids last fall. You and Nick both failed at getting her back from Second Sight when she was right there in your grasp, and neither of you bothered to tell me she was in trouble in the first place."

Damascus wanted to wipe the smug look off this man's face but instead, he took a deep breath. "I recall Nick *did* come to you, right after he found out Noory smelled of dark magic. Remember that? He came to you when he was scared.

"But yes, sometimes those you love do hide things from you. Noory's been doing it. The real question here is why are you not at home looking in the mirror and asking yourself why people are keeping things from you, instead of running off my tasty boyfriend? Come on, handsome. You and I are ancient and smart enough to know when we are kidding ourselves. If we keep getting in the same situation with different people, then the one common denominator is . . . ?" Damascus looked at John and opened his palm like an answer was forthcoming. "Huh?"

John simply stared at him like he wanted to kill him as the low rumble of club music drifted through the night.

"Well, you still look bewildered, so I'll clue you in. It's you, dumbass. Maybe being one of the chosen all these years has gone to your head, but if you are having issues with everyone around you doing the same damn thing, then you can bet your sweet ass the problem is with you."

"I won't take advice from the likes of you."

"Me? What about me?"

"A demon. I was there when the Master Rabbi cast your kind out, on more than one occasion. You are not to be trusted. I won't have you near my family. Stay away. I won't keep telling you."

"Noory would already be dead if it wasn't for me. I threw away the bullshit leads that would have definitely gotten her killed. You didn't bother to tell her about the scion bounty on her head. How the fuck could you not tell her about that? She had at least a dozen names of magical practitioners on that list who would have killed her the moment she stepped through their doors because *you* neglected to tell her about the bounty, and you strong-armed Nick into silence, too. She couldn't come to you because of this little self-righteous act you have going. She was scared. Scared of losing Nick, scared of losing *you*—though I cannot fathom why—but couldn't tell you because *you don't listen*. You think you know everything. You've become unapproachable." He watched John struggle to remain calm.

"Stay the hell away from my family. Last warning."

"You know I'm right," Damascus said before turning his back and walking away.

But the next thing John said cut him deep. "You know, if she could see what you truly are, she wouldn't be able to look at you anymore."

Tears clouded Damascus' eyes, but he refused to turn and let John see them. He also couldn't help but wonder if maybe John saw him most clearly.

He knew he'd walked through the ages, smearing bloody footprints as he stumbled through time.

CHAPTER 20

While Noory waited on her mother to come get her for their "appointment" that she was to dress in tactical clothing for—not worrisome at all—she watched Grace sitting on their couch, feet tucked beneath her, reading a book on neuroscience and metaphysics. The crossroads of the Second Sight lab.

Noory wasn't sure if she should be happy Grace was reading to learn about ways to take their enemy down someday or worried that Grace might get too chummy with Locus or Lorien and might submit herself to tests in order to understand what was happening to her. She could see her desire to know more. Yet who in this place could they trust? She'd have to ask her mother about that today while they were away from prying ears. Noory cringed as she thought about just how many conversations Second Sight might have been privy to when she thought she was having a private dialogue.

"So," Grace began, "your mom is a professional . . . what? Assassin? That's so badass," Grace said before burying her nose in her book again.

"No. It isn't. She's trapped here."

"I'm sorry. You're right. That was insensitive of me."

"S'okay." Noory rubbed her arms briskly, sat back down on the bed, then leaned over her boots to make sure they were double knotted.

"What are you afraid of?" Grace asked. "I mean there's the usual: being trapped in this place, evil corporation, blah, blah, blah. But there's something extra vexing about this for you. Yeah?"

"Yeah. I'm never sure what I'll be expected to do. What my mother will expect from me."

"If you'll live up to her expectations?"

"Maybe."

"That is the good thing about having no family. There's no one to disappoint. Well—" Grace lowered her book and looked at Noory for a few seconds "—that's not entirely true. I always hated disappointing you."

Noory laughed. "Could have fooled me!"

"Well, then clearly I did."

Noory looked at Grace and felt as if she were seeing her for the first time. She'd been in and out of her shelter for years as a teenage girl, and now, she believed a woman was sitting in front of her.

"Sorry I gave you so much grief."

"What's happening?" Noory looked around the room.

"Stop it. I'm serious. You always . . . tried. Thank you."

One of her kids thanked her. They actually *thanked her*.

A knock at the door yanked her from her moment.

Noory opened the door, and her mother stepped inside. Noory watched a huge smile stretch across Grace's face. "What?"

"You two are definitely related." She gestured toward mother and daughter.

Noory turned to stand in front of her mother again, and the resemblance hit her. They were dressed alike, their posture was the same, the look on their faces. She'd even chosen to put her hair in a braid like she did. The only differences were that her mother's hair was black while Noory's was blonde, and Catherine was perhaps an inch or two taller. Otherwise, they were like yin and yang mirror images of each other.

One side of Catherine's mouth quirked up. "Hmm," she said. Noory thought she looked pleased by Grace's observation.

Noory turned to look at Grace. "Be back in a little bit."

Grace nodded. "Kill somebody worth killing," she said and went back to reading her book.

Noory pulled the door closed, Catherine turned right in the hallway, and Noory followed. "We need to stop by my office first," Catherine said.

Jericho fell in line behind them. Catherine had informed her they always sent a handler to make sure she returned and reported any issues. Farther down the hallway, a woman with a scar on the side of her head, and a patch of hair that appeared to have been burned off, passed her. When she did, she looked into Noory's eyes for the briefest of seconds and horrific images slammed into Noory's brain. She saw the shelter she ran downtown in flames. The windows and doors were closed. Hands reached up from the floor and slid slowly down the glass as if those trapped inside were becoming overwhelmed by smoke inhalation and would soon burn to death. *They can't get out. They're trapped.* Panic seized Noory. She struggled to breathe. She turned and watched the woman disappear around the corner they just passed.

Catherine turned to her. "You okay?"

Noory tried to breathe deep, get herself under control before answering. She looked down the hallway again, unsure of what had just happened.

Catherine whispered, "Did that demon Janus show you something?"

"The woman that just passed us?" Noory answered, wrapping her arms around herself, then quickly putting them back down when she realized Jericho was watching and didn't want him to see the demon had affected her so. "Yeah. She did."

"Ignore it. They always pull shit like that when they know you are about to head out on a mission. It's their way of reminding you not to run."

"Did they show you horrible things about me and John?" Noory's voice sounded small in her ears, and it made her angry. She cleared her throat, as if that were the cause.

"They did," Catherine said in a strained voice.

"God..." Noory breathed. Twenty years of being reminded, harassed.

"It's bullshit. Don't let it bother you. We'll head in here first." Catherine pointed to a different hallway that led to the public face of Second Sight. "In here," she said as she brought them into an office that had a name plate by the door that read, "Catherine Abramson, CEO." When this place staged a ruse, they went all the way.

"CEO?" Noory laughed at the absurdity of it. The laugh had a manic edge she couldn't deny.

"Yes."

Catherine opened the door, and they stepped inside. Jericho

remained outside the office. The place was gorgeous. The large desk was all glass and boasted a sleek laptop and nothing else, and the chair was black, soft, buttery leather. On the wall, near the ceiling were monitors with newsfeeds from Rio, London, Dubai, Seoul, and Tokyo.

"Well, you don't actually run this though."

"Much of it. Yes."

Noory's mouth fell open, and she stood there opening and closing it a few times. Once they were inside, they both sat on the small couch across from her desk. Noory pointed to her ear and around the ceiling and walls.

"Ah, no. No listening devices here. I've . . . made an arrangement."

Noory was afraid to ask what that was but took her word for it.

"How do you . . . Why?" Noory gestured at the sleek desk. "Can they literally make you sit behind a desk and work?"

"When they pulled me away from you and John it was bad enough, but once they *threatened* you, they could make me do anything, but I chose to work my way up to CEO so I could be more than hired muscle. I may not be able to leave, but I can wield power from inside. To truly ensure you aren't fucked with, you have to be brawn and brains. If you lack either of those components, they will eat you alive. If I'm ever gone for good—" her mother's eyes darted away "—you make it your business to sit in this chair."

Noory swallowed hard. There was something savage there in her words. She understood it, but it made her a little sad too. She nodded. "While it's just you and me, I need to know who I can trust. It isn't just about me or who I have to protect on the outside. Grace is here now. These people here are a little too interested in her gift." She didn't elaborate hoping her mother would offer information.

"Ah, I understand. You're very protective of her. Lorien won't hurt her. He'll do all he can to protect her, too. I trust him. I always hoped my blood could help him. He wanted to find a cure for himself and others of his kind that wanted so badly to be free. When I first arrived, he was so excited; he even thought he might be able to cure cancer with my blood. It hasn't happened yet, but God bless him for trying."

Noory realized what he'd meant when she first arrived, and he'd asked her what right she had to withhold something that could help others. Catherine stood and walked over to her desk. "But keep her away from Locus at all costs. He'll manipulate her under the guise of helping her."

Noory nodded. Some part of her felt as if she were talking to a colleague who she didn't know that well.

Catherine got a candle out of the drawer with three gold, bas-relief Hebrew letters on it: Aleph, Vav, Resh, and sat it on top of her desk.

Together they spelled a word Noory knew well. "Light," she said softly.

"Yes. Like you."

Noory caught the sparkle in her mother's eyes as she looked at her. She felt cherished. Catherine lit it and stared at Noory for a few moments. She cleared her throat and then spoke. "Well, this ritual grounds me before I leave on a mission. I thought . . . maybe you might . . ."

It was the first time she'd seen her mother look vulnerable since she'd arrived there. Noory smiled. "Of course, show me."

Catherine stood in front of the candle, turned her palms up, closed her eyes, and began speaking in Hebrew.

The cadence was soothing and familiar. A memory surfaced from her childhood; John used to have her recite prayers with him on Friday evening. She remembered complaining. Did he give up because of her whining? What were these words? Suddenly, the Hebrew began to translate and flow into her mind. "*You will not fear the terror of night, nor the arrow that flies by day . . . A thousand may fall at your side, ten thousand at your right hand . . .*"

Her mom was reciting Psalm 91, a prayer for protection. Images of mob bosses flashed through her mind. They went to church and confession, devout Catholics who went out and slaughtered in the name of power, money, drugs. Dear Lord! Was Catherine like a Jewish mafia boss? No. There was a difference; her mother never asked for this.

"*. . . See the punishment of the wicked . . . With long life I will satisfy him and show him my salvation.*" Catherine took a deep breath and exhaled slowly. She opened her eyes and looked at Noory. "Must seem strange, yes?" Her mother looked uncertain, waiting for judgement perhaps.

"No, not strange. It's your connection beyond this place." Noory gestured to the candle. "This is a thing they can't contain."

Catherine answered with a soft smile and a nod, blew out the candle, and placed it back in the drawer, then straightened her shoulders and spoke, "Now, let's go crack some fucking skulls."

CHAPTER 21

Catherine and Noory sat in the back of the SUV with the windows tinted so dark Noory could barely see the streetlights through the glass. Jericho drove them through the city toward their destination.

Her mother said, "The mark is a businessman who's been overcharging the company for years. When our new accountant took over, they caught the discrepancy, looked into it, and realized he'd been keeping a cut for about four years now. Second Sight will not beg the legal system to take care of shit like this. I've been sent to take care of it."

"He's a thief. That doesn't mean he deserves to die."

"He also sleeps with underage girls. Grooms them too. He's already paid off two families to keep their mouths shut."

"Well, I might not feel too bad about this one then. Do you always find something like this on them?"

"One minute," Jericho called from up front.

The timing felt a little too perfect. She guessed Jericho was listening, and Catherine was likely glad for the out. What else could she do? What would she do if they threatened Grace or Nick? She knew she would kill for either one of them, and Second Sight *was* threatening them. They'd just not made her take the shot . . . yet. A chill skittered up her spine as she followed her mother out of the car, into the night, and watched her place a hand on the pistol strapped to her hip.

"All right. Remember. Stay behind me," her mother whispered. "No going off on your own. Don't act without my go-ahead. Absolutely no being a hero if he or anyone else gets me on the ground. I've gotten out of scrapes many, many times. Do you understand?"

"Yes." Could she just watch if her mother needed help? Not likely.

Catherine waved behind her for Noory to follow, and they disappeared into the brush lining the side of a yard and into the shadows where the floodlights coming from the corners of the garage and streetlights wouldn't find them. Now they were in the backyard of a three-story house. Noory wondered how they were going to make it past possible motion sensor lights, and what if this man had a dog that might start barking and give them away?

The back windows were dark except for a softly glowing lamp in the window of the second floor. Catherine motioned for Noory to stay down, and they moved straight up the middle of the yard. Perhaps to avoid the motion sensors, Noory thought, but she felt exceptionally exposed out of the tree line. When they reached the basement door, her mother ran some type of device along the edge of the door before she exchanged it for another that she placed over the lock, and Noory heard what sounded like a deadbolt sliding. Even as quiet it was, it made Noory jump at the snap it made.

Catherine listened for a second, then opened the basement door and motioned Noory in behind her and softly shut the door. Damp basement assaulted her senses. Luckily, there was still enough light filtering in through the basement windows for them to see their way through.

Noory remembered doing this sort of thing with Nick as they tracked the kids who needed help. An ache bloomed in her chest. She always felt safe with Nick. If her mother had lasted this long doing what she did, then she had no choice but to believe she'd be safe with her now. Still, it all felt different when she'd been doing this kind of thing for the sake of her kids. But this was vengeance for the sake of Second Sight. Then again, this guy had hurt young people, or was it just a lie her mother told her or that Second Sight planted on these people to make it easier for Catherine to make the hit? Noory felt nauseous. Down that rabbit hole lay only torment. She was sure her mother had followed that line of logic as well. How could she not have after all these years?

Soon they were on the second floor where Noory had seen the lamp in the window. They traveled down the hallway of wooden floors with a soft runner covering the length of it on nearly soundless feet. Noory and Catherine both froze when they heard soft voices echoing from the far end. A man walked from the room, closed the door behind him, and strode into a puddle of light coming from the staircase opposite of where they'd entered.

Her mother looked around wildly from where they stood in the shadows of the hallway. Noory was sure she was looking for an open doorway for them to duck into, but the doors were closed and trying to open one of them would only confirm to whoever it was that they were there. The man started to turn to the right and head down the stairs when he hesitated and peered into the darkness. He took two steps forward. Noory knew they'd been spotted but he drew no weapon. Noory had a sick feeling that the body count had just doubled. "I see you. Come out and state your business."

He seemed way too calm for someone who'd just discovered intruders in the house. She could tell that this wasn't the mark. His hair was blond, and he was taller. Her mother drew her weapon but before she could even aim it, it was yanked from her grip. Another second and Catherine's upright body was sliding across the hallway rug, which tangled around her feet for a second before her body lifted a fraction higher. Noory saw her surprise but also saw her shut it down a second later and simply go with it.

When Catherine reached the man, she softly said, "Hey, baby," as if she were in a lover's embrace. Almost faster than Noory could track, she'd drawn a knife from her hip strap and plunged it between his ribs.

The man grunted and yanked it free without moving his hands. Catherine looked down and lunged to the side, anticipating he'd stab her with it. Noory ran forward to help her, but it suddenly felt as if she were hitting a wall. What the hell? She felt upset that there were supernaturals around who wielded this kind of power. It would never be a fair fight. Noory looked everywhere for the gun but didn't see it. What had he done with it? Finally, she spotted it beside a potted Ficus. As soon as she could move, she'd . . .

As her mother and the telekinetic grappled, he lost his hold on Noory, and she lunged for the weapon with the silencer on it. She grabbed it, hating the way it felt in her palm. She'd never liked using a gun. As she turned in time to see her mother against the wall with the man choking her without even touching her, she knew she had to do something. Panic raced through her. What if he were just defending himself against people who'd broken into his house? Maybe he wasn't guilty of anything other than defending his home. This wasn't who they'd come for. But as the man squeezed harder and Noory saw that her mother couldn't breathe, she pulled the trigger and the man dropped to the ground. That's when she realized her mother had used none of her abilities to get free. Noory had felt a similar fury as when she was fighting Jericho. So, why hadn't she felt the pull of energy that she had before? She realized the only answer: the telekinetic could block it.

Her mother slid to the floor and gasped for air. Noory watched an uneven circle of red grow against the fabric of the telekinetic's t-shirt. Had she killed him? He wasn't moving. Her mother was now beside her and holding out her hand for the gun. Noory gave it to her, and Catherine stooped down beside the man, felt his pulse, and then shot him in the head. "You always make sure. Never assume," she said softly without looking Noory in the eye.

Noory felt bile rise in her throat but swallowed hard and looked away. Logically, she knew her mother was right. Still, this man was dead now, and Noory didn't know his connection to the target, what his life was like . . . Now was no time to ruminate on it. She heard a shuffling from inside the room he'd just been in. Their intel had told them only the target was home. They'd been wrong once already. How many people needed to die tonight?

Catherine signaled for Noory to open the door while she lifted the body. As soon as Noory opened the door, her mother threw the blond man into the room and followed. Noory thought it was an adequate distraction. It was certainly freaking her out. No sooner had she thrown him in than she shot her weapon two more times, and Noory heard another body hit the floor. Catherine looked to where Noory stood in the hallway and nodded. Noory came in and saw her mother checking this man's pulse as well. Judging from the bloodstain blooming across his chest, her aim was true to the heart.

Catherine walked around to the desk and looked beneath it while running her hands along the underside of it. "Always check for silent alarms. They're often beneath desks where they can easily be pressed. I don't think there's anything here. He likely thought his telekinetic was enough."

As they made their way through the back yard beneath the silver moonlight, a dreamlike separation from what had just happened gripped Noory. Had this been Catherine's life for the last twenty years? How did she continue to live like this?

They got into the back of the waiting SUV, and Catherine muttered something to Jericho before they drove away. Noory felt cold all over followed by a rush of warmth and panic as she thought about what had just happened. She suspected the reality of it would be even worse when she woke the next day.

They were halfway back to Second Sight before Catherine spoke. "Are you okay?" she asked softly.

"Yes. I'm fine."

She felt her mother's eyes on her as if waiting for more, but Noory couldn't even begin to process how she felt about all of this. They drove into the parking garage, got out, and entered a service elevator that Catherine had a key for. On the long ride up, she felt her mother looking at her again but said nothing. Once the three of them got out of the elevator, Jericho followed them to the armory where the armorer on duty signed Catherine's weapons back in. After, Jericho went one way, Catherine and Noory another. Catherine walked Noory back to the room she shared with Grace, then paused before the door. Catherine asked, "How far would you go if you knew it would save Nick's life?"

"All the way," Noory replied.

"Then, please, don't hate me. Get some sleep," Catherine said. She nodded at the guard, and then walked away as Noory went inside and sat down on her cot. Noory unlaced her boots and let them hit the floor. One thud for each of the men they'd killed.

Chapter 22

Catherine could hear her heart beating in her ears as she answered. "I don't have it."

Janus glared at her. "The head of the priest is non-negotiable. Malachi won't tolerate this."

"I don't answer to you." She'd trained decades to hide her fear around these people, but she guessed they had sent her on one last hit, kept her around just long enough to show Noory the way of things, and now they were done with her. She'd be punished for letting Father Roy go.

"You've been getting entirely too bold, Catherine. Don't think the boss doesn't notice. You were number one bitch for a very long time because only you had the goods but there's another who has it. There always has been. And you've finally pushed far enough for us to go get her."

Catherine saw spots before her eyes and fought to keep her knees from buckling as the door to the conference room slowly opened. They'd officially brought her into this world. There would be no turning back for Noory now. One simply did not walk out the door of Second Sight. She'd failed her. She only hoped she had bought Noory sufficient time to become powerful enough to deal with being here. Now that they had Noory, they wouldn't need her anymore. She said a silent prayer they wouldn't execute her in front of Noory just to prove a point. She knew she had to be strong for her daughter. She'd held the wolves at bay for two decades. That wasn't half bad. Her conscience had caused this. She knew killing the priest would hurt Noory. Not killing him was about to hurt her more.

Two handlers dragged Noory into the room. Both had glowing hands just as she had thought they would. Noory was stronger than them both unless they were spelled. No Jericho this time, which was telling. She could call him down. Catherine stood stock still, just staring at her. At least she had gotten to see her daughter, face to face, before she died.

"I'm sorry," Catherine said. An avalanche of emotion constricted her throat. She could tell by the sheen of sweat on Noory's face she'd already tested them and found she couldn't best them while they were spelled.

"It's okay," Noory whispered. "I just don't understand. You've done what they asked. All these years."

"I refused one command. I wouldn't kill the priest."

"Roy," Noory whispered.

Catherine nodded and began praying as the executioner approached her. At least it wouldn't be a bloody death in front of her child. She'd seen it enough times to know. This plump old dowager with eyes appearing to be covered by cataracts, yet who seemed to see perfectly, would simply place her hand over Catherine's heart, concentrate, and she would fall to the ground. The last thing she would smell would be cookies, old money, and evil.

Noory struggled in the grip of the handlers, but the spelled hands that held her were just too strong, even for one of her lineage. Catherine's heart pounded in her ears. "I love you, baby."

"I love you, too, Mom," Noory sobbed.

"Tell John I love him."

"I will."

Catherine looked at Noory and then to Lorien, who'd followed the executioner into the room, and mouthed, "Please."

Lorien nodded once, walked over to the handlers, grabbed Noory by the arms and told them to release her.

"No, we have orders for her to stay for this."

Catherine heard a loud hiss and knew Lorien's features had changed into the scariest fucking thing they would ever see in their lives. Short lives if they didn't comply. They feared him, and he liked it that way. "The camera is over there," he said, knowing the camera was trained on the execution not the rest of them. The boss wouldn't know Noory was gone. He walked Noory out, and Catherine relaxed. But only a little. Noory was crying, which hurt worse than knowing she was about to die.

Catherine fought the urge to close her eyes as the executioner made her way closer. It felt braver to die with her eyes open.

When the blinding white light appeared, she almost wished she had shut them.

Father Roy appeared between her and the executioner. He was part flesh, part spirit, and in his arms, he carried a brazier of fire. He closed his eyes for the briefest of moments. Everyone in the room except for her looked to be in another dimension though they stood in the same space. He was not subject to the muting of powers that any other person entering their doors was. He cooked every person and demon in the room and left the brazier in the other realm. God, the man is powerful. No wonder they couldn't tolerate keeping him alive, she thought.

"Let's go get Noory and Grace," Roy said. As he turned to go, he stopped, tilted his head, and a look of horror swept over his face.

"Father? What's wrong?" Catherine's brain swam with possibilities. Anything could happen to him here. He could have been spelled from another location or, God, she didn't know.

"I can't hear Him anymore. We have to go."

"But Noory and Grace! Father, snap out of it!" She grabbed his shoulders and squeezed. She had a chance with him, a chance to free them. This was the break that was too good to be true.

"I cannot hear Him, Catherine!" He wrapped his arms around her, shifted them both into spirit form, and carried her to stand before John's shocked and trembling mien.

CHAPTER 23

Noory walked into the lab with Lorien in silence. He'd held her in his vise-like grip, holding as tight as the handlers had, refusing to let her go. Now, even the deep bruises they'd given her as she struggled against their grip of steel had gone as cold and numb as her heart and mind. Shutting down was much preferred to dealing with this nightmare.

As soon as the lab door closed behind them, Lorien flung a long arm across the table before them, sweeping it clean of notepads, pens, a laptop, and various reports. They hit the floor as a sound of anguish escaped him, deep and primal, not quite a scream or a growl. It was grief and fury looking for an outlet but finding none as it folded in on itself. He placed his palms against the edge of the table and went dangerously still.

"How could you just let her die?" Noory asked softly, not caring that she was poking a coiled snake.

"I've been here for *twenty years,*" he said, as if each word cut him. "She would've never made it out of the building."

"I grew up without her. I never . . ." How could she confide anything in this . . . creature? She wasn't even sure how to classify him and was torn between understanding why he didn't act and wanting to blame someone.

Lorien walked across the lab, took something from a cabinet, and came back. "One decent thing can come from being here," he said. "We have something you've been searching for." He held out a vial to her. "Here. Live. Live long enough to make it back to Nick. Have an eternity with him."

Noory just stared at it. "I waited all my life to meet her. I finally did, and you just took her from me."

"I didn't take her from you. I would have never done something like that, but I've learned to accept what is, what I cannot control."

"So, this place can be reasoned away with one big Serenity Prayer?"

Lorien sighed and extended his hand containing the vial closer still. "This will ease the pain. I wouldn't give you something that would hurt you. Drink it."

She wasn't so sure she believed that, but she wasn't sure she cared either. Futility washed over her. The mother she had waited so long to know and understand was right before her, then gone in an instant. She'd fallen in love, true love, but now Nick was gone. God only knew when she'd see John again. She grabbed the vial without thinking, opened it, and turned it up.

It felt as if every cell in her body were being washed with . . . light, strength? There was no word quite right to describe it. She looked up at Lorien. "What is this?" Her own voice sounded strange in her ears, ethereal somehow.

Lorien gave a sad smile. "It's a little light, a little dark. When you think about it, isn't that what we all are?"

"Yes. I guess so."

"You'll want to sleep now."

Lorien placed a hand on her back and guided her out the door. When they reached the farthest corridor, smoke drifted from under the door of the conference room they'd previously occupied. From the other end of the hall, she spotted Grace.

"What are you doing out?" Lorien asked.

Grace scoffed at Lorien. "I go where I please, bloodsucker."

Noory watched Lorien flinch as if slapped before heading toward the door to see what was happening. She cringed, afraid the mode of execution had been to burn her mother alive, but no odors accompanied the smoke, and they'd had her in there with her and wanted her alive. Something else had happened.

As Lorien approached, a security guard strode down the hallway and felt the door handle. "It's cool," he said. "The sprinklers didn't even go off. This must be something business related." Noory guessed that was code for *more weird shit that can't be explained logically so the normal rules don't apply*.

He took a handkerchief to cover his mouth and switched on his flashlight. He shined the beam around in the room. "The room is intact," she heard the security guard tell Lorien. "There's a little smoke but no damage. Not sure what this is."

"Bodies?" Lorien asked.

"No."

Grace slowly turned her head in Noory's direction and smiled. "She's alive."

Noory hovered somewhere between hope and despair. Too wrung out to experience either.

CHAPTER 24

John stared at Catherine with his mouth hanging open. He watched Father Roy slowly loosen his grip on her and back away. John noted that his friend, the always-confident rock of faith in his world for the last six months, now looked stricken, unsteady. But John couldn't address that right now. Not when the love of his life stood in front of him, looking as if she might shatter at any moment.

He took one step toward her, his instinct to heal and calm with his gift, his healing touch being almost too much to bear, too much to resist when his wife was in pain. He knew she knew it too when her palm shot out. "No! Don't. It happened. I failed her. I don't deserve . . ." She shook her head.

"Catherine. No. You did all you could."

"I did not. I got weak. I came to see her last year, and now she's paying for it. She's paying for my weakness by taking my place."

"Don't run again," John pleaded.

Catherine turned and surveyed her surroundings. She'd never been in his home. He'd moved there after her supposed death. "I won't run. There's nowhere for me to go."

The hopelessness in her voice was crushing him. He realized she had absolutely nothing but the clothes on her back.

"I just . . . need a minute." She turned and walked out the front door.

John hurried to the window and watched her. She looked around the property before making her way across the yard and into the barn. His mind spun with questions. Was she planning on sleeping in the barn, for God's sake? Everything in him wanted to run to her, but he knew she needed to be alone for a while. He didn't want to take his eyes off the barn for fear she'd run off again, but she'd said she wouldn't, and he had to honor her word. Badgering her would only alienate her. Instead, he turned his attention to someone who hadn't run off but appeared to need a friend. God knew Roy had been there for him without fail since the day they'd met.

He didn't want to push him, but he couldn't help but ask. "Did you see Noory? Any chance to bring her back? Talk to me, Father."

"I'm not sure I deserve that title anymore."

John's mind automatically conjured Nick saying that very thing dozens of times throughout the centuries.

"I'm completely sure that's not true. Can you tell me what happened?"

"Catherine was sent to kill me. When we were destroying the relic last year, I burned several demons while I was in the in-between. A couple of those demons were on the board of Second Sight. They wanted my head. Since Catherine was due for a test of loyalty after visiting Noory last year, she was sent to retrieve it. I gave her permission to kill me. Made it easy. She couldn't do it. She's assassinated before—" John winced even though he knew it was true, given what she'd said that night "—but she couldn't kill me."

"Why didn't you tell me about that before now?"

"It would only grieve you to know Catherine was in anguish and hurt you to know I might die soon, especially by her hand." Roy sat down on the couch and scrubbed a palm over his face, looking truly exhausted for the first time since John had met him. He barely ever slept. Something about his returning from being on the other side so long kept him from needing it.

"They sent the executioner to kill her, and now that Noory is there, they don't have to keep someone they can't trust. I don't regret saving Catherine. Of course not, but John, I cooked a room full of people and demons to get her out of there. I don't know how to begin to process this or how I square this with the other side. I knew what my mandate was. There are certain things I'm not supposed to interfere with, but the other side . . . it whispers. It used to be so beautiful, and I trusted so deep. Until it told me about Catherine. Why would it tell me these things if I'm not to interfere? He tells Nick a child is in danger and Nick gets to do something. He tells me Catherine is about to die and informs me that I am simply a *catalyst*. It sounded holy before. Pure. Meaningful. Now?" He threw a hand in the air and the tears finally spilled over and ran down his cheeks. "I'm nothing more than a mere shit stirrer in the grand scheme of things. This was a test, and I failed. God help me. I would've brought Noory, too, if . . . if He hadn't fled from me for my weakness. I was afraid to do more. To make things worse."

He felt frustration that Roy couldn't have saved Noory, and Grace, too, before having his panic attack over the silence of heaven, but this was everything to the priest. John looked toward the barn again as a cloud scuttled across the sun, leaving a long shadow replaced quickly by midafternoon glare again. "The longer I live, the more I realize that none of this is as cut-and-dried as that, Father. If it were that easy a pattern to follow, any damn body could stay on track. Don't flatter yourself to have had it all figured out. Maybe your so-called failure today is as much a part of the plan as anything you've done thus far."

"But you don't understand," Roy said as tears streaked his face. "I can't hear Him anymore."

John recalled something else he'd heard Nick say before: *His ways are infinity more painful.* "I don't know why the radio silence, Father, but I know a good man when I see one. I've never had the same kind of connection to the other side as you do, so I don't know what that's like, but don't lose heart. You haven't been abandoned."

"How can you know that?" Roy asked like a small child grasping at hope.

"Because I'm still here, and *Lord knows* I won't abandon you."

Chapter 25

"How old were you when you stopped aging?" Grace asked as Lorien removed the last bit of sticky gel from her scalp where the leads had been attached for the EEG. He'd run a neural scan while asking her questions about cards she couldn't see and random number generators he was using to have her guess which number he was seeing. She cooperated for him without a fuss because he asked for her permission—didn't demand it— and truth be told, she was curious about the results as well. She wanted to know more about her gift. She'd never been great at anything. This made her special. It didn't hurt that his hands were gentle as he worked, and he was beautiful. She had to remind herself he was the enemy.

"I should have had you guess before I took the leads off your head. It would have been interesting to see what your brain would have done with a question like that, since you know I've been around a very long time, but you are technically asking about my human age, in your terms. That being the case, I'm twenty-two."

"What did you do to Noory?"

Despite his kindness to her, she wasn't naïve. They were gathering information on her for their purposes. She was only finding out as a byproduct of their interest.

"I gave her what she was looking for," Lorien said.

"Shit! You made her an immortal?"

Lorien tilted his head to the side as if considering the question. "I finished the job."

"Oh, fuck me! Did you bite her?"

Lorien looked half insulted, half amused. "No. Of course not. I simply mean that all the scions are halfway there to begin with. The elixir that she took is the same thing that allowed her mother to stop aging. A regular human could take it, and it would not work. In Noory, and some others that are halfway there—" he looked at Grace in a way that made her feel he was fishing around inside her brain, her body, without her permission "—it finishes the job that has already begun."

"I see."

"I'm curious about you. Were you at all clairvoyant before the incident with Jonah?"

"The incident? You mean when that son of a bitch let me flat line and turned me into a Styrofoam cup to stuff souls into and ferry across an eternity bridge? 'Incident' makes it sound as if it was almost an accident. It wasn't. You people don't get to just use people up and toss them when you're done. I'm a person. Do you hear me? A fucking person!" Grace had gotten to her feet and started yelling. When this had happened, she didn't know. Where the well of rage came from was a mystery as well. She'd considered herself fairly laid-back.

Lorien stared at her without anger. In fact, if she didn't know any better, she'd swear it might even be compassion. She just stood there with her chest heaving, looking around the room, refusing to meet his eye. Not knowing what else to do, she sat back down.

He spoke gently. "You are a person. You have worth. I didn't mean to imply that you did not. Grace, I don't drain people. The reason I don't is *because* they are people."

"Then why are you working here? Why are you letting them hold us here? Why did you let them keep Noory's mother from her all this time? Did you know they kept Catherine here by threatening to hurt Noory?"

Lorien hung his head before answering and wouldn't meet her eye. "Yes."

"Then fuck you," Grace said in a tone that she hoped conveyed all the anger and none of the hurt before storming from the room.

Grace watched Noory punch a speed bag until her fists were a blur. Sweat dripped down her face. She wondered if Noory even knew she'd entered the room, but Noory had been so frustrated since they'd been held there, she was likely just getting out enough aggravation to carry on a decent conversation. Grace grabbed a bottle of water from the minifridge, walked over to her friend, and held it out.

Noory gave the bag one last punch. It broke free of the metal ring holding it to the board above and sailed past Grace's face. "Whoa!"

"Shit! I'm sorry. You okay?"

"Yeah, but I'd like to ask you the same question."

"I . . ."

Grace narrowed her eyes at Noory. She knew when a lie was coming and surely, she wasn't going to try to lob one at her in this place. There was no way to paint a silver lining on this fucking storm cloud.

"I am not."

"Thank you."

"For what? Getting you caught up in the disaster that is my life? For getting you stuck in this fucking prison for deranged weirdos looking for people they can turn into super villains?"

"No, thank you for telling me the truth. Thank you for making me an equal."

Noory took a huge gulp of water and nodded before speaking. "Your hair is all janky."

Grace reached up to smooth it down and remembered Lorien's touch on her head as he gently pulled the leads free. "Yeah. Pft. Lorien." Grace laughed. The look on Noory's face was one of utter shock. "Dear God, Noory! I didn't screw a vampire. He gave me a neural scan. They enjoy playing around in my head. Although . . ." Grace smiled just to mess with Noory. She was still seething over her conversation with him.

"Oh, no you don't," Noory scolded.

"Well, shit! If we're gonna be stuck here anyway. I mean, he's lonely. I'm lonely. He's hot. I'm . . ." She tilted her chin, looked to the side, and raised her hand for emphasis. "I'm like a classic Victorian Gothic—"

"No, no, no, no, NO vampire tail for you!"

"Well, you're no damn fun at all."

"Besides, what about Elliot or that priest in training, Thomas? Weren't you on a mission to talk him out of becoming a man of the cloth?"

At the mention of Elliot, Grace shuddered. Funny how she could spend time with a vampire and feel less distressed than at the thought of Elliot. "Elliot was connected to something that caused me a lot of . . . I don't even think pain is an adequate word. There are just too many terrible memories there. He'd been trying to contact me before we came here. I don't really blame him for what happened with Jonah. He was as young and stupid as me, but I'm ready to move on. Now that I'm away from everyone, I think the thing with Thomas was me trying to connect with someone that understood where I'd been. I don't really know that we were compatible. I shouldn't have been trying to talk him out of his calling, however boring," she said with an eye-roll.

"I get that. By the way, stay away from Locus. That dude is bad news."

"Noted, but you don't think Lorien is?"

Noory unwound the tape from her hands, making circles around her hands until they were free and faint lines remained on her skin.

"Oh, I don't trust him either, but I think there's some chance there's good in him. I think there's *no chance* of anything good in Locus. There's something *deeply* wrong with him. And whatever that wrong thing is, it's ancient and settled in all the way."

"And yet, I want to learn from him."

Noory made a face. "Why?"

"There's a lot I don't understand about my gift."

"When we get out of here, I'll find you a better mentor than that!"

"At Gifted Psychics R Us?"

"Yes. There. I mean it. Stay away from Locus . . . Please."

"I will." As much as she might have wanted to know about what was going on inside her head, she had to admit, if only to herself, Locus scared her too.

CHAPTER 26

Grace lay in bed listening to Noory's steady, even breath. She was glad she'd finally gone to sleep after a fitful night. She'd listened to Noory flip and flop like a fish until about three in the morning. An extra bed had been moved into Noory's quarters after she had vowed to make everything difficult for an eternity unless Grace could room with her. Noory's mothering was relentless, but sweet.

She cringed into the darkness of the windowless room when she thought of Noory, Nick, and John having to come get her from the clutches of Blake, the man she'd traded herself to for money. That had only been six short months ago. Though she couldn't imagine doing such a thing now, she knew it would take a while for them to see her as anything other than the same messed-up teenager they'd known.

A soft knock at the door made Noory stir. Grace hopped out of bed in hopes she would stay asleep. She made her way to the door, adjusting her sweatpants and t-shirt on the way. She started to open the door when Noory spoke behind her, "Don't open that. You have no idea who's out there." Noory clicked on the small bedside lamp. So much for her sleeping.

"And if we don't open it, we have *what* as recourse? We're trapped here with no defense. I think we have to open it."

Grace slipped her feet into her sneakers just in case she needed to run, though where she'd run to, she had no idea. She opened the door and found a young woman in blue scrubs with a pleasant oval face, brown eyes behind thick glasses, and hair tucked under a surgical cap. "Grace?"

"Yeah?"

"Hi. I'm Manda. You've not eaten anything this morning, correct?"

"No, why?" She didn't care for where this was going at all.

"You're due for a quick test this morning."

"You're mistaken."

"Yeah, you're very fucking mistaken," Noory said from behind her and then in front of her as she took Grace by the arm and positioned her behind her.

"Not to worry. This won't take long at all. It's a very simple procedure."

Noory fell to the ground. A small dart stuck out of her chest.

"What the hell?" Grace said.

Jericho, the biggest wall of muscle Grace had ever seen, stepped up beside Manda. He placed a small gun in his pocket that didn't look like any pistol she'd seen before. She assumed it was the dart gun that had tranquilized Noory.

"What did you do?" Grace said through clenched teeth.

"It's not a big deal. She'll wake up in a couple of hours," the muscle said.

"Not okay!"

"You—" he pointed at Grace, "—we're not allowed to tranq, unfortunately. Not good for the test." He picked her up and threw her over his massive shoulder, knocking the wind out of her. He clamped his arm across her as she struggled.

He took her into the lab and practically laid on her as she thrashed and screamed while Manda tried to get her arms and legs into the restraints. "What are you doing?"

"Stay calm. When you wake up, you will be just fine. I promise," Manda said in a tone calm enough to only anger Grace further. "This is just a test to see how your brain functions under anesthesia. That's all. You'll go to sleep for a little while then wake back up. You must be still though. You're making it hard to find the vein. Please stop fighting me."

This reminded her way too much of when Jonah had put her under to have her cross over into purgatory and ferry the souls of dead SS officers back to the mortal realm. He'd allowed her to flatline in his desperation to drag information back from the beyond. Perhaps even worse, the great behemoth's weight on top of her reminded her of one of the foster homes she'd lived in, when she'd been attacked by an older boy . . . The anger morphed into stark fear.

Jericho kept slamming her arm down on the table as soon as she freed it. She could barely breathe beneath his weight and started getting lightheaded. "I can't breathe," she rasped out. His weight and her subsequent lack of oxygen were making her weak. She felt the sting of the needle. *No!* She heard shouts coming from the other side of the room.

Hot tears streamed down her face, making her angry with herself. The last thing she wanted was to show weakness in front of these assholes. Whatever they'd given her in the IV was working. She was lost. Lorien appeared in her field of vision. *Angry.* "You didn't even tell her you were doing this today? You just went and took her from her bed? What the hell is wrong with you?"

Manda said nothing but Jericho started yelling about following orders. Lorien made a hissing noise that stood the hairs at the back of Grace's neck on end. As he looked away from Jericho—having made his point—and turned to look at her, she caught a glimpse of his face before it morphed back into something human. His eyes glowed golden, and she caught a glint of teeth before they slid away. She didn't care that he was something else, or that they had fought the day before. As her brain became foggy, Lorien's face was an anchor she clung to in a storm.

"I don't wanna sleep." Her words were slurred as she spoke to him, and the drugs pulled her under.

Even though the last thing she'd said to him when they fought was "fuck you," he didn't seem to be holding it against her as he placed his hand on her shoulder and said, "I'll stay and watch over you. I'll keep you safe." It was the last thing she heard before the darkness claimed her.

When she woke, she lay in a bed with the back elevated. She had been moved to what seemed to be a type of recovery room. It was smaller and deserted, except for Lorien, who sat at her bedside.

"How are you feeling?" he asked softly.

The effort it took to turn her head to the side and look into those untarnished bronze eyes made her head swim and ache. "Head hurts," she answered with a dry voice.

"I'll get you something for it." He walked over to the cabinet and brought back a syringe.

"What is that?" She heard defeat in her voice. She was only asking out of vague curiosity. The fight had gone out of her.

"A mild narcotic. After the morning you've had, you could probably use it for more than the headache. I was going to put it in your IV, but I can get you some plain aspirin if that would make you more comfortable."

"Are you kidding? Fill 'er up."

Lorien gave a soft smile as he slowly injected the medication. He walked over to the red sharps disposal attached to the wall, deposited the syringe, and then sat back down beside her. He poured her a glass of water from the bedside carafe. When her hands shook, he wrapped one of his own around hers and helped steady the glass as she drank. "I'm sorry, Grace. I didn't know."

There were so many things she wanted to ask him, like why he was working for an evil corporation when he seemed to be a good man, vampire, whatever the hell he was. Why would he try to look out for her but not help her escape? The very thought of getting into something like that right now made her head hurt worse and her heart hurt even more—she was just too scared of what the answer might be. So, she looked into his eyes and went with what her heart believed about him and begged God it was true.

Chapter 27

Grace finished getting dressed in the bathroom adjoining the recovery room then walked back out to the bed where Lorien stood waiting on her. He was watching her closely as she placed a hand on the wall.

"Feeling okay?"

"Oh, yeah. Yeah, I'm fine."

She knew he didn't buy it when he guided her to the chair.

She said to him, "Stop fussing, Mom. I'm good."

He gave her a long-suffering look. "Placing one's hand on the wall for support after anesthesia does not scream, 'I'm good.'" He helped ease her into the bedside chair.

She leaned forward to put her shoes on but felt as if she would just keep falling forward and perhaps through the floor. The vertigo was intense. Lorien was suddenly on his knees in front of her, pushing her body back into the chair. His warmth enveloped her like a blanket, and she didn't want him pulling away. Whoever had said vamps were cold was way off. He was close enough that she could feel his breath on her face. Vertigo be damned—he was doing things to her insides. Lovely things. He pulled away too soon to suit her, reached for her sneakers, and picked up her left foot.

"No. You do not have to dress me. Oh, my God."

"I absolutely do. The vertigo will pass soon but for now I can't have you falling over and cracking your skull. Besides, who's the doctor here?"

After he got her shoes on, he said, "Stay here," walked over to a closet, and pulled a wheelchair out.

"Oh, no. Not happening. Too weird."

"You have extreme vertigo. I can't have you walking like this."

"But you have wicked fast reflexes and an ungodly amount of strength. You can walk me back to my room."

He sighed. "Fine, but you have to tell me if you start to feel faint."

"Done."

They slowly made their way back to the room she shared with Noory. "How long was I out?"

"Two hours."

"Did you learn anything?" she said, having trouble keeping the snark from her voice.

"Yes, actually. Your brain is remarkable. Again, I'm sorry you were not informed. I wasn't either, and it's technically my O.R."

"You going to share this remarkable information with me?" she asked as they arrived in front of her door.

"Yes, I will. It's your knowledge to know and you will, but for now, you need rest, and I'm sure Noory is worried about you."

Grace tried the door but found it locked—a sham of privacy, to be sure. Second Sight had a key to every door here. "Noory, it's me," she said through the door.

The door opened, and Grace stepped inside, followed by Lorien.

The lights in the room flickered, and the furniture vibrated. Uh, oh, Grace thought, maybe they should have kept Noory in one of those Faraday cage lined rooms. Noory's hair lifted from her shoulders as she looked at Lorien. "You son of a bitch."

Oh, hell! She was going feral again. "Noory. Stop! Lorien didn't do this to me. He tried to stop them."

Noory didn't seem to hear her. Grace said, "Lorien, just leave. I'll be fine."

"Absolutely not. I need to tell her what she needs to look for since you share a room and are having vertigo." Grace turned to look at him and found the juxtaposition between his calm voice, glowing eyes, fangs, and body that had slid into a defensive mode in a blink, both hilarious and terrifying.

She stepped in between them. "Stop it!"

Noory snapped, "Move, Grace!"

"No!"

"Stop. Defending. Him."

Grace couldn't decide who was scarier. Noory with her hair rising from her shoulders like wispy Medusa snakes while the furniture inched toward her as if she were some sort of living, breathing black hole or Lorien looking like an actual, fucking vampire. But it didn't matter, and she decided he didn't scare her. There was something about him. Maybe she was a fool, but . . .

Noory didn't seem to notice she'd pushed Grace out of the way. Grace stumbled and fell. She was a hair's breadth from hitting her head on the floor when Lorien caught her, faster than any human could have, even Noory. "Jesus, are you okay?" Lorien's face had lost its battle vamp edge before he propped her against the bed. He gently lifted one eyelid, checking for dilation before he was yanked off his feet and thrown across the room.

The vampiric battle face was back, descending on him like a cloak. "Get a hold of yourself, Scion. When you slip into battle form, you must remain anchored in your humanity, or you will lose yourself. Take it from someone who knows." He gestured to his face, a mix of human and vamped out canines extended, eyes dilated.

"Do not attempt to school me, bloodsucker."

"You require schooling, Noory. You almost knocked someone you love to the floor, and you don't even realize it."

"You don't know what you're talking about. Fight me, you abomination."

"No."

Noory ran at him, and he stepped aside at the final moment. She stopped just short of hitting the wall. By the time she turned around, Lorien was already back at Grace's side. When she came back to drag him away again, he was on her before she could mount an attack. He locked both her arms beneath his own. He glanced up to where Noory and Grace had both guessed the camera was in their room and spoke so softly that Grace could barely hear. She figured he must've known how loud he could talk before they picked it up. "Listen to me, Scion.

I've been with your mother the entire time she's been here. I've watched them manipulate, use, and turn her emotions against her. Get. Yours. Under. Control. You almost hurt an innocent."

"You're one to fucking talk," she spat as she seethed in his grasp.

"And you work for Second Sight now, too. Am I to assume you are about to go around gleefully hurting the vulnerable every chance you get? Yes, it's complicated as hell, but your mother wasn't a monster. You don't have to be either. Now don't pretend you know me, and get your shit together, and for God's sake don't shove someone that just came out of anesthesia."

She said nothing.

"Are we clear?" He gave her a little shake.

"Yeah," she said quietly.

Lorien released her and turned back to Grace.

"Doing okay?" Lorien said to Grace.

"I'm okay," Grace said softly.

Grace noticed Noory wore a pained expression as she looked at her.

Lorien said, "Noory, please watch Grace. If she becomes nauseous, starts throwing up, if her vertigo gets worse or doesn't improve in the next couple of hours, please come get me. I'll be in the lab." He helped Grace get settled on the bed, asked her if she needed him to bring her anything, and then left.

Noory seemed to have calmed considerably as the door closed. She walked over and sat down next to Grace. "I'm sorry. I wasn't thinking about what they might have done to you in there. I was thinking of our conversation about him and how you mentioned how hot he was and that you might be taking up for him because of that. I didn't even consider what might have happened to you, and that was wrong. When I was falling in love with Nick, John was always on the defensive. Anytime I took up for Nick, anything I said, he just . . ."

Grace looked up, becoming aware that someone might be listening and spoke in a whisper. "Ain't nobody falling in love over here. So, calm down."

Noory laughed but made no further comment.

"I hear all kinds of judgment in that silence, Noory."

"He's so much older than you. You don't know him," Noory whispered.

"Not that it matters, because I'm not in love with him, but he's not so much older. He's only twenty-two."

"Pft. No. He's probably like seven hundred or something."

"Oh, okay. You wanna go there? Let's go then. Nick is thirty-ish, and you are only twenty-seven. And he's like from what century now? Four hundred AD, some shit like that? Don't even play this game with me."

"It's different. I'm twenty-seven. You are seventeen! You can't handle this!"

Grace laughed out loud. "I've lived on the streets, died, came back, went back and forth to purgatory and ferried evil souls across the rainbow bridge. And I'm not exactly inexperienced in the sack. I ran my own business, or have you forgotten?"

"Yes. I remember pulling a demon-possessed slime bag off of you after he bought you in the business that you ran. I'm surprised you'd bring that up as a point of pride." Noory got up and walked over to the fridge and retrieved a bottle of water. She twisted the cap off and handed it to Grace.

Grace drank a little of it. "I'm not proud of it. I just mean, I'm not your typical seventeen-year-old. Any chance of that is long gone, and we both know it."

"I do know it, and it hurts my soul."

Grace scooted over and patted the bed next to her. Noory settled in and Grace put her head on Noory's shoulder. "You two were like the clash of the titans in here," Grace joked.

"It's nice to be loved, huh?"

"Huh, it's terrifying when it's you people. Besides Lorien doesn't love me."

Noory said nothing but Grace heard her snort.

Chapter 28

Grace sat on a stool in the lab turning a test tube this way and that as a viscous substance clung to the sides of the glass. She looked over the top of the tube and watched Lorien study the clipboard in his hand. Since no one had waylaid her as soon as she stumbled out of bed to drug her and test her like a rat, she'd wandered down the hall to find Lorien. Besides, Noory had gotten up, drank a cup of coffee, and started wailing on a brand-new heavy bag—the speed bag still hadn't been fixed. She was terrible company right now. Lorien was alone like she hoped—no *thought*. Like she'd thought, she corrected herself.

"Okay, so what did you learn about my head? Hot stuff?"

Lorien turned to look at Grace with wide eyes.

Grace laughed. "Come on. It's my noggin. I've got a right to know what goes on inside my own brain, right?"

"Hmm. I thought it possible you might not want to know."

"Nope. I'm a curious sort. Lay it on me, Vlad."

Lorien sighed long and deep. "I am neither Russian nor Slavic, and right now I do not gloriously rule anything, which is what the name would imply." Lorien flung the clipboard onto the counter. It made a loud clatter as he scrubbed a hand through his thick, dark hair.

She froze a couple of feet in front of him, wondering if she should go. "I'm sorry. I didn't mean to upset you. I have a habit of trying to joke when things are—"

"No need to apologize. You haven't done anything wrong. I'm the one hooking you up to wires and drawing your blood. If anything, I should be . . . doesn't matter. We can't change any of this."

Grace sat on the stool at the table across from him. "Wrong," Grace said.

"What?"

"I said, you are wrong. It can change."

"There's little room for baseless optimism here."

"Baseless? No, of course not, but I got all kinds of bases, baby." She winked.

Lorien extended his arms, placed his palms on the counter, and laughed but it sounded like pure exhaustion in Grace's ears.

"How can somebody that doesn't age sound as tired as you?" She slowly extended her hand and placed it on top of his.

He straightened suddenly, as if her hand were a snake. "You shouldn't."

She spoke softly. "My hope is not baseless. When I look into our future, I see us here a while longer, but then it gets fuzzy. Do you know what that means?"

"Tell me," he said in a voice so soft she could barely hear. He glanced at her then. It was the first time those eyes had looked as if he might need something from her. The need in his eyes slayed her, making it hard to find her voice. But she leaned forward with all the confidence she could muster and said it, because it was true: "It means whether we remain here is not set in stone. Let a little hope in."

The hope might kill me.

"Did you say something?" she asked. His mouth hadn't moved but she heard him speaking clearly.

"No."

She held his eyes for a moment, and he looked away, cleared his throat, and did what most people did when they felt exposed: changed the subject. "Stay away from Locus. He's dangerous."

She laughed. "Yeah, I'm hearing that a lot lately."

"From Noory? Well, there's good reason she's warning you. He's dangerous, Grace. Very, very dangerous. He has no regard for human life, and I think he might be attracted to you."

The second Lorien said the words, adrenaline shot through her. She knew what that meant. She knew Noory didn't think she knew. But she'd lived on the streets and bounced from one home to the other. She knew it meant everything just got way more dangerous. She swallowed and avoided Lorien's eyes.

"Well, I shouldn't hedge when it comes to him," Lorien said. "He *is* attracted to you."

"How do you know this?"

He hesitated before answering.

"Cagey? Why?"

"If I tell you, why, then you will become self-conscious around me. It's happened before, but you'll badger me until I tell you, right?"

Grace nodded.

"I can smell pheromones."

Fuck! He looked at the floor when he said it. If he smelled pheromones, then he knows I'm attracted to Locus too. Too? Am I attracted to Locus? Shit! I am. At least a little bit. Why? God, why? This just got confusing.

"And there it is." He pointed at her. "Now you're self-conscious around me. That's how fast it happens."

"Okay. True, but I've had to get over a lot of awkward things in my life. I haven't had a typical teenage experience. I can work with this." She waved a hand as if to brush the knowledge away as inconsequential.

He laughed softly. "You do roll with things better than the average person. Most people would not be in a room alone with me. *At all*." He held her eye a second longer. Her insides did a flip flop, and she knew pheromones were rolling off her in waves. Was he trying to see if she would blink first? He shook his head as if trying to clear a trance.

Gotcha, she thought as he looked away. "See? I don't care. Phero-mones. Every-damn-where." She made an exaggerated motion of smell-ing the air. "All right. Now, back to my fascinating brain. What exactly have you found out?"

She thought she detected a faint smile as he shook his head before answering. "Okay. Well, there are these things inside our brains called microtubules. Inside these microtubules are superluminal photons. It's light, basically."

"I like that. That's a nice thought."

"I agree."

She liked the way he smiled at her like they were sharing a secret.

He said, "We believe this is where consciousness is stored. When we're awake, the light emitted from these microtubules moves slower. When we're under anesthesia, it moves faster."

Grace snapped her fingers. "Like that theory . . . what is it? A proton is nowhere until it is observed. Then it slows down, and it's *somewhere* once it's seen?"

"Yes, there's a connection. So, we are all experiencing consciousness by observing and placing things. However, when we looked at the light inside the microtubules in your brain, it was much brighter than it should have been. The same is true for Locus."

Grace grimaced. "He should really be doing better things with the light in his head." She remembered the way Lorien had looked at her as she drifted off under the anesthesia. How reassuring his presence had been when Jericho was scaring the hell out of her.

"Hmm." Lorien nodded. "What we believe is that you are both able to observe this light in different places and follow it to its, perhaps, brightest place."

"Where it will be observed next?"

"Yes, like, perhaps the light scatters when the future is uncertain in someone's mind or in the collective unconscious, but when many minds are heading toward a certain inevitable conclusion, then maybe you see that bright spot on the horizon. We're theorizing at this point. What we do know for certain is you have more light inside you."

For some reason the idea brought hot tears to her eyes before she could hide them or make a joke of it. *Damn it.*

He spoke softly. "Yeah, it's a good thing. And this," he pointed at Grace, "is exactly why Locus is dangerous. It would never strike Locus as a beautiful thing to bring a person to tears. His first thought would be how he might exploit his gift."

Now it was her turn to clear her throat and change the subject. "So, are you a neurosurgeon or something?" She hopped up from the stool and went to the dry erase board on the nearby wall, picked up the black marker, and began drawing a rough sketch of Jericho.

"Yes."

"I just threw that out there. I didn't really know."

"I figured. I'm also a geneticist."

"Really?"

"Yeah. I've always wanted to understand what's wrong with me."

"Wrong with you?" Grace drew horns on the picture of Jericho.

"Yeah, the vampirism."

Grace tilted her head. "There's nothing wrong with you. There's something wrong with him." She pointed to the picture of Jericho.

Lorien laughed.

Grace continued. "But there's nothing wrong with *you*. It's just what you are."

"Grace Turner. In all my 700 years, that's the first time anyone has ever said such a thing to me."

"Really? I would think it should be obvious. My head is a damn light bulb or whatever. Noory is a descendant of the Jesus H. Christs, Nick is the immortal Santa. You get to know enough anomalies and it turns into just what you are, right?"

"Not really for my kind. We've been hunted to near extinction. Not always without cause either."

"Well, there are plenty of evil humans. With no excuse whatsoever. You know?"

"True enough."

"Why are you here?" He froze when she asked. "Uh, oh. I'm sorry. Is it classified? Or are you afraid my opinion will change? My opinion has never mattered before. I'd be shocked if it did now." She laughed.

"Working here is an excellent research opportunity," he said, but he looked at her and down to his notepad and tapped it with his finger. She walked over and stood beside him. On the notepad he wrote, "Supply closet." He got up, and she followed him inside. He shut the door behind them.

"There are no listening devices in here." A thrill ran through her to be in such close proximity to him, even though it was just a closet full of alcohol wipes, latex gloves, extra syringes, and other supplies. *Oh, yeah, he'd be getting another nose full of telltale pheromones. Oh, well, no help for it. Drink it in, baby.*

He looked at her before continuing, as if he were about to cross a bridge from which he couldn't go back. "Catherine and I are in the same position. They're holding my sister. My service ensures her survival."

"I'm sorry. Where are they holding her?"

"I don't know the exact location, but she's sleeping under a spell. The human body couldn't handle the atrophy that would take over the body from years of that, but the vampirism preserves her just fine. Whenever I get out of line, they show her to me from wherever she is. She's completely helpless there."

"All that power and she can't help herself."

"Exactly."

"My God, Lorien. How long have you been here?"

"I arrived right after Catherine did. I was brought here specifically to study her. She tried to kill me at first."

"I bet! If she's anything like Noory."

"She's *just* like Noory. It's spooky how alike they are, given Noory probably has no memory of her."

They both stood in silence for a moment. Suddenly out of the words that had flowed so freely just minutes earlier, Lorien's phone rang. He took it from his pocket and swiped a thumb across it. "I have to take this."

As Lorien opened the door and walked off, Grace walked over to his notepad, scrawled a message on a scrap of paper, and handed it to Lorien on her way out. She heard him pause in his phone conversation midsentence. She pictured the note and smiled.

The hope won't kill you.

Your sister's name is Anna Belle. An ally wakes her soon.

Chapter 29

Nick walked into the shelter with his heart a leaden weight in his chest. He knew he had to face John soon. They'd worked so hard to restore their relationship. Now . . .

"Hi, Ava."

"Hi . . . whoa. You okay?"

"Yeah, just not getting much sleep. Noory is still checking out that school in Virginia."

"Ah. It's hard to sleep without her. That's so sweet! What will you do if she decides to take those classes? She'll be gone for a while."

He hated that he'd been lying to the woman. It was about to get worse. Damascus was going to come in today and cast a spell so Ava would believe Noory had been accepted, wouldn't be back for a while, and never question it. He'd already done so with Grace's aunt. Why tell her the truth? She couldn't fight Second Sight, and trying would only get her killed.

Nick walked into Noory's office, sat down, and powered up the old computer. He looked around, seeing her everywhere. Her well-worn hoodie hung on a hook by the door, a framed photo of them at his penthouse sat on the desk. She's insisted they take a selfie when the sunset was particularly beautiful outside the floor-to-ceiling windows of his dining room. Their faces had a glow. "Magic hour" she'd said. As he looked at their faces side by side, he could almost smell her hair and feel her warmth. Another photo of her and John on the day of her high school graduation sat beside it.

As an ache in his chest bloomed, he looked away from the photos. He sat, head in his hands, as the computer booted up.

Knuckles rapped on the door frame. He looked up. Orange eyes looked back at him with sympathy. Nick motioned for the demon to take a seat on the old threadbare couch in front of the desk.

"It's done," Damascus said. "She thinks Noory's been accepted to the school in Virginia and already moved there, leaving you in charge."

"Thanks," Nick said softly. "I spoke to Roy the other night. Since that whole bit with the other side going quiet on him, he won't go out on rescues with me anymore."

Damascus rolled his eyes. "Oh, hell! God *never* talks to me, and I'm doing just fine. Tell him to buck up. He'll get used to it. Do I need to go have a talk to him?"

Nick studied him for a moment and realized he was only half kidding, and Damascus didn't seem to catch the irony that a demon was offering to go talk to him since God wouldn't. There was some true sincerity there.

Nick smiled at him.

"What?" Damascus said.

"You just . . . made me feel a little lighter is all."

"Light? I don't get *that* much."

"Maybe you should." *What has my world come to?* Nick shook his head as if to clear it. "We need to talk to Catherine. She knows that place better than anyone else on the outside, but John is so mad at me he can't see straight. I doubt he'll want me talking to her or planning anything.

"Oh, screw him!" Damascus said.

Nick gave a tired laugh. "Sometimes you're a breath of fresh, sulfurous air."

"I have my moments." Damascus looked at him. "I fear they won't let Catherine live long on the outside, Nick. She knows too much."

"I worry about that, too, but she lives with two skilled fighters now, and she's lethal all by herself."

Evan poked his head in the doorway. "Hey, Nick! Ava said you were back here . . . Oh, sorry. Didn't know you had a guest." He looked at Damascus with curiosity.

"It's all right. Please meet Damascus." Nick watched Damascus fight to regain his composure. His orange eyes had grown huge as he stared at the boy.

"Oh, yes. It's lovely to meet you," Damascus said as he took Evan's hand.

Evan reluctantly shook it. Nick couldn't tell if that had to do with Damascus' odd appearance or if it was because of the way Damascus was looking at him.

To the kid's credit, he recovered quickly. "Nice to meet you, too. I'll come back in a little while."

"Sure. I'll be here most of the day," Nick said.

Damascus watched the kid until he had gone down the hallway and away from view. Then he turned to Nick and whisper-yelled, "Holy Hades! You didn't tell me you had a freaking magus living here. There are so few legitimate magi alive in the world today. This must mean . . . something."

"Evan? A Zoroastrian priest? No. And why are you so rattled about it even if he was?"

"You're not as ancient as me, but you should know this. Typical, only paying attention to the Judeo-Christian shit. The old magi, the ones born with the magic, only show up when something major is coming to pass. How did you not see the sheer power radiating off his aura?"

"I didn't look, and for your information magi *are* part of Judeo-Christian tradition. Three of them showed up at Noory's great uncle's birth."

Damascus rolled his eyes. "They were around long before the frankincense and myrrh peddlers."

"Yes, they were. Anyway, I don't think the kid knows what he is. I don't even know if it's the best idea to tell him. I mean what would he even do with that kind of information? Besides the Zoroastrians technically forbid sorcery."

"What is it with you people and your ignorance-is-bliss theory? That kid is as powerful as a djinn! What if something finds him before anyone tells him, and he isn't able to defend himself because he doesn't even know what the hell he is? Other entities will sense him. I sense him. I can tell you right now he has elemental powers like the old, old, ollllld effers did. I bet you anything he can read the stars like a mother too!"

"Well, you make a good point." Nick conceded.

"What if he ended up here because you're *supposed* to help him?"

Nick nodded. "I need to study this some more. His powers would be elemental, right?"

"Yes." Damascus rose and walked to the door. "You tell him, or I will." It wasn't spoken like a threat, just a statement of truth, and he was right.

Nick sighed. Evan already couldn't have a normal childhood. His father was gone. He lived in a shelter. Hopes of normalcy just got further and further away for some people.

"I'll tell him," Nick said. Yet another worry niggled at the back of his head, that he'd not told Even because he was just afraid to. It was hard enough to protect an average child, much less a powerful one.

Chapter 30

Noory knocked on the door to the lab. Grace had said that's where Lorien would be; she always seemed to know where to find him. There was way more pride-swallowing going on here than she was comfortable with, but it couldn't be helped. Not only was she in need of more serum, but she also wanted to thank him for looking out for Grace when she couldn't.

He opened the door and motioned for her to come in. She got what Grace saw in him. He was striking with his bronze eyes, and that hair almost glowed. It was brown but with highlights that seemed to have collected energy from a sunset somewhere. He wore a lab coat over a blue dress shirt, black pants, and leather dress shoes. Everything about him spoke of taste and sophistication, yet he wore it without a shred of arrogance. Yeah, it was hard not to like him, and yet, she wanted to hate him for so many reasons: working here, not helping her mother escape, treating her like a child in need of a good scolding . . . well, that one was justified and the reason, partly, for her visit.

Lorien walked past the tables supporting a laptop and paperwork, tests in various stages of development, she assumed—judging by the measuring cups, beakers, scales, microscopes, and so on—and around the corner to a sitting area with a coffee table surrounded by a couch and two comfortable chairs. He motioned to the couch, and he took one of the chairs.

He sat back, crossing one leg over the other. She sat on the edge of the couch and forced herself to breathe. She guessed the serum was wearing off. Her hands were starting to tremble. She wondered if she should be angry at him for that, but it was what she wanted, and her mother had taken it and seemed fine. She wouldn't start with that though. It felt far too loaded a subject to begin with. Luckily, she didn't have to begin the conversation.

"How's Grace this morning?"

"She's doing very well. Seems to be back to her old self."

"Good. I thought she would be. Again, I didn't order them to take her like that. That was scary for you both, and I'm sorry it happened that way."

"You're sorry for the *way* it happened, not that it happened."

"Grace wants to know about what's going on with her gifts, and I promise you, I wouldn't perform any tests that would be harmful to her."

She believed him, but wondered just how much he could control. How much control did anyone here have? "Listen, I'm sorry about how things went down when you brought Grace back the other day. I didn't handle it well. Your advice was . . . appropriate and—" she waved her hand in the air searching for the right word "—correct." She quickly put it down when she noticed it trembling.

"Thank you. It looks as if you are in need of another dose."

"I thought that might be what this is." She held her hand out in front of her.

"You will stabilize, eventually. I must warn you that first your body will grow addicted and then you will have to kick the habit. After that, you will maintain your cell renewal forever. The only thing that can kill you would be something drastic like separating you head from your body or the blackest of magic."

"Sounds like something you could have told me before I started taking it."

"We'd been watching your search for immortality since it began. Would a surgeon general's warning label have made a damn bit of difference after the stuff you'd ingested at the various shamans and witch doctors' huts? I wasn't spying on you personally, but you know how it is here. How it is with your family."

She nodded.

Lorien got up and walked to a cabinet, opened it, then ran his fingers across a glass panel in a combination she couldn't decipher. It opened a small safe. He took a vial out, opened it, and brought it to her. For a moment, she wondered if she could trust him. Maybe this was the thing that would kill her. When she drank it last time, she almost didn't care. She'd thought her mother was dead and she would never make it back to Nick. Now there was more to live for, but as her hands shook with a need that she felt brushing the bottom of her soul, she knew she would take it regardless.

"I've no reason whatsoever to harm you, and every single reason in the world to keep you alive."

She drank the vial and handed it back to him. He placed it in his coat pocket. "I won't push you on when to kick the habit, but don't let it go on too long. It will be harder to break the longer you let it go."

"How long do I have to take it before it works?"

"It probably started working with the first dose. You likely didn't even need that one."

"Then why in the hell did you let me have it?"

"Because, despite yesterday, I've grown to consider you a friend, and when it's time to abstain, you won't be my friend. I'll be the gatekeeper of the thing you want more than anything, and you'll try to kill me for it."

"How do you know?"

"Because your mother did. First, she begged me to keep it from her, then she begged me to give it to her. When that didn't work, she tried to kill me, and you will too. That's okay. I've been through this before. You won't succeed."

She tilted her head and looked at him, really looked at him for the first time. He appeared ancient in his exhaustion, and his pain seemed so close to the surface she felt she could reach out and take it from him. He reminded her of Nick, and she understood something all the way down to the bone.

She knew exactly why Grace had fallen in love with him.

CHAPTER 31

Damascus walked into Robert's office like he had a hundred times before, but this time, something felt different. He tried to trace his emotion to its source. What was it?

Oh yeah, he felt . . . good. There were times he'd felt hopeful when walking into his office, like when he knew Robert needed someone bumped off, something Robert had neither the stomach nor the power to do, depending on how strong the person was. *You're only hopeful if he's going to use you. That's some toxic shit.*

"Damascus! I'm so glad to see you." Robert walked up and kissed him. *Kissed him!* That never happened before, either. "Champagne?" Robert asked. He pulled a bottle of Cristal from a small wine fridge and filled two flutes already sitting on his desk.

"What are we celebrating?"

"Second Sight has asked me for a favor, and this time, delivering shouldn't be a problem." He handed Damascus his glass, they clinked them together, and drank. "I only need a small thing from you. Nothing for someone of your talents."

Here it is.

"I know you've been spending some time with Noory and her people to keep an eye on them. 'Keep your enemies close.' That sort of thing."

Damascus nodded. It might have started out that way, partially. Though to be honest, the second he saw Noory . . .

"Anyway, Second Sight has dismissed their CEO. That bi—" Damascus guessed that Robert had started to talk about Noory's mother beating the hell out of him last year, but apparently his pride still wouldn't allow him to admit a woman had done it. Instead, he said, "That bastard that went off on me after I put my heart and soul into the tower project.

Anyway, they say if I can deliver that priest who's taken up with John and Noory, I'm back in. That's where you come in. They've sent their CEO to apprehend him, and they failed. They sent their demons, and they failed, but they haven't sent you. They don't know how amazing you are." Robert leaned in and gave him a long, lingering kiss.

This time, it didn't pack the same punch. He even, dear Lucifer, resented it a little. A lot, actually. Although . . . it had been a while since Robert had wanted something from him this badly. It had also been a while for other things . . . He had no intention of bringing him the priest, but it felt good for once to be in control. He didn't need Robert anymore. That thought sank in deep. *He didn't need him anymore.* Yeah, he still loved him on some level. Maybe always would, but the days of groveling were over. Freedom was settling in.

His orange irises flashed, and he beckoned Robert with a curled finger. Tonight, the man would do *his* bidding.

CHAPTER 32

John stood in the doorway of the barn, watching her. She'd abandoned her heels and blazer and now stood on the worn wood floor in bare feet, flinging a hatchet at the largest support beam in the center of the barn with all her might. It landed with a solid *thunk*. She walked up to the post, dislodged the blade, and returned. Without looking, she spoke, "Don't try to make me feel better."

"I won't. It didn't work with Roy. I don't expect it to work with you." *Sometimes presence is all we can offer.* Roy's words came to him from last year when Nick had shown up at his door, broken, alone, trying to figure out what to do about the entity that had taken up residence inside of him. He couldn't let it go for fear it would find its way back to Noory, but he knew it was changing him, scaring him, and Nick was already pretty damn scary by most people's standards. They didn't know what to say to Nick that night. They could only offer presence.

Catherine turned to look at him with the hatchet in her hand. Her chest heaved from exertion. Strands of black hair stuck to her face. It was a cool spring day, but she'd worked up a sweat. He couldn't imagine what she'd gone through. The years of isolation and fear. Now he was fearful too, afraid he didn't truly know the woman before him anymore. He'd lived long enough to recognize the look she was giving him was a challenge. This woman was used to being in charge. So was he. He sat back against some enormous stacks of hay and stared at her. Her move. If he tried to treat her the way he had before she'd "died," they'd have no chance. He had to watch, wait, and let her make the first move. It wasn't that he didn't care. He wanted to run to her, but the rules had changed.

She looked hungry. Predatory. He'd never been with a woman like that. He never thought he'd want to be, but he sensed nothing evil in her. Maybe that was it. He thought a woman with that depth of hunger would be soulless. Not so. He felt it. She was still Catherine. His Catherine. He had to push the soles of his shoes against the planking to keep from moving toward her. Now wasn't the time, no matter how many years he'd longed for her.

She leaned against the post and crossed her arms. "The first thing they'll do is give her the serum. Word has spread around the office that she has been looking for a path to immortality. They can give it to her. You see, now it won't be a simple matter of threatening her with hurting someone she loves. They have that, sure, but they also have the immortality key. At least for our kind."

"I take it this is why you look younger than you should?"

"Yes."

"So, you're an immortal now?" Despite the sorrow of Noory being held captive at Second Sight, John couldn't help but feel joy at the idea of Catherine being able to spend her existence with him.

"Yes."

There was so much more he wanted to ask her. So many details he'd like to know. He knew there was a powerful serum that granted immortality. Fine. He'd seen some wild things in his time. He was immortal himself. But when she'd died, her body was cold by the time he arrived. Her spirit was absent from her body. She was well and truly gone, but he could tell she was in no mood to talk about it.

John sighed. "Our daughter is in love with an immortal. She can't bear the thought of letting him go someday."

"No," Catherine looked deeply into John's eyes, making him have to fight to avoid shrinking beneath her gaze, "she can't bear the thought of *him* having to let *her* go someday. When we were together . . . before, I often thought of you having to go on without me and what that would do to you. It hurt me far worse than the idea of my death. You would have to remain and mourn."

John felt guilty for accusing her of not caring when he'd first run into her twenty years after he thought she'd died. "Well, when she's finally free, she'll be able to spend eternity with Nicholas." He wanted to say the same about him and Catherine but again, now was not the time.

"She'll have to rid herself of the addiction first," Catherine said and looked away as if she didn't want him reading the pain of the memory.

"Addiction? You mean if she stops taking it, she won't be immortal anymore?" Panic raced through him when he applied the thought to Catherine too.

The look she gave him was grave. "No. She's immortal now that she's taken a dose, and I'm sure she has or will. Second Sight won't pass up a chance to make her beholding to them. But coming off it is horrific. The absence of it is like acid eating into your soul, and only another dose can make you whole. Because the serum is half light and half dark; it feels like it is taking everything and leaving a chasm in its wake. It's perfectly balanced as long as you're taking it, but the body has a hard time balancing eternity on its own, so as it wears off it feels like it's ending you. In a way, it is. Every cell in your body must transform to accommodate eternity. The serum does it for you as long as you take it. As hard as it is physically, emotionally it's worse." Catherine looked into the distance as if lost inside a painful memory. "It feels like you're tumbling into an abyss, being pulled apart."

"How did you get through it? Why did you bother when you were so alone? It must have felt like there was no reason to even try." He extended a hand to her but stopped when she looked at it as if it were a foreign thing or perhaps just something she didn't think she deserved. When she'd sat with him in his patrol car the night he caught her creeping around Noory's apartment trying to make sure she was okay, she accepted his touch as if she were hungry for it.

"I always believed an opportunity would rise and when it did, I didn't want to be tempted to return because of the addiction. That's the biggest problem we face now, John." She turned and threw the hatchet with expert precision, exercising her rage. He wouldn't want to make her mad right now. "Even if we can manage a rescue, once she's addicted, she will willingly return to cool the fire in her veins. Believe me, it's that bad. Your love won't be enough, not even Nick's."

"So, we have to find a supernatural detox."

"That isn't our only problem."

John raised his eyebrows.

"Her first kill will be coming up soon."

John rubbed a hand across his face. The more the woman talked, the worse things got.

CHAPTER 33

Nick, John, Roy, and Catherine sat around John's coffee table one step away from despondent. Roy had convinced Nick to come over despite John's anger toward him. But he could tell it was all Roy had in him. The light had gone from his eyes. It hurt to even look at this man who had been holding them together in more ways than he'd realized until that energy was gone. Roy currently sat at the table looking like he'd lost everything. From his perspective, he had.

"I can't believe you escaped with your life," Catherine said.

John looked directly at Nick. "I can't believe you didn't take me with you."

The tone of John's voice wasn't angry anymore. It was just . . . sorrowful. John didn't argue anymore about why Nick didn't bring him in the failed rescue attempt. He didn't fly into a fit, didn't give him a speech. He just sat there, looking defeated. It must have been such a head trip to finally get what he wanted—only when he got Catherine, he lost Noory. But it wasn't just John and Catherine who felt like they'd failed; everyone in the room was a sorry sight, including him.

"I wanted there to be someone we could trust on the outside if we all got stuck there. I knew you'd come looking for us."

"That can't happen anymore. If we are going to get her out of there, we have to start working together. It's going to take all of us," John said.

Nick was glad to hear him say that. They still had issues after him going to Damascus instead of John, but he could see that there was hope.

"So, if her first kill is coming up, maybe we could intercept her while she's out and—"

"They'll still have Grace," Roy said.

"They won't kill Grace," Catherine said. "She's a powerful psychic.

Second Sight won't give up a treasure like that. Noory will still go back for the serum, though."

"But if we could just reach her, maybe we could help her detox."

"We have no way of knowing when they'll send her out for the kill."

"We need a dream walker," Catherine said.

"I know you don't want to hear it, but Damascus is a dream walker."

John said, "You're right, Nick. I don't want to hear it. We don't do business with demons."

"That demon saved Noory's life."

"They always have a dark motive. I won't be a part of asking a demon to dream walk my daughter."

"Not even if it could save her life?" Nick asked.

"We'll just find a better way."

"We're listening," Catherine said.

Nick watched a look pass between them. No way this was the same relationship they'd had twenty years ago. Catherine was setting new boundaries for him.

She said, "We may not have a lot of time. You'll have to be flexible, John."

"There are some things we shouldn't compromise on."

"John," Roy began, "I do think Damascus has Noory's best interests at heart."

"Dear Lord, Father. Not you too!"

"He works in mysterious ways. It may be a tired cliché, but it's true," Roy said.

"I need to go think," John said and left the room without another word. Nick looked out the kitchen window and watched him head toward the field.

Catherine sighed as she followed John's progress through the tall grass. "Nick, go call Damascus and have him walk through Noory's dreams tonight. For all we know, they could send Noory out tomorrow. We can't wait out John's stubborn streak."

Nick nodded. He didn't want to anger John, but the Disciple's word wasn't law either.

"I'll let you know what he finds out."

Chapter 34

Damascus slid into bed and looked at the clock. It was 2:00 in the morning. He got comfortable and began deep breathing as he focused on Noory and drifted into sleep. Before long he felt his mind begin to float.

He found her sitting at a desk flipping through a large, ancient text. Her soft rhythmic breathing in real life was superimposed upon the dream. He was seeing and hearing both at once. "Hey, girl. Whatcha doing?"

Noory turned to look at him. "I'm looking for answers."

Damascus leaned over and tried to read the pages of the book. There was nothing there. She wasn't focusing. He gently closed the book. "Will you make me a chair to sit on please?"

"Okay."

"Please give it a lighter shade of inlaid wood with a checkered pattern."

She complied.

"Blue please."

The chair turned blue.

"I'd like it to have orange legs." He sat down in the chair she'd conceived. "This is wonderful. Now that I have your attention, who does Second Sight want you to assassinate?"

He watched sorrow and guilt twist her face. She looked away before she spoke. "Robert."

An ache bloomed in Damascus' chest. He felt it in the dream and from where his body lay in bed. This was his fault for not giving up Roy. Then again, it was time for the cycle of usury to end with Robert. He couldn't have come as far as he thought if this was an alternative to, say, having a serious conversation with the man. *Whatever, no help for it now. Once a demon, always a demon.* He'd thought it before. This time it didn't sit right. *I've become so soft. Fucking, humans.*

He pushed forward with his questions. "What day and time will you be going to Robert's house to assassinate him?"

"Tomorrow at midnight."

She still avoided eye contact. "I'm so sorry. You'll hate me after I do this." She began sobbing. The kind of ugly crying she would have never done in front of anyone. She had no idea he was dream walking her. Once she got out of this mess, he'd have to teach her dream walking. Yet another skill she should already know. John could be such a tool.

"No, honey. I won't," he said, though his heart did ache a little. "What did they threaten you with to make you do this?"

"They told me they would kill Grace."

Damascus nodded. "Who exactly is they?"

"A man named Malachi. I haven't seen his face."

An ancient then.

"Okay. Get some sleep, love." Damascus thought back on what he'd heard Noory talk about that seemed to make her happy. Nick? That would likely grieve her. He conjured a beautiful beach for her, sun, sky, swaying palms, but as he started to leave, the waves became enormous, and she backed away in terror.

"We've got to get you out of here." He snapped his fingers, and they were at John's farm, in the field with the sheep. She closed her eyes and smiled, letting the sun warm her face. Before he left, he whispered, "Don't worry, babe. I'm gonna help you. Don't tell anyone I've gone so fucking soft."

Damascus stood below the office window of Robert's Buckhead estate. "There he is," he whispered. A soft glow emanated around the heavy curtain. He could hear Robert talking through his Bluetooth headset, but no one else could. Not even the best parabolic mics could get past the wards Robert had him put in place years ago. It was a good thing since the handlers who had been sent with Noory were one street over and through the tree line. Damascus sensed no presence in the home other than Robert's.

Robert's wife had left him recently, which made this whole thing easier. He used his key to get into the basement door farthest from where Robert was. It would take longer to reach him but make less noise.

Finally, he reached the hallway where his office was and felt another presence of some power. It was a confusing mix of light and dark energies. Though formidable, he sensed it could not overpower him. Just three feet from the office, he came face to face with Noory.

They stood looking at each other. "You're not supposed to be here yet!" he hissed.

"I knew it! You *are* a dream walker! No fair! That is so not okay," she whisper-yelled.

"I can't let you do this," he said. "And why do you read light *and* dark now? You used to read all light?"

"Never mind that! This hit is my responsibility. I have to protect Grace."

"Why? Because some prick at Second Sight says so? You weren't made for this, Beh—Noory." Damascus looked away, realizing he'd almost called Noory by his sister's name. "I'll do it."

The look on Noory's face was one of pain and empathy. It made him love her even more. *Love her. Shit, when did that happen?* He had to get away from these fucking people.

"You love Robert," she whispered. "You cannot do this."

"And he's used me from day one. It's time I got free. If he's alive, that can't happen."

"Not like this." Noory put her hand on Damascus' arm. "This will damage you."

"Noory, I'm over two thousand years old. I've killed more than you can fathom." He realized it was time to make a statement, "I've maimed. I've tortured." He unsheathed his claws and ran one beneath her jaw. "*I am a destroyer.*" If he had to scare the shit out of her to save her innocence, he'd do it.

Noory's shaking hand passed through a shaft of moonlight streaming in from the skylight window and grabbed his wrist. "Then why are you are crying?" she asked.

Fuck.

From inside Robert's study came a grunt and a thud. Damascus slowly opened the door and in the glow of the desk lamp, he saw Nick standing over Robert's body. Robert's head twisted at an unnatural angle. Damascus felt his brain racing to catch up to what his eyes were seeing. He was no stranger to death. So why was his brain refusing to process?

Nick looked at Noory in a way that Damascus knew Robert never had, never would, and now, never could look at him. Nick would do anything for her. He would kill to spare her conscience, and Damascus couldn't hate him for it. He was about to do the same for her if Nick hadn't beat him to it. He envied the shit out of that kind of love. When did that tricky bastard even get inside? He'd sensed no one in the house other than Robert.

Nick tore his gaze from Noory and looked at him. "I'm sorry."

"I know," Damascus whispered. Grief ricocheted through his chest, competing for dominance with the relief he felt over not having to deliver the killing blow. Somewhere deeper still was a relief to be free of the burden of unrequited love. But the leaden weight on his chest . . . it begged him to go home, curl up, disappear, for how long he couldn't say.

"You can't fight my battles for eternity, Nick," Noory said.

"Eternity?" Nick whispered as he studied her face. He walked toward her slowly, cautiously, as if he were afraid to believe, to hope that it could be true. That what he had with her might last. He reached up with a shaking hand and looked into her eyes. "My God. It's true."

Chapter 35

Noory placed a hand on Damascus' arm and looked up at him. "Take all the time you need."

"I'm fine," he said softly, never taking his eyes off Robert's body, which lay on the office floor. He'd arranged him in a peaceful pose and closed his eyes.

Damascus noticed the way Nick and Noory looked at each other, and it made his chest ache in a different way. She had to return with Robert's body to Second Sight to confirm her kill. But why couldn't she and Nick have some time together first? "Tell you what, I'll ward the house and show an illusion of him still walking back and forth, talking on his phone in front of the window. They'll think you are still waiting for the right moment and don't want him alerting whoever he's talking to. It'll only buy you a few hours. Go, spend some time with Hot Santa before you have to go back."

"You can't just sit here with his body while Nick and I are together."

"Noory, the whole time you're with him, you'll know you have to return to Second Sight in a few hours. Trust me, I know very well I won't be the only one in mourning."

When Noory and Nick materialized in his penthouse kitchen, the mood was somber, but she was glad to be back in his home. He paused before turning to look at her. She could see it in his eyes; he wanted to ask her about her immortality. He was afraid to ask, and she was afraid to tell him. Maybe her mother already had. She knew she needed to distract him, and it wouldn't be hard. Mixed in with the questions in his eyes was something far more urgent—hunger, lust.

Noory stepped toward him with the idea to distract, but it only took one step in his direction for the misdirection to morph into something far more genuine. The dam burst, and all the fear and sorrow she'd held tight within for the last two weeks broke free, and she reached for him like he was a lifeline in a hurricane. A sob tore from her throat as he closed the distance. She pressed her mouth to his and tried to convey the longing, fear, love, anger, devotion. His mouth claimed hers with equal ferocity as he wove his fingers through her hair and tilted her face to meet his. He said, "You don't belong to them. You're mine."

Fire shot through her core and scorched her veins. His words reminded her of things he'd said while possessed by the demonic entity last year. Only this time, it was all Nick and damned if that didn't make it sexier. "Yours. Only yours. Forever. No matter where I am. When. What century." He took her by the hand and looked around the kitchen, searching. God, she hoped he was looking for a place to bend her over and—

"Island," he said, as he seemed to lose the ability to speak in complete sentences. He pulled her shirt off and threw it to the floor, walked backwards to the island, and then unbuttoned her pants, turned her around, and pulled them down. She heard his own belt and zipper loosen. His big, warm hand slid across her back, stopped at her bra, unhooked it and yanked it away as if it offended him. His two hands slid beneath her breasts and held them as he groaned. Then he freed a hand to rub between her legs, and he ran a tongue along her earlobe as she moaned. She felt his smile along her cheek. Clearly, he loved the power to make her moan. The cool marble of the island contrasted with the heat coming off his chest now curved to fit around her body perfectly.

Two fingers entered her, and she whimpered.

"Miss me?" he asked.

"Horribly."

From the corner of her eye, everything about him was slaying her now, even the way his large hand grabbed her smaller wrist. "Good. I'm going to give you something you won't forget for an eternity." He tilted his head, locked eyes with her, and entered her. She sucked in a breath.

Her other hand smacked the countertop like a wrestler tapping out, only she wasn't about to surrender. He was warm, big, exquisite, and all hers. Deeper he pushed, and she angled herself higher and pushed back to meet him until the impact almost made her see stars. She didn't care. The last two weeks had felt like two years. When he reached between her legs to touch her, she couldn't believe how fast she came. She immediately felt him lengthen within her and, with one final push and growl, he relaxed.

His warmth and weight covered her before he moved away suddenly. "I'm sorry. I don't know what I was thinking. I could've cracked some bones leaning you over this marble. Are you okay?" he asked, sliding a hand over her ribs.

Straightening up slowly, she felt a bit of an ache from the countertop, but the bliss outweighed it by far. She smiled. "It's all right." She pulled up her pants and watched him dress with shaking hands. She spoke softly. "You okay?"

"Yeah. Listen. You aren't taking Robert back to them. We've all been talking, and your mother thinks they won't kill Grace. She's worth far too much to them alive."

Noory felt panic wash over her.

Nick reached over and pulled her to him. "It's okay. Grace will be okay."

She felt guilty when she realized Nick thought the panic was for Grace. Noory realized with a dash of shame that the panic was for herself. She didn't want to be away from the serum. She hadn't even thought she'd had time to become addicted to it, but it wasn't just that. It was Grace, too. "I cannot, I will not, leave without Grace."

"I won't teleport you back to Robert's house."

"Then I'll go myself."

"No."

"You cannot run my life for me. Grace will sit there thinking surely I haven't left her, then days will go by and she will slowly come to understand that I just *left her there*. God, Nick, I can't do that to her. It's wrong of you, John, all of you, to expect that."

And then there was the serum. They had her, and they knew it. She wanted to hate Lorien for giving it to her, but she couldn't. She would have taken it if she'd had to steal it, knowing everything she did now. It was her chance for an eternity with Nick, even if the next several decades were stolen while she fought for a way out.

"Noory, I can't lose you again. I don't know if I'm strong enough. You're my everything." He held her closer, and she felt a tear dampen her ear. This might hurt her more than the withdrawals.

"Every moment hurts." She pushed the words past the lump in her throat. "Maybe we shouldn't draw this out. It's too hard." Her voice cracked.

"I still don't think you should go, but I won't control you. Give me one thing before you go." He walked over to the laptop sitting on the kitchen table, clicked a few keys, and then soft music filled the air. He held out his hand. "Dance with me," he whispered.

She took his hand and curled into his warmth as they swayed, and she listened to his breath, then he pulled her hand in the air and turned her in a slow pirouette. He gave her a sad smile as he looked at her. When the music stopped, he wrapped his arms around her, and she found herself in Robert's office again.

Damascus stood a few feet away with a hat box. Noory felt perplexed for a moment until she noticed the body was wrapped in plastic and shorter than when they'd left it. "Oh, God. Is that his he—"

"Yes. In a convenient carrying case," Damascus said.

Noory swallowed the bile threatening to rise up her throat.

"And that was awfully quick, you two." Damascus pointed to Nick. "Are you a rodeo cowboy who thinks eight seconds is enough?"

Nick sighed as if the exhaustion reached through the ages.

Damascus lost his smirk and gave them a sad smile. "Well, may as well keep it light because there is no upside to this shit show."

Noory nodded and appreciated the attempt at levity. She turned to Nick. He touched his forehead to hers and spoke softly. "Promise. Promise me you will never stop trying to get back to me."

"As long as you promise me you won't give up and fall down that hole you were in when I found you."

"I promise," he said, then leaned in and kissed her with ferocity. The shaking was increasing, but whether from the lack of serum or the heartbreak of leaving Nick, she couldn't tell. Both, she guessed. "I love you," she whispered.

"I love you, too, Light. Always will."

She grabbed the hat box from Damascus but refused to turn around and look at Nick again. It hurt way too bad. But she did hug Damascus and whispered, "Thank you. Keep an eye on him. Please."

"Hell, girl. I can barely look away now," he said with a devilish smile that didn't reach his eyes. "Please. Take care of yourself and get the fuck out of there the first chance you get."

"I will." She turned and left with the box. Once out of the office, she let the tears flow as she walked out of the house and into the cold spring night.

Chapter 36

Roy sat by the little stream at the back of John's property, watching the water flow softly over the rocks. The light made its way through the branches and leaves overhead, creating dappled, intermittent patterns on the water. He savored the coolness of the spring air, soaking in the moments on the Earthly plane . . . while he could.

"Father?"

Roy turned and gave Catherine a sad smile.

"May I sit with you for a while?"

"Of course."

She sat down beside him on the mat of dried leaves, pine needles, and moss and hugged her jean-clad legs to herself for a while before speaking. She was a hard woman to most of the world, but he felt it, beneath the surface, a reservoir of light and love as pure and constant as the stream in front of him.

Her voice was soft as she spoke, "I never really thanked you for saving my life. I was so busy being distraught over having failed Noory I didn't stop and realize what you had given up in that moment. We're a sorry, guilty pair. Aren't we?"

Roy ran a hand across his face. He wanted to laugh and cry all at once. Here he sat, a priest returned from purgatory, on the farm of John the Beloved, talking to a descendant of the Holy Family. He'd had it all: a holy commission straight from God to fight alongside these people while hearing the very voice of God—or perhaps a spirit guide. Whatever it was, it sounded beautiful and spoke in impressions, colors, light, music. It was beyond anything . . . "The silence is killing me." His voice cracked on the words, and the anguish poured from him and felt as if it were ripping him apart from the inside. "It would have been better if I'd never known. If I'd never heard His voice. Now I'm here, in hell."

Catherine wrapped an arm around him and pulled him close to lean on her shoulder, just as he'd done for her the night she'd been sent to kill him. He gasped and sobbed. She put her other arm around him and rocked slowly, softly, as if he were a child, and he did not resist. Somewhere a soft, distant thread of what he'd heard in the now-silent voice of God resided in her, and he could feel it weaving its golden thread through his weary soul as she spoke, "Our humanity got the best of us. I just wanted to see my daughter. You just wanted to save me. It isn't too much to ask. I thought I'd never be able to forgive myself until this very moment. I don't know why you can't hear Him anymore, but if you are being punished for trying to save someone you love, then He is not God, and you shouldn't worry about whether He speaks to you again."

Her words felt blasphemous and true all at once. He laughed in her embrace, sat up, and wiped his eyes. "Thank you, my friend."

He watched her look up and to the side before speaking again. "Have you ever thought that maybe He didn't stop speaking but you stopped hearing because you thought you were no longer worthy due to what you did?"

"No."

"Who in the world would stop speaking to you?" She took his hand. "I believe you're wrong about what is happening to you. You're a wonderful soul."

"I have to find out. I can't live in this world without my connection to the other side. I don't know how anymore. I'm going back, Catherine, and I'm going to search that plane and call out to Him until He answers me."

"'Jacob said to the angel, *I will not let you go until you bless me.* He wrestled the angel and won, and was given a new name, Israel, the man who struggles with God,'" she quoted from Genesis.

"Maybe I know how he feels."

She nodded. "I know this is selfish, but we need you now more than ever."

"I can look out for you from the other side. I can find out even more maybe, but I can't keep living like this. Every moment is painful now."

"I can't tell you not to go, but John and Nick, they will miss you so badly."

"Nick should be able to find me if he needs me. Can you do me a favor?"

"Sure."

"Please don't tell them I'm leaving. Everyone will try to talk me out of it, and I have to do this. I just have to."

Beside him she sighed and nodded.

"I know. It's a lot to ask. I know it's unfair. They'll want to say good-bye, and John will want to control this. He's a good man. The best. But he thinks he knows what's best for everyone, and I can't let him steamroll me on this."

"Yeah, I get that. Okay. I won't say anything, but, if at all possible, please come back to us. Consider that your frail humanity is part of a bigger picture, and it's okay to simply have to live on faith like the rest of us, huh?" She gave him a playful punch.

Her words stung a little, mostly because they rang true. It had crossed his mind more than once that he was no better than the rest of humanity to go back to finding God in the silences, in the faces of each other, in the joy, in the pain, but at the bottom of it all was the terror that he'd broken some sacred trust, and he'd been abandoned entirely. "I have to do this," he whispered without looking at her.

She put her hand on top of his. "I know. I'll be here when you get back."

He was surprised when she didn't get up to leave, but instead lay her head on his shoulder, sat with him, and listened to the wind through the trees and the water flowing in an endless stream over the rocks before them.

Chapter 37

Father Roy's absence permeated the farmhouse, and Catherine felt a small sense of guilt for not telling John, but she knew as well Roy did that it was for the best.

"I just can't believe he wouldn't tell me," John said.

"He knew you'd try to talk him out of it."

Catherine squirmed a little beneath John's gaze, the one that always peered straight through to her soul, but she refused to look away. As soon as they'd reconnected, she'd remembered his weakness: control. There was a time when she thought his need for control had to do with him trying to put a permanence on things when he'd watched almost everyone he'd ever loved pass away, but now she wondered if he'd been that way since the beginning. It didn't matter. Her heart still did somersaults when he turned that ancient, dark gaze her way.

"Catherine?"

"What?"

"You know something."

"Does it matter? If he wants to go, he's a grown man and you can't stop him."

"You could've warned me."

"He asked me not to." The hurt look on John's face made her chest ache. "That's just an indication that he knows you love him and would try to keep him here."

"Damn right. He's just on a guilt trip. You can't chase God down and force Him to speak to you."

The anger in John's voice told her this was about more than Roy. She reached across the table and took his hand. "You know what it's like to feel abandoned."

"I'm not abandoned. There's a reason I'm still here."

"But you don't know what that is and sometimes it must feel as if you've been forgotten."

John whispered, "Maybe . . . now and then." She wondered if he'd even realized he'd whispered the words, as if on some level he was afraid the Almighty would hear his lack of faith and be hurt.

"I know a little about that, too." And there it was, that bond, one of the many reasons she loved this stubborn fool. That, and those damn eyes. She kept gazing into those eyes, and he gazed back.

Their cups of coffee made thin trails of steam between them through the soft golden light of sunrise coming in through the kitchen window to fall softly on the old oak table. Since she'd returned, they'd not been able to truly reconnect. Moments of passion so strong it made her knees buckle would overcome her. Flashes of him pressing her against the barn wall a few days ago took her breath away. She thanked God every-day he'd not found someone else while she was away. Every couple of days, they'd kiss with intense ferocity before guilt would overcome one or the other. And then, either out loud or with a loaded silence, they'd express the guilt that kept them from experiencing the joy of being together again. How could they when their daughter was captive? Her body ached with decades of pent-up need, love, desire. Even more than that, she longed for comfort. His touch could do that.

"John," she said with a tremble in her voice. She didn't know how he knew, maybe the hunger in her eyes or the need in her voice that she couldn't conceal, didn't want to conceal. He said nothing but shoved his chair back from the table, strode forward to grab her hand, and they walked to the bedroom together. He laid her down on his bed and placed his palm on the side of her face and she said, "I've been alone for two decades. I can't do it anymore."

"I can't either," he said before his mouth found hers. He eased his weight over her.

She set her guilt aside and they began their forever again.

Chapter 38

Grace walked into the lab to find Lorien, but he wasn't there. She walked into the room just off the lab where extra supplies and refrigeration were stored but still no Lorien. When she walked back out, Locus stood there. He'd come in and closed the door behind him so quietly he could have been a ghost.

Grace jumped. The silvery tone to his skin didn't help in the ghost department.

"Looking for someone?" he asked. He removed the cufflinks from his pristine tailored shirt. Locus was a man who liked fine things. That was one of the features that had initially attracted her to him, that and he looked at her as if he understood her, knew something about her, and damned if that wasn't sexy. But lately, he'd been showing up in her path far too much to be coincidence and looking at her in a way that made her nervous.

"No." She attempted to walk past him, but his arm shot out.

He said, "Let's talk some more."

"I don't want to."

"I think you do. You just don't want to admit it."

"And I think no means no."

"You and I could form such an alliance. We could practically be running this place. Noory may have brawn, but she does not have the brains. You and I hold all the keys. People like Noory don't even know what target to strike without people like us."

He pulled her to his side with his arm around her as if she were a long-time girlfriend. She knew from experience that running would escalate the situation very quickly, but staying put would encourage him to continue. There were no easy outs for women in her situation.

"Let me go, please."

"I can give you everything."

"I don't want anything from you." She attempted to pull away, but his arm was like a vise. She felt panic roll down her body and knew, at least at the moment, she would trade in her mental gift for Noory's brawn in a heartbeat. He was a good-looking man, beast, demon, whatever, and ironically someone she would have sold herself to in her earlier life, but now she had a healthy dose of self-respect and had to get away from this creature. The problem was, she didn't know if she could.

He turned to her and leaned her back over the countertop.

"Let. Me. Go," she said through clenched teeth.

He said nothing but pressed his body against hers. She could feel his erection pushing against her stomach. She squirmed and thrashed. But it was like being pinned by a wall.

"Don't fight me. I can give you everything you've never had. If you resist, I can take everything. In here and out there. You'll learn to love me. It won't always have to be like this. Besides, you owe me for what your friend did." He gestured to his scar as his body pinned her in place.

She wondered if there was any way at all to stop him. Unless someone came wandering by, how would anyone even know they were in here? Noory had been sent out on some errand. Lorien worked in the lab a lot. Maybe he would come by. In time, though? At the thought of him, she remembered that she'd heard his thoughts once before and wondered if it might work in reverse. She screamed in her head for him and showed him the clearest picture she could of where she was and what was happening to her. She poured all the fear, the dread, and even the pain of the countertop biting into the small of her back into the thought, with little hope of it working.

"You're beautiful, but I bet you don't realize just how much, do you? Your eyes are so green, like a glistening morning in Galway. We could trade this slouchy teen angst get-up I always see you in for clothing more suited to a woman of your caliber." He ran a hand down the side of her breast. "It's time you lived up to your potential and realized just how powerful you are. The things I could show you, buy you. We could go anywhere and do anything. I've waited so long for someone who understands the power, the potential. It could be you."

He grasped her chin and swiveled her face toward him. "Stop looking at the door and relax. I've locked it down. No one can get in. Even with their passkey." So even if Lorien got her message, he wouldn't be able to get in. Her mouth went dry with terror. Could she just go somewhere else in her head like she did sometimes back when she had sold herself? She had left all that behind, only to find herself here at this bastard's mercy.

Grace's ears felt as if they were imploding as the metal lab door flew across the room. From her periphery she saw a body leap to the corner of the ceiling beside the door where she knew the camera was, and before she could even calculate what was happening next, Lorien was on Locus' back. Locus roared at him.

"Look away," Lorien said. His voice was so forceful and distorted from his canines being extended that she complied out of shock but then turned back to see. She wanted to know Lorien, really know him. In a rush of clarity, she knew this was what it meant to know every aspect of who he was.

Long white fangs sank into the back of Locus' neck as he tried to turn and get Lorien off him, but it was too little, too late. Even though Locus was bigger, his was a power of the mind, and Lorien was preternaturally fast, strong, walking death. Grace heard a crunch that could only be Locus' neck snapping. She looked away again before Lorien could know she'd witnessed the killing bite. Locus' head had blocked his view of her. A wave of nausea washed over her because of the blood and the unnatural way Locus' neck fell to the side, but it changed nothing about how she felt about Lorien. He was still a good person, coming to her aid the best way he knew how.

The pressure on her body released as she felt Lorien yank Locus off her and drag his body into the storage room. It had all taken mere seconds. She realized this must have been why a being as strong as Locus had backed down from Lorien when they'd first arrived. Locus could see turning points ahead. Perhaps he'd sensed his death in Lorien's hands someday.

She followed him inside and stood there fighting guilt that she'd dragged Lorien into this situation and anger that she should have to feel bad about something that wasn't her fault. Lorien's face was back in its usual state, though his pupils had overtaken the bronze irises entirely. "Stay here," he said to her.

He ran to the metal door that had hit the wall, picked it up, raced to the doorway, and jammed it back in place. He got on the intercom next: "There's been a biohazard breach in the lab. No one is to enter until the all clear is given." He also shoved a massive cooling unit against the door in case someone decided to enter anyway. Then he moved so fast back to Grace's side he was a blur.

"Are you okay?" he asked. He put his hands on her shoulders and looked her up and down frantically.

Something inside her wanted to burst into tears, which pissed her off to no end. She was proud of how strong her years on the street had made her. Then a new thought hit her: maybe she was just touched that he would value her this much. She opened her mouth to speak, but nothing came out. She nodded instead.

"I'm sorry you had to see this," Lorien said as he gestured to Locus' body with blood pouring from his broken and bloodied neck.

Then the words came. "I'm not. Screw him."

"There she is," Lorien said as the shadow of a smile played about his lips. It was then that she noticed the splatters of blood on his white lab coat. He stepped away and began rummaging through the shelves.

"I'm sorry for you," she said.

"What? Why?"

"You once told me you don't drain people. You said you were looking to understand what was wrong with you. That you didn't like being . . . I get the idea you don't like using your vampirism in this way."

"This is one of those times I'm grateful for it."

He said it so matter of fact, with no caveat, that she believed him. He'd given into it, let it take hold of him for her.

"There," he said, taking a couple of white emergency candles from a box he'd found on the shelf.

"What are those for?"

"For summoning a Reaper. Of course."

Chapter 39

"A what now?" Grace asked.

"A Reaper. You should know how to summon one. With the gift you have and the kind of people you know, you are bound to end up involved in things you can't explain to the police and bodies you won't so easily be able to hide. Doesn't mean you've done anything wrong. Like today was not your fault. But here we are." He gestured to Locus.

"What does a Reaper do? It is a being, more or less, that will come and eat the energy left in the cells of the body. Everything disappears. If the body is too old and there is almost no energy left in it, the Reaper will either refuse or ask for some other form of payment. That won't be a problem here. Locus has massive amounts of energy."

"Should I go? Is it okay if the Reaper sees me?" Grace couldn't trace why, but she felt . . . guilt.

"Why?"

"Well," Grace said and wrung her hands, "I don't know, I . . . This wouldn't have happened if I hadn't—"

Lorien's voice took on a deep, serious tone. "Look at me."

She forced herself to make eye contact with him. He said, "This isn't your fault. The Reaper doesn't show up and hold a trial. It doesn't care. It just reaps. That's it." He tilted his head and looked at her more closely. "You're still not okay." He sighed. "Why would you be? We'll get this taken care of, and you and I can talk about this."

Grace nodded.

Lorien sat the candles up beside the body, lit them, and began chanting in a language that sounded very archaic to her. After a minute, a breeze came from nowhere, and a being stood at the foot of the body. Grace had expected an ominous being in a long black robe with hollow eyes and pale skin. Instead, the Reaper was roughly 5'8" and rather androgynous looking with light brown hair shaved above the ears and neck and hanging off to one side, covering one of their hazel eyes. They wore jeans with holes at the knees and a loose gauzy button-up. The Reaper enjoyed comfort.

"What have we here?" they said and sniffed the air. "Oh, fuck!" They backed up a few steps until they bumped into the shelving and put a hand back to brace itself. "Mind if I call a couple of friends to join me?"

Grace looked at Lorien.

The Reaper looked at Grace. "Don't worry, Seer," the Reaper spoke gently. "I'm not summoning them for you. I can't contain all of this," they said gesturing to Locus. They tilted their head and concentrated, then snapped their fingers twice. Two individuals appeared beside them. One was a middle-aged woman with brown skin wearing a bright yellow sari. The other was a younger, short man in a business suit.

"Oh, my," the woman said, seeming pleased.

The man in the suit nodded his approval.

The Reaper who appeared first said, "We approve of your offering. No further payment is requested."

The three closed their eyes and extended their hands. The air between Locus' body and their palms wavered like heat radiating off the pavement on a sweltering hot day, though the room was cool. He disintegrated bit by bit, his matter evaporating like a vapor. In a matter of seconds, the formidable power that he was simply vanished, leaving only his pristine dress clothes and shoes. Even the blood trail leading into the supply room and the blood splatters on Lorien's coat disappeared.

"With our thanks," the original Reaper said. The three bowed their heads. Their images wavered for a second, then disappeared.

They both looked at the spot where Locus had lain just moments before, where now only his garments lay. She didn't know about Lorien but the surreal quality of it all just wasn't sinking in. She wasn't sure if it ever would. But, at the moment, she just felt deep remorse that she had gotten Lorien into trouble. She'd gotten him into something that she should have been able to handle herself. What would they do to him if they found out he'd killed Locus? "I dragged you into this. I'm so sorry. I don't have anyone on the outside who could suffer for my actions, but you do, and I'm very, very sorry that I might have just pulled you into something that could place your sister in jeopardy. I really—"

"Stop, Grace. I saw the panic in your head. I know what was about to happen to you. You couldn't just stand there and let him rape you. He's done it before, you know."

"No. I didn't know. I've seen many things since my brain got all rewired, but I've never wanted to see into his. Was it because I knew on some level, he was a bad person and I wanted to remain ignorant about it? Jesus, Lorien. I'm so disgusted with myself. When I first met him, I was actually attracted to him. What's wrong with me? What does it say about me that I would feel that way about this monster?"

"You didn't know what he was. Most women are sexually assaulted by someone they know. Do you think there's something wrong with them? Are they bad people?"

"No."

"Then give yourself a break."

"Will you get into trouble for this?"

"I don't think so. It's likely they just won't know where he went." Lorien's cell phone began ringing. She heard him talking into it as she walked out of the supply room and into the lab proper, keeping a hand on her lower back, which was getting more and more painful by the moment.

Lorien disconnected the call and walked over to her. "You're in pain. Let me get you something for that before people arrive with questions and hazmat suits. How painful is it? One to ten?"

She tried to bend forward a little then back up and gasped as a stabbing sensation tore through her lower back. Heat gathered behind her eyes, but she quickly blinked it away before Lorien could see. "An eight," she said.

Lorien walked over to a cabinet, came back with a syringe, adjusted the dosage, emptied into her arm, and put the syringe in a sharps container on the wall. "Do you mind taking the fall for a little container spill? I have to find a reason for ripping the door off its hinges."

"Not at all."

"Okay. So, you spilled some ammonia, and I smelled it wafting under the door. I was afraid someone was in here overcome by fumes. It turned out it was you. You are fine. The spill is cleaned up. We replaced the door. We're done. Got it?"

"Got it." Whatever drug Lorien had given her was starting to work. She was feeling woozy. "If they start questioning me, I'll just tell them I was trying to see if I could recreate one of those science project volcanoes like you make in middle school."

"That'll work. Ready?"

"What about the cameras? I saw you take it off the wall when you came in, but they'll see what he was doing, know that the camera cut off right after that, and maybe put two and two together."

"I suspect he already disabled the camera before he attacked you, I just went ahead and took it out as a precaution. I wouldn't worry about it." He gave her one more look and whispered, "It's okay."

She nodded. He dumped Locus' clothes and shoes into an incinerator unit and then moved the refrigeration unit from the door and slid the broken door aside.

As predicted, a security team arrived shortly thereafter and asked her a few questions. Then she went back to her room and laid down.

More than anything she hoped Noory would walk through the door. She felt alone and isolated now that she wasn't with Lorien.

She knew it was a selfish thought, knew she should hope her friend escaped, but the thought kept circling around, what if Noory didn't return?

Chapter 40

Noory walked into the room she shared with Grace at around 2:00 a.m. with a heavy heart. Lorien had met her when she arrived, saying they were all up late because of a chemical spill. Her bullshit detector was going off, and the way Lorien looked at her said he knew she knew he was lying, but there were still a couple of people milling about. Clearly, he couldn't talk about it but gave Noory another dose of the serum. She got the feeling they would have talked more about that as well, but he seemed a bit rattled.

The pain in her heart over leaving Nick kept coming at her in waves, but seeing Grace asleep just a few feet from her was a balm. She knew she'd done the right thing by returning. Now she stood over her, watching her sleep and wondering how she went from protecting her at the shelter to getting her in this situation. When would it end? How would it end?

"You were right about Locus," Grace whispered. She sat up with a wince and turned the bedside lamp on.

"Sorry. I didn't mean to wake you." Noory sat on the edge of the bed. "I saw Lorien. Something seemed off."

Grace looked at Noory and pantomimed writing. Noory nodded and went to gather a pen and paper from her nightstand and brought it to Grace.

Grace told her everything. Afterward she said, "I owe him," and grimaced as she rubbed her lower back.

"He wouldn't want you thinking about it that way."

"No. He wouldn't. He's a good person like that."

"I think so. Yes. I'm so sorry that I brought you into this screwed up—"

"Stop. You've saved my ass so many times. You have nothing to apologize for. I'm where I want to be right now. If you were stuck in here, and I didn't know what was happening to you, I'd go crazy."

Noory had to fight back tears. Grace was worried about her as well. It was so similar to her own thoughts all evening.

"And now, I can get more information about what's happening to me." Grace leaned her head lower onto Noory's shoulder and spoke into her ear, "And Lorien makes a wonderful ally. There are worse situations to be in."

"Indeed." As horrible as it all was, they had each other and one scary strong friend in a lab coat.

Grace continued whispering, "I should have listened to you about Locus. Now, Lorien had to use the thing he hates most about himself to save me."

"He didn't mind doing it for you."

"That's what he told me, too."

"We're going to get out of here someday. I promise."

"I won't leave without you *or Lorien*. Never ask me to."

Noory nodded. "I won't." That might prove one of the hardest promises to keep. If Grace had a chance to leave, she wanted her to take it more than anything, even at the cost of her own loneliness.

Noory kicked her boots off and went into the bathroom, flipped on the light and soaked the paper they'd written on until all the ink was unreadable and then began washing up for bed. She brushed her teeth, splashed her face with water, and stood with her arms braced on the sink as the water dripped from her chin. All the power she possessed, and she couldn't just walk out. She looked into the mirror and could barely recognize the person looking back. She didn't look quite the same anymore but damned if she could pinpoint what had changed. It was both comforting and disturbing. Comforting because the old her couldn't survive here but disturbing because she wasn't quite sure what she was becoming.

CHAPTER 41

Nick walked through Centennial Olympic Park with Evan. It was a beautiful spring day, but the pain of running the shelter without Noory was always with him. He had so much power and yet, what good did it do him? Now here he was, about to tell this kid that he was a powerful being, and why? It would likely just get him into trouble. Would it drive him to drinking too? No, he had to tell him about all the good he could do with his gift. He couldn't let Evan lose sight of that.

While the kid was gazing at the huge Ferris wheel at the top of the park, Nick inspected Evan's aura. At first, it was harder to see than the average person's, almost like looking through a microscope that he couldn't get into focus. Was it somehow cloaking itself? When it coalesced . . . it was beautiful. It appeared to have green flames emanating from it. In all his seventeen hundred years, he'd never seen the like.

"Haven't seen Grace in a while. Has she moved?" Evan ate another bite of the hotdog Nick had bought him and pointed to a bench by the reflecting pool.

They sat and Nick ate another bite of his, but it was sitting in his gut like a stone. Would this kid think he was insane? Nick unscrewed the cap from his water and took a drink. Was it okay to pretend it was ouzo or was imagining a type of gateway drug unto itself? Oh, yeah. Evan was asking about Grace.

"She's been helping her aunt a lot lately." Dear God, was Damascus going to have to spell this kid to make him think Grace was somewhere else too? Would a spell hold on a magus? He'd never dealt with one before.

"Hmm. She's a good kid."

Nick stifled a laugh. "So, do you consider yourself more of a skeptic or do you believe in supernatural things?"

"Well, my mother says it's best to leave that stuff alone, but I think it's all around us. I mean why else can humans concentrate really hard and make it rain? Why can we move fire a little when we're trying to toast our marshmallows, but then we're afraid to move it any farther in because we don't want to burn our eyebrows? Why can we pull a warm spot to us when we get in the ocean, and it's a little too cold? That sounds like we're moving nature around, right? I mean, why does God let us do those things?"

Nick started choking on the water he'd drank. Evan patted him on the back. "You okay?" Nick nodded but kept coughing.

"Evan, people can't—" he started coughing again. "Damn it. Sorry. Regular people cannot do all those things you just mentioned."

"Of course they can."

"No. They can't."

"Oh, stop it."

"I'm serious. Have you ever asked your friends, your mother, if she can do those things?"

"Well, no. I just assumed . . ."

"There are supernatural beings in this world, but what you're describing, the average human cannot do those things. What if I told you there's a reason you can? Would you be okay with that?"

"Would it help me with the ladies?"

Nick slapped a palm across his face. "Lord, help me. I swear. Evan."

"What? I need game!"

"No, you need to just be yourself, and no, you can't run around telling people about this. Look at it this way though: there's something to be said for a man with quiet confidence. It's the sexiest thing in the world. Trust me."

"I do actually. You landed Noory, and she's *hot*!"

Nick laughed. "Okay, so you know my friend Damascus you met the other day in Noory's office. The—"

"Oh my God! Yeah, the one with the freaky orange contacts?"

"Yeah, those aren't contacts. He's . . . different."

Evan gazed into the distance before looking at Nick again. "Things make more sense now. So that's why he buzzes."

"Buzzes?" Nick asked.

"Yeah, you know how certain people's body gives off a faint buzzing? Like their body is vibrating. I guess everyone describes it differently, but we don't often run into someone like him."

"He doesn't buzz around me."

"You sure?" Evan said, his eyes big.

"Yup."

"Huh. Well, it always reminds me of this level I found. I used to play with it and watch the bubble go back and forth. For some reason, when I meet someone who buzzes, I think if I could put the level on their head and balance them, they'd stop buzzing. Like maybe, they are out of balance in this world."

"Dude, you are fascinating," Nick said.

"That's the first time anyone has told me that. They've told me I'm a big ol' nerd, kinda weird . . . but *fascinating*? Not so much."

"It's true. I didn't notice myself until Damascus told me. I didn't even think to look for it, but your aura gives off green flames with a little blue mixed in.

"Why?"

"You're a magus. One of the magi."

"Magi? Like one of the three wise men? Those are the only magi I know."

"Yes, like that. Yours is more like a genetic heredity thing. We think you are descended from an ancient line of Zoroastrian priests. The religion is still around today."

"Well, what does this mean? What am I supposed to do with this?"

"We think you were born to herald a great event of some sort. Damascus was the first to notice. I think it might be wise to introduce you to someone that can help you learn to hide your aura."

"Why would I want to do that? It sounds awesome to me."

"It wouldn't be awesome if the wrong person found out and tried to use you for something bad."

"Your aura is blue and white mostly. When you look sad, it gets black streaks. I can tell you're worried when that happens. I've never been able to see my own."

"Me neither."

The two of them finished their hot dogs, got up, and began walking.

"You're something different. Aren't you? And Noory too? I know she's different because I've never seen an aura like hers. It has this pulsating core of white surrounded by this soothing pink and green, but here's the fascinating part that I've never, ever seen before in the same person, there's red hovering about the edges, just waiting, hanging out in case it's needed." Evan shuddered. "I have a feeling that hot chic could mess you up if you crossed her."

Nick laughed. "Yes. Yes, she can."

"What are you?"

Nick ducked in behind a maintenance shed and breathed deep, allowing his power to unfurl. "Okay, now please don't feel threatened." Two daggers with a soft blue glow appeared in each of Nick's hands. They disappeared just as quickly.

"Whoa! Can I have that power?"

"We don't exactly get to choose, but I'm thinking if you can move the elements a little, then with practice, maybe you could move them *a lot.*"

"I bet Grace would think I was cool if I could do that."

The two walked and talked for the next hour. Nick told him his origin story.

"So, there is a Santa Claus. I knew it," Evan said.

"Such as it is. Yes."

"Well, you're way cooler than the story I heard when I was a kid."

Nick chuckled, but almost cried as well. This boy's sense of wonder and innocence made him feel humbled, everything seemed simpler. Evan needed him. He could do this.

They'd made their way almost back to the shelter when the hairs on the back of Nick's neck stood on end. He turned to look and a man whose face was obscured by a hoodie broke from the crowd on the street and darted away down a side ally once Nick had spotted him.

Evan was still chatting and didn't seem to notice.

Yeah, the boy needed training, and fast.

CHAPTER 42

Grace marveled at what a strange thing it was, running into some-one who had saved your life—at least that's how she saw it. Had Locus gotten his way, she'd have been a slave to him. She sat across from Lorien now in the cafeteria, eating lunch. She stared down at her half-eaten chicken salad sandwich and wondered, how in the world to tell him thank you or look at him the same? It's such a massive debt. She'd tried, but she could tell it made him uncomfortable. Also, she was curi-ous about a couple of things, though. "How were you able to hear me?"

"I'm afraid the answer will anger you."

"Try me."

He shoved his salad away and exhaled. "After they came to get you that morning to put you under anesthesia, I realized their interest in you had become a frenzy, an obsession. I've rarely seen our boss push like this before. I knew I had to do something to protect you. Then when you left me that note about my sister, I realized you had heard me talking in my head earlier. Do you remember that day?"

"Yes. For the record. I wasn't snooping in your mind. I wasn't trying to eavesdrop. I've never been able to hear thoughts like that. So clear, I mean."

"I believe you. It's my vampiric blood. We don't know why, but psy-chics can sometimes hear vampires, and we can hear them too, if we ingest a drop of their blood. This is where you freak out and run from the room. First, please understand that I did not bite you."

"I understand. Continue."

"The next time I drew your blood, I ingested a couple of drops so that I could hear you if you were ever in trouble. I'm not listening in on your thoughts, and it doesn't work unless you are having a very forceful thought, the kind of thoughts that come from being terrified. I didn't do it to spy on you. I did it because I know how dangerous Locus is and how dangerous this place is for you. I would say I'm sorry, but that would be a lie. I did the best thing I knew to do in order to protect you."

She placed her hand on top of his arm. "I know you did."

"Still, I'm not happy about it, but I don't regret it either."

Grace looked up to find Janus staring at her from across the room. The woman's gaze made her want to squirm, but she wouldn't give her the satisfaction of knowing she made her nervous. She removed her hand from Lorien's arm and sat back. Lorien wasn't facing Janus but still seemed to know what her reaction was about. "Yeah, stay off her radar as much as possible. If she's walking down the hallway, go the other way. Avoid talking with her whenever you can. By now you know what she does, right?"

"Yeah."

He lowered his voice to a whisper. "You're safe because Malachi is so interested in you, but she was in love with Locus and might have known that he was interested in you, to put it mildly."

"Ah. That's just great, and so not my fault."

"I know, but you can't reason with a psychopath."

Grace nodded and looked around warily. "And this place is full of them."

"It is. Be very careful."

Grace kept her back to Janus but felt her eyes on her the whole time. It was all she could do to ignore the impulse to run.

Nick knocked on Damascus' door early on a Saturday morning. When he didn't answer, Nick knocked louder. Finally, Damascus opened the door. His hair stuck up at odd angles and he wore a pair of pajama pants with flaming chili peppers on them. No shirt. His amazing abs were on full display. "You're out annoying bright and early," Damascus said, squinting into the light. "It can't wait?"

"No."

"All right. Come in. I'll make you breakfast."

Damascus shut the door and Nick followed him to the spacious kitchen. The beautiful scent of coffee beans kick started his brain cells as the demon poured them into an elaborate hammered copper and machine brass modern version of a 1920s style espresso machine, and before long it came to life hissing and steaming. Next, he took eggs out of the refrigerator. "Talk to me," Damascus said as he began working.

"I want you to dream walk Noory again. Find out when they'll be sending her out next. I'll be there. Enough playing around with these people. I'll show up and kill whoever is guarding her and take her home to detox. Yes, I'm going to hold her against her will. Even if she ends up hating me. I don't care."

"Okay."

"Now, I know what you're thinking. I—" Nick began.

"What? I said, 'okay.' We've tried going into their turf. It's just too well-warded. We can't use our power there. She's most vulnerable when she goes out. You gonna tell John and Catherine?" Damascus asked as he set a frying pan on a burner and opened a package of bacon.

"I'll tell them, but I won't be asking their permission. I'll let them know right before I go in case they'd like to provide backup. They don't get to decide what I do."

"Finally. If he knows I'm involved at all, he will lose his mind. I don't guess he told you about his little stunt at the club where he scared off my date?"

"No."

"Yeah, he showed up in uniform going on about, 'You're a demon. The Rabbi used to cast your kind out,'" Damascus spoke as he waved a spatula around imitating John. "Anyway, I let him have his little rant. He's just mad because people don't come to him with things. I told him he needs to think about why the hell that is," Damascus said pointing the spatula at Nick for extra emphasis.

"Funny. I told him the exact same thing."

"Hmm," Damascus flipped the bacon and beat the eggs with a whisk. "When do you want to do this?"

"As soon as we find something out."

Damascus poured the eggs into another frying pan, then went to retrieve the espresso. He sat a steaming cup in front of Nick. "Saints and demons sit down to breakfast together. Whatever is the world coming to?" Damascus laughed.

"Hell if I know. I never have," Nick replied.

Damascus moved the eggs around the pan, and then slid them onto two plates. "I guess that's where faith comes in."

Nick looked at him and felt that suddenly the world made an odd kind of sense. "Out of the mouths of demons . . ."

"Cometh wisdom?" Damascus asked.

"Now and then. Yes." Nick lifted his coffee cup and nodded.

<h1 style="text-align:center">CHAPTER 44</h1>

Catherine sat in the spare bedroom of John's farmhouse as the smell of cedar drifting from Noory's old trunk permeated the room. Photo albums, a graduation gown, old playbills, ribbons from science fairs, and other mementos from Noory's childhood lay scattered about her. It hurt. At the same time, she couldn't stop. She'd smile, then tear up. John walked in and sat down beside her.

"You okay?" he asked.

"I missed so much."

"I'm so sorry. All this power to heal and comfort, but I couldn't help you. It's been the only time in my existence where I've been truly angry at God."

"You and me both." She sighed deeply, looking in futility at all the years she would never get back. She heard a knock on the door.

"I'll go see who it is," John said.

Catherine picked up one of Noory's old term papers from an engineering class at Georgia Tech. She had just begun reading it when she heard Nick quietly speaking with John. She set the paper down and went into the living room.

John turned to her and spoke. "Nick is going to intercept one of Noory's assignments downtown in about an hour. He wants to know if we'd like to provide backup while he kidnaps her."

Catherine ignored the sarcasm and jealousy in John's voice—she knew he wanted to be everything to his daughter, and his fundamental problem was that another man was stepping into his territory as protector.

"I know she doesn't want to leave Grace, but if we can just keep her long enough to find a way to get Grace out of there while Noory detoxes maybe we'll have a shot."

Catherine nodded, though in her heart, she didn't believe it would be enough. She also knew she couldn't ask them to stop trying. The hope it would have given her to know someone on the outside was trying . . . that someone on the outside had even known she was alive. She asked Nick a question. "How did you find out where she would be?"

"Damascus dream walked her."

John's olive toned face turned an angry red. "No! Absolutely not. I warned him to—"

"Zip it, John," Catherine said. "Stop missing the point and listen. We have a chance to help save our daughter."

"First of all, 'help.' I don't need help."

"Yes, you do. You didn't have this information," Catherine pointed out.

"Any information coming from a demon cannot be trusted."

"It worked before," Nick said.

"He's been in her head before?"

"Sure has. I intercepted her assignment to kill Robert Billings after Damascus dream walked her to find out about it. I took Robert out myself so she wouldn't have to. If I hadn't been there, Damascus was going to do it."

Catherine spoke, "Not everything is black and white. I had to kill to keep you all safe. You know that. You gonna toss me out now?" Catherine advanced on him. "You wanna hear about the people I killed?" Catherine felt it—the perverse itch to tell him about the kills she'd made. *My God where did the urge come from? Was it some desire to make sure he'd still love her if he knew? Some twisted loyalty test like the kind Malachi used to demand? Was it remembering, after all these years, how harsh his judgement could be, and wanting to force him to see the gray area? She'd had to. There was no choice for her. Why should he get to live in the convenient black and white world where everything fit into neat, clean categories?*

"No."

"You sure? I think you should."

"Catherine," John warned.

"No. I'm serious. You overlook what I had to do because it's me. Because I'm human. Do you think it was his choice to be a demon? He was born one. Demons are djinn. A race, at least to some degree. They get used, trapped, for centuries even, exploited for their power."

"Now you're going to feel sorry for him?"

"No, but people come into our lives for a reason, John. You know this as well as I do. Why am I in yours? Why is Damascus? Grow or whither. There have never been any other choices."

Catherine felt sorry for Nick as he looked from her to John and back. He was caught in the middle of them trying to catch up on twenty years of change and trying to adapt to the new normal. But he was no fool. He knew. Nick reached into his pocket. "Here's the address and time. There might not be enough detail here to save her from making the kill. But I think we can grab her and take out the handlers." He gave them a final nod and vanished through his portal.

John was looking at her as Nick disappeared. He still wasn't speaking, just staring. This was either going to be a speech about dealing with demons or—

He spoke suddenly as his voice shook, "You're all I've ever wanted. All I've ever needed. Nothing is more important than you, not my pride, not my opinion. I waited so long . . . now you're here, but you feel like you're so far away sometimes."

"John, I'm saying all this because I want you to know me. Really know me, and you can't if we pretend my time at Second Sight didn't happen, but it's a lot to absorb. I'm sorry."

"Don't be. It's not your fault. I want to protect everyone I love. I want to make the choices easier for everyone, so it will be safer. I just make everyone mad." He sat down on the couch and propped his elbows onto his knees and looked into his hands.

Catherine walked over and sat down beside him.

"I'm the one that should be apologizing," he said.

"Your heart is in the right place," she said.

"Have you ever noticed that when someone has to say that about someone, it means their head isn't?"

"Well, maybe, but you've done so much good all these years: on the force, with your healing, the time you've spent with Nick."

"Please don't leave me."

This was only the second time she'd seen John this vulnerable. The first time was in the squad car the night he'd found out she wasn't dead after twenty years of being gone. "I'm not going anywhere. I think we've both become a bit harder over the years." Catherine placed a hand on his back. The warmth coming off him felt so good. "If you're willing to put up with me then I can deal with you, you big pain in the ass."

John's broad shoulders shook with repressed laughter. He turned to her; all hint of mirth gone. He lifted his hand and slid it to caress her cheek and leaned in to kiss her long and slow. She felt the kiss all the way down to her core, igniting an ancient ache and setting her on fire. When they pulled apart, she was almost shaking with need but knew they couldn't indulge. "Well, I'm glad we're going to get Noory. All this pent-up passion will fuel me well in battle."

"You'll have to expend it some other way. You can't go."

There went the tender moment. "The hell I can't!"

"Think about it. We already fear Second Sight will come after you for breach of contract. You know too many company secrets. If you show up to take their 'substitute you' away, what do you think will happen? Their rage will know no bounds. You are just asking for their wrath. Please. Think about it. I'm not trying to be an ass, and you know it."

She did know it, but she wanted to smack him anyway.

CHAPTER 45

Nick took a deep breath to steady his nerves as he materialized in the parking garage of an apartment complex near the High Museum of Art. A light mist had begun to fall, lending a chill to the spring night and pulling the damp into the concrete structure.

Nick had left early hoping he could get there before Noory had to hurt anyone, but truth be told, he also didn't want John intercepting her first. He felt a small sense of shame. It shouldn't matter who arrived first, as long as Noory was safe, but he wanted her with him. There, he'd admitted it to himself. It was the truth. Was that so bad? He loved her and wanted her to be with him. Well, John did too. He doubted he could handle it any better if he were a father. Some fool that you'd seen at their absolute worst takes all your daughter's attention away. Yeah, he wouldn't be any better than John.

He breathed in the air, smelling of cool damp concrete and made his way to the stairwell. John would show. That much he was sure of. Catherine shouldn't. There was no reason to anger Second Sight even further when it came to her, but he wouldn't tell her what to do. That was a decision she and John had to come to on their own. He began the climb up to the fifth floor. He didn't want to just pop up to where he knew Noory would be. It was best to know what waited between here and there. The elevator was a no go. He could get trapped in there. There were several ways to sabotage an elevator, especially if it was lined with a Faraday cage.

When he reached the floor where the target's apartment was, he immediately caught a trace of Noory's scent, along with wood polish and high-dollar room spray. Almost two thousand years of life had made him aware of every nuance of existence: subtle energies, smells, auras. There was so much more to the world than the average human had enough time to even begin to grasp. There was no other identifiable scent. John wasn't here yet. He looked up at the security camera, and there was no soft blinking light as there should have been with the model he was looking at. Noory, or someone else from Second Sight, had already disabled it.

He tried the door Damascus had directed him to. It was locked. He held his hand over the lock, directed his energy at the mechanism inside until it gave a soft click, and let himself in. Once the door shut behind him, he called forth his daggers. They gave off a pale blue glow, and if one looked closer, they had ancient Aramaic script that read, "The word of the Lord." That was it. Nothing more.

He was glad almost no one saw the daggers unless they were about to die because he didn't enjoy explaining what the inscription meant, because, truth be told, he didn't know. He could only speculate. He had come to believe it was almost like Christ calling himself "I am." He remembered the first time it hit him with shocking clarity. *I am whatever I say I am.* You are whatever you say you are. Words are powerful. You tell me, he thought. Maybe using the moniker "I am" was God's way of conveying just how important it is to know ourselves and be careful what label we used.

Nick knew if he ever cut someone it was because they'd killed a child. So, if he came after them and the daggers had been given to him by God, well, then, hear "The word of the Lord" and bleed, you sadistic son of a bitch. That's what it meant to him. He knew such a concept would be controversial, but the blades were given to him knowing full well how he thought.

Thumps came from somewhere in the back of the apartment. Nick felt his heart quicken. He hated the idea of Noory having to kill. Even worse, he hated the idea of her getting hurt. He made it to a back bedroom on soft feet. The first sight he saw was Noory leaning over the body of a man who looked to be ten years older than her. As soon as she heard Nick, she rose and drew her pistol. He didn't think he'd ever get used to seeing her with a gun. She'd never liked using them. It was but one more thing Second Sight had made her compromise on. Nick backed up and raised his hands, daggers still gripped.

She sighed and lowered her weapon. "You cannot keep trying to save me. You'll only end up getting trapped too."

Nick flicked his wrists, and the daggers disappeared. "I'm taking you home. Our home." He wouldn't take no for an answer. Not even her loyalty to remain with Grace would prevent him from seeing this through. Nick saw the beginnings of protest, then her eyes grew wide as she looked at something just over his shoulder. Fire lanced through his back, and he collapsed.

CHAPTER 46

As Nick fell, Noory thought back to her mother's words: "You will look into their sick skulls, find out their weaknesses, and shove it up their asses with the heat of a thousand suns."

The creature that stood behind him had glowing red eyes, eyebrows that arched up into points, and dark hair that flowed back from his face like flames. Noory spared a quick glance at Nick and noticed smoke rising from his back. "Where is the magus?" the creature said in a voice that seemed to hiss and crackle as he spoke, as if fire fueled his voice.

"What?"

"The magus. I've seen you with him. Give him to me, and I'll let you live."

Rage flooded her being. She'd just killed for Second Sight like an attack dog they threw at their problems. Yeah, the man she'd wasted was no prize. He'd robbed dozens of pensions and had plans to rape her in retaliation for breaking into his house. She'd looked into his mind just as her mother had advised. She still hated it, but it made her job easier to know these weren't good people. This still didn't change the fact that she was no killer. Now this creature had attacked the man who loved her more than himself. She looked into his soul . . . dark, ancient. Older than Nick. Older than John. He started advancing toward her. She began backing up. What *was* he? She probed deeper. A battlefield spread out before her in a vision so strong she felt as if she could reach out and touch it. It was all she could do to stay grounded in reality as she looked around inside it. The same creature stood on the field, burning victim after victim who fought back. Many were human, but others fought him with water, earth, and wind.

"The magus!" he roared.

Beyond the vision, she saw a young boy in the hallway. *Dear God! Evan.* What's he doing here? Evan looked up at the ceiling, focusing on something she could not see, lifted his hand, gripped it into a fist in front of him, and yanked down. The sprinkler came on. The creature cursed and screamed as every drop of water caused steam to hiss and rise from his body where it fell on him. His form twisted into a fiery vortex before becoming a tight ball of flame that slammed into the window. Glass shattered in his wake. Noory turned to watch him plummet several stories down then dart underneath the parking deck. Apparently, the falling mist was not a favorable condition for the fire being.

When she turned back around, John was beside Nick, healing his wound while Evan looked on in wonder. She tucked her gun in its holster and ran over to crouch on the floor beside them. "What the hell was that about?"

Nick sat up with a grimace. "The boy can't be out in the open anymore," Nick spoke through gritted teeth as John kept a steady healing touch over his wound. "How the heck did you get here anyway?" he said to Evan.

"Well, you know how when you sometimes fall asleep and dream about a location where something big is about to happen to someone you care about?"

"No. People don't—"

"Oh, so this is like cooking the marshmallow?"

"Yes," Nick nodded.

"People don't?"

"No. Not so much."

Nick straightened his shirt, stood, and then turned to look at John and Noory. "Anyway, he's a magus. Damascus thinks he's one of the ancient line of the magi."

John looked at him with awe. "He can come home with me," he said immediately.

"No. I won't leave my mother," Evan said. Noory marveled that the immature swagger had fled when he worried for her.

"She can come live with us too," John said without appearing to give it a second thought. She wondered what in the world made John so loyal so quickly to this child and his mother.

Nick got to his feet, looking as if all traces of pain had fled under John's healing. "We need to leave. I'm sure the handlers will be along any minute."

Noory nodded. "I'm surprised they aren't already up here. I don't want Evan becoming their next project."

John said, "They aren't coming. I knew Nick would take care of things here. I took care of the two in the limo."

"What? How?"

"Does it matter?" John asked.

"No," Noory answered.

John patted Nick's back. "You good?"

"Yes. Thank you."

Noory heard the tension between them but didn't have the bandwidth for it. He'd trusted Nick to take care of matters up here. That was a good sign.

She said, "When I looked into his head, I got the sense there isn't an army of whatever he is, and it may be why he wants Evan so bad. Also, I think Evan is . . ." she tilted her head and looked at him, "more than he is, somehow." She also got the sense that the creature might have even been his father, but she didn't know if she was right or how much Evan knew, so she kept it to herself.

John said, "I'll go to the shelter and talk with Evan's mother. Nick, you'll get Noory home." He looked toward Evan again with that same awed expression.

"Yes. Of course."

So, he was still miffed at Nick, but not protesting that Nick was taking her home. Getting to spend more time with him was a gift. Still, he had a surprise coming if he thought she'd abandon Grace. And whatever Evan was, it was beyond huge for John to relent so easily.

Chapter 47

John, Catherine, and Evan's mother, Maria, sat at the old oak table in John's kitchen drinking coffee and talking well into the night while Evan played games in the living room on one of Noory's devices left behind years ago when she went away to college.

Catherine had met John at the shelter after he'd called. When John had arrived with Maria's son, called them into Noory's office, explained what had happened, including some of the supernatural details, the woman immediately started packing and demanded her son do the same. This looked like a much-repeated scenario.

There was no wringing of hands or fretting about whether they should go. She simply walked to her partitioned off section of the shelter, pulled her suitcase out from under her bed and started packing up what little possessions she owned with the resignation of a woman who'd become used to such a life on the run long ago. When Evan didn't immediately leave to go do the same, she stared at him as if he'd suddenly sprouted another head. That's when John explained who he and Catherine were, even the Biblical lineage. If she didn't flinch at the supernatural stuff, they might as well go for broke. Then he explained why she and her son would be safer with them than on the run again. Their home had been triple warded in order to protect Catherine now that she had gone rogue from Second Sight. The same wards should now be sufficient for Evan.

Catherine couldn't help but notice that Evan seemed surprised, while Maria did not. There was a story there.

"I simply cannot believe that beast hadn't tracked you to the shelter already," John said.

"The orange-eyed demon took care of that," Maria said casually.

Catherine smiled, and John froze.

"What?"

"Yes. He came to me as soon as he discovered what Evan was and offered his protection. He cast a ward about the shelter so that . . . the creature . . . couldn't sense him."

"That's good," Catherine said. John gave her a sharp look. She smiled in return.

"What did he ask from you for this protection?" John asked.

"Nothing. I asked him why he would want to help me. He said he knew what it was like to be different, to be feared or hated for it." Maria shrugged, then lifted her mug and drank another sip of coffee. "It was the first time anyone had acknowledged what Evan was. The next day, Nicholas had a talk with Evan." She sighed and ran a finger along the edge of the table. "I'd kept it from him as long as I could. I figured if he didn't know, he wouldn't be tempted to tell anyone. He'd likely tell that cute little Grace just to try and get her to go out with him, in case you all haven't noticed how he is yet."

Catherine had noticed, and it was adorable, but she understood what the woman was saying—she wanted to wait until he matured a little, but clearly time was up. "Please don't be angry with Nick. He thought you didn't know what Evan was and didn't want him blindsided when someone came after him for his power."

"I'm not angry. I know Nick's intentions were the best. They always are," Maria said.

Catherine couldn't help but notice the woman looked at John as she said it. Maria was seriously perceptive. Maybe Evan's father had chosen her for a reason. Catherine didn't want to pry but also didn't want to be surprised if they were going to be helping these two. Maria would have to be honest about Evan's parentage, but she was avoiding something. Of course, she could just look into her head and take the information, but she'd vowed to only ever do that with those who'd forfeited their rights already by hurting the vulnerable. "Maria, why is Evan being hunted?"

Maria slowly lowered her cup and sat it on the table. "Fifteen years ago, I was going to school in Santa Fe, waitressing on the side, when this tall, gorgeous man, maybe Persian, kept coming into the diner. My gosh, all the women there stopped what they were doing just to catch a glimpse of him, but he always made sure to sit in my section. He talked to me. Listened to me. Really listened. You know? His name was Milad. When I look back on it now, I realize he didn't talk about himself very much. It should have been a red flag. It's like I was half asleep during our relationship. Now, I think that might be true in a sense. My ancestors on my mother's side might call him a trickster or something like that. We saw each other for a couple of months after that, and then, one day, I stopped hearing from him, which was especially scary since I was pregnant by that time."

Catherine winced. "Sorry."

"Yeah. Well, the real and literal nightmares started after that. I had dreams of being chased by him. I questioned what the reality was. Was it when I was with him or the nightmares after he was gone? The sense of presence and power in the dreams permeated all the way through my very bones." Catherine watched Maria's fingers gripping her mug turn white. "I fear thinking about him too much even now might . . ." She waved a hand and continued. "A few weeks before my due date, my grandmother came to me saying that she'd had a terrible premonition that I would die, and my child would be taken. She was sobbing as she told me I had to leave. I had to get far away from Santa Fe."

"Was she always a seer?" Catherine asked.

"More or less. People would come to her asking for readings, wanting to know their future, who they should love, who they should avoid. She never sought it out. They always came to her. Anyway, I've been running ever since. I called home a few times. No one has ever answered. I've always been terrified to find out what happened, if they moved or if he came looking for me and—" she swallowed hard "—and when they had no information, he killed them. I don't know. I'm afraid to know."

"How in the world did you end up here? At the shelter? It can't be a coincidence," John said.

Everyone looked up when Evan spoke. "Well, that was the easiest part. We just followed the brightest star in the sky."

"Well, it's more than a little on the nose but yeah, that's essentially what we did. The last place we lived in New Orleans wasn't bad. A kind woman named Madam Boudreaux said she felt led to take us in."

Catherine and John exchanged a look. Catherine knew John still didn't know how to feel about the woman, but Catherine knew there wasn't a thing in the world the voodoo priestess could have done to help Noory if Second Sight was holding her grandson, and it was wrong of John to hold bitterness toward her.

"You know her?" Maria asked.

"Yes," Catherine said. "It was very kind of her to take you in. Did she teach you anything about her craft? I understand she is a legitimate practitioner."

"She told me I was a type of medium who had a gift for moving on lost souls who were stuck or trapped in this plane of existence. I guess that makes sense. It explains the dreams I've had of people I didn't know asking me for help. When I woke, I thought I sensed a presence in the room. Anyway, she believed that was how I was able to "host" the child of a powerful magi. She didn't believe just any female could. She said she would help me develop my gift, but I was afraid it would, you know, light me up or something and draw Milad to us. She also disagreed with me not telling Evan. She was keen to teach him some things, ways to protect himself. I asked her not to reveal too much to him. I was always terrified him knowing would also pull Milad to him."

She shook her head and sighed. "I see now it didn't matter. He would have found us no matter what. Boudreaux was right."

"So that man that was looking for someone tonight, the one that burned Nick, that was my father, wasn't he?" Evan asked.

She held out her arm and Evan came to stand beside her where she sat as she wrapped an arm around him. "I didn't see him, but yes, probably. I'm sorry."

"S'okay. It's not your fault."

She leaned her head over on him and continued her story. "We lived with Madam Boudreaux for almost a year before coming here. Then one night she dreamed that we were no longer safe there. When I asked her where we should go, she said that Evan would know. When I asked him where, he said he felt guided by light. When we got in the car, he looked up at the stars, then he told me every turn, every exit to take until we arrived at the shelter." She looked up at him and smiled.

Evan picked up where she left off. "When I heard Nick call Noory, 'Light,' I knew we were where we were supposed to be."

Chapter 48

Nick grabbed Noory, and they faded into the in-between. She knew the serum would wear off, and she'd want to leave. Right now, though, all she wanted to do was go home with Nick and be his. She calculated how long she had before she would need another dose. She could hold off for a few hours.

They had dinner together and then shortly thereafter it began. It came so much quicker than she thought it would. She thought there would be more time with him before it started, but it showed up like a thief and tore at her. He picked her up and carried her into his room. The shaking felt as if it would rattle her bones apart. He laid her down on the bed and went into the bathroom, wet a washcloth, and came back to wipe her face.

"Thank you," she ground out, trying desperately to steady her voice. "How did you do this, Nick?" She clung to him like a lifeline. "It's going to take everything from me," she sobbed. "I tried to hold off a few hours at Second Sight and couldn't do it. I know what's coming."

He got on the bed with her, leaned against the headboard, and pulled her into his arms. "I know it feels like it will kill you, but it won't. I promise."

"Our cells regenerate faster. We recover from wounds so much quicker. Why not this? So much of it is physical."

"I've wondered that too. I've often thought maybe it's because something in the brain triggers the craving. It isn't just a body ailment. Or maybe it's a choice that cuts off some regeneration inside us. Like maybe we can only recover from things that we didn't choose. Then again, my liver would have been Swiss cheese if that were true, right? I don't know. I just wish I could take it away so you wouldn't have to feel it."

"Distract me. Please." She yanked his shirt from him and pulled him on top of her. "Please."

He kissed each eyelid. "I love you. Always. Always." He moved to her neck and slid his lips along her soft skin. Then he pulled her jeans and underwear down and touched her softly, gently until she ground her hips against his hand, longing to forget, for distraction, until he moved his fingers against her in response to her frantic need. Soon she cried out against the release, the freedom his touch brought her, if only for a moment.

Chapter 49

Nick looked through the peephole but didn't need to—he could sense the demon on the other side. He opened the door and motioned for Damascus to come in. After the last twenty-four hours he'd had, he could use a friend. The hell spawn with a backpack slung over one shoulder halted at the threshold.

"What?" Nick asked.

Damascus gave a small smile. "Careful, hot stuff, you're looking at me as if I were . . . human."

Nick nodded slowly and motioned for him to have a seat at the dining room table. They sat down. Nick ran his hands through his hair and scrubbed his face.

"How's she doing?" Damascus asked.

"Not good," Nick said. "Though I know it isn't so, damned if I don't feel like I'm aging. Hell, I've thought about breaking into that place, taking my chances with turning to dust, and stealing a few vials of that stuff just to make it easier to wean her off it. The physical pain is worse than anything I've felt or seen with any other drug."

Damascus reached into his backpack and pulled out a small case containing four vials. "I have something that will help with that." He opened the case, and Nick's eyes teared up.

"How?"

"I'll tell you how, but first I'll tell you a quick story. Until 1590 I had a sister. Her name was Behar. She was strong, funny, caring but she was never as powerful as me. She was summoned by the Algonquin to find out what was going on at Roanoke when the English first arrived there. I believe the Algonquin summoned her because they were more matriarchal. I wish every day of my existence they'd called me. I'd have rained down hellfire when those Puritan sons of bitches tried to come at me. The English took one look at her, saw something they couldn't understand, and . . . burned her, broke her . . . You and I both know what has to be done to destroy an immortal. So, of course she regenerated, and they had to have killed her more than once. If I had been there, at least after the first death . . ."

Nick thought of John and what would have happened had he not been there after John was burned at the stake with the other Templars, the horror of a painful death and regeneration only to find someone standing there, about to behead you. It was unthinkable.

Damascus looked out the window and continued. "She'd kept me . . . good, stable, sane, I guess. When I found out what had happened. Well, there's a reason Roanoke is called the Lost Colony." Damascus spread his hands, unsheathed his claws, and flames spread between them. "I obliterated that place. They can speculate till kingdom come. They won't ever find a fucking thing." He watched the flames for a few seconds longer. They danced in his eyes, which bore a faraway, haunted look that should've been scary, but instead, broke Nick's heart.

"When I met Noory . . ." Damascus' next words caught in his throat. The flames disappeared. He covered his mouth as tears spilled over and ran down his face.

Nick waited without speaking. He looked out the window, trying to give Damascus his dignity.

Damascus swiped at his eyes with his shirtsleeve. "She looks nothing like Behar. But she looks at me like maybe, maybe she thinks there's something worth salvaging, just like Behar did. In her eyes, I see my sister. I'd do anything to keep Noory safe."

Nick nodded and spoke quietly to Damascus. "I understand. It's exactly how Noory looks at me."

"Anyway, this was a chance for Robert to get back in Second Sight's good graces. He gave it to me a while back when she first began her quest to become immortal. I was to get Noory hooked, and she'd have to go to Second Sight for more." He tapped the case holding the vials. "But I was never going to do that. You'll use it to wean her off the stuff."

"So, they know Robert was going to use you as the go between?"

"Yes." Damascus watched him piece it together.

"They'll want to know where these vials are. They'll ransack his house when they can't find them, then they'll come looking for you."

"Yes. Likely."

"You sure you can let that happen?"

Damascus slid the container even closer to Nick. "Noory changed me. I owe her. She looks at me like Behar did. Robert looked at me like I was something he needed to scrape off his shoe. He was a bad man, and *I know bad.*" Damascus' eyes glinted as he made the statement. "Hide this shit and don't let her know where it is. You know she'll manipulate your emotions to get to it. To make you feel sorry for her."

"Please, you're talking to the king of the addicts. I know how this works. She won't trick, pry, plead, beg—"

"Or blow?" Damascus said with a devilish grin.

"Language, demon!" Nick said in a Cajun accent as he gave a perfect impression of Madam Boudreaux.

Damascus laughed. "Spot on. No worries, dude. She'd blow you regardless. I'm sure of it."

"Dear God, man, you gotta stop that shit!" Nick shook his head but was trying to hide a smile.

"I need for her to be okay," Damascus said as the impish smile left his face.

"She will be. I swear it."

Nick watched Damascus stare out at the Atlanta skyline. He felt as if he weren't even looking at the same person he'd met last year. Thanks to Noory, neither one of them was the same.

CHAPTER 50

Nick watched Noory drift in and out of sleep on the couch. He was going to offer her some of the serum, but it concerned him. How would she react when she knew he had it and was keeping it from her? He forced himself to wait another full twenty-four hours before considering giving her any of the serum Damascus brought. He knew the temptation to let her burn through it would start the moment she knew he had it.

She sat up slowly and gagged. She reached a shaking hand to her ribs. "God, I don't think I can handle one more vomit."

He walked over to the couch and sat down beside her. "You may not have to. We can wean you slower now. I managed to get a hold of some of the serum." He didn't dare tell her it was Damascus who'd gotten it. She might go after him later. He might try to get more just to help her and end up getting himself killed trying to sneak back into that building.

Nick pulled the half-filled vial out of his jacket. "This is a weaning, Noory. We have very little of this. You must be strong and remind yourself it won't last."

She took it from him and unscrewed the top with shaking hands. He watched her drink it and hold the vial upside down for a few seconds to get every drop out of it. "Do you feel better already?" he asked.

"I feel it taking effect. Yes." She leaned back, eyes closed, and he knew what she was doing. Right about now, she was so relieved to have it back in her system that she was savoring it, trying to hold on to the way it felt. He remembered it all too well.

"How'd you get it?"

He knew he had to answer carefully. "Back when I was helping Robert with the tower project, I remembered him saying he was given some for a client flying in from Dubai. He was really proud of himself, but they never showed."

"Seems like they would have come back for it. They keep this stuff under lock and key."

"Yeah, well. My guess is they left it with him in hopes of luring you in. Whatever the case, it was a shot in the dark that it would still be in his safe, but it was."

"They're going to come after Mom."

Nick knew that was likely true. "Just focus on getting better. Your mother doesn't want you worrying about that right now. She just wants you to get well, not beholding to Second Sight."

"I heard them talking before I left. If she comes through the door, she'll die. They say they've painted the doorframe."

"Ah, how very biblical of them." Nick realized they were making use of the Old Testament story, where the angel of death swept over the Egyptian land and only those with the blood of the sacrificial lamb over their door were spared. It was a reversal of that tale.

Nick knew he had to change the subject. Noory wasn't well. In the short time she'd been there, she'd tried to escape four times—he'd had to bring Damascus in to watch her when he went on calls, the sleep deprived demon never complained, even at 3:00 a.m.—fought him to get to the door and vomited everything she'd eaten. She was thinner than he'd ever seen her. Her face was looking gaunt. While she had the serum in her body, he intended to get her to eat. "I'll order from your favorite place. Fried chicken and fried green tomatoes? I can also cook if you'd like."

"Fried. I want fried."

"You got it." Nick got his phone out and placed an order.

After they ate, she kept the food down for the first time in a long while. Then he picked her up and took her to the bedroom where he made love to her, gently, with all the fear that she'd run back to Second Sight expressing itself in every touch and stoke. He cherished her and couldn't lose her to this. He held her in his arms and drifted off for the first time in over two days. He woke to find her gone and someone making noise in his kitchen. He looked at the clock and realized he'd been asleep for five hours. "Oh, God."

He raced through the living room to find the couch cushions on the floor unzipped. In the kitchen, he found her rummaging through cabinets and drawers. He rubbed his eyes and watched her. "You won't find it, sweetheart," he said softly.

She sat on the kitchen floor in his oversized sweatshirt and her yoga pants and blew out a frustrated breath. She refused to make eye contact with him. He sat down on the floor in front of her. "I love you. Your freedom is everything to me. I know what it's like to be a prisoner. I don't want that for you."

"So, you're going to watch me suffer when you could alleviate it. I already feel it wearing off."

"I'm doing this *because* I love you. You know that."

"You heard what my mom said. This is a hundred times worse than detoxing from alcohol."

"I heard her, and I believe it, but I don't have an endless supply. That's why you are only going to get enough to wean you off of it. I talked to your mother extensively about how to do it."

"You all are talking about me when I'm not around? Like I'm a child? That's not okay."

"How many times did you talk to John about me when I was struggling?"

She said nothing.

"I know you did, and that's okay. You both love me. Now that I'm sober, I can see just how lucky I am to have people that would care enough to go behind my back and plot to get me well. So many people don't have that, Noory. I love you too much to let you destroy yourself." He leaned against the cabinet and pulled her into his lap. She sighed against his shoulder and relaxed. He felt her kiss his neck. She ran a hand up his bare chest. He felt himself get hard in response to her touch.

She took his big sweatshirt off to reveal her beautiful bare breasts. He ran a hand over them slowly, deliberately, and watched her shiver at his touch in the dim undermounted cabinet lights.

"God. Your hands are warm." She raised up on her knees and pulled her yoga pants down and moved one knee and pulled a pant leg off, then the other. She reached for the band of his sweatpants. "Make me forget," she said.

He lifted his thighs as she tugged his pants down. He swallowed hard and wondered if it was okay to be with her in this way. He throbbed and ached but didn't want to—a moan escaped his lips as she wrapped her hand around his shaft. He closed his eyes and forced himself to speak. "Noory, you're having a tough time. Maybe we shouldn't . . ." He felt her slide down onto his length, so warm and soft. She began rocking on top of him.

"I love you, Nick."

He put his lips to her ear and said, "You're the love of my life, and that's saying something. You know how damn old I am."

She laughed, and he felt it vibrate through her body. He watched her on top of him as she moaned and rocked. He placed his hands on the floor and pushed his hips up. She gasped like he knew she would, then gave him a wicked smile. Nick glanced up at the island counter he'd bent her over the first time she'd returned home after being at Second Sight. The very thought of it almost drove him over the edge. She planted each of her palms on the cabinets behind his head and increased her rhythm. He watched her, transfixed, and pushed himself up once more with a deep groan and emptied himself inside her.

She leaned forward slightly, ground herself against him, and cried out. She lay on him panting. She was so much lighter than when they'd met. He worried about her but reminded himself that she was immortal now. It just didn't feel like it.

Nick rubbed her back lazily as she lay on him. "You told me to make you forget. What were you trying to forget, Light?"

She spoke from where her head lay on his shoulder. "I wanted to forget, for just a little while, that they told me my mother is still under contract. It's a life for a life. Lorien told me this means they'll either have *me* or kill *her*. I can't let that happen, Nick. The building is spelled now such that if she walks back in, it will kill her instantly. She can't just go in there and trade her services now. They don't trust her anymore, and every moment Grace is there without me feels like I've betrayed her."

His hand stopped moving on her back, and he felt like he couldn't breathe for a moment. "What are you saying?"

"I'm saying I'll go back before I'll let them kill my mother. She gave up her life for me for twenty years. Maybe it's my turn to give mine."

Nick felt his heart shatter all over again.

She was already gone.

Chapter 51

Noory and Catherine sat in the kitchen sipping coffee and watching through the window as Damascus coached Evan on how to wield his fire. Evan could wield all the elements, but the control Damascus had over one was applicable to all. John had grudgingly agreed to it.

Noory took a sip of her coffee, gripping it tightly to keep it from shaking. She'd rather her mother not see it; she held enough guilt already. The detox was almost complete. So many times, she thought the craving would kill her, but Nick had been steady as a rock. Her rock, and she knew she would love him forever.

She watched as Damascus nodded at Evan. She didn't need to hear to see the tension in everyone's posture. John stood by with the garden hose at the ready—he'd been burned alive back when the Templars went to the stake. Thus, he understandably had an issue with fire. Nick crouched like a boxer, shifting from foot to foot. Evan's mother peeked between her fingers.

Manipulating an existing fire to cook a marshmallow was way different than calling it forth by working air molecules into a frenzy that Evan didn't yet know how to control. So far, he'd left several charred patches in John's pasture. Damascus showed him the fire between his palms for a few seconds. Evan nodded, gave a thumbs up, and sprouted a huge ball of flame. They all backed away. Damascus held his hands up as if coaxing a man with a weapon to lower it. Evan took a deep breath, and the fire got bigger rather than smaller as he exhaled. Damascus pointed at the target of bottles set atop an old metal milk can.

Evan started to throw it in that direction, but Noory noticed Damascus' mouth move and she watched in horror as Evan turned around in mid throw to look at Damascus for further instruction. The fire turned with Evan's pivot and swept over Damascus. Noory and Catherine both jumped. Evan's eyes became round and horrified. Damascus laughed as the flames licked his body and burned through his clothes. He lifted his hands and slowly made fists. The flames receded with the curling of his fists, as if he were pulling the flames in and snuffing them out.

She also noticed John hadn't bothered to put out the flames. Either Damascus had told him not to or John thought it a convenient way to be rid of him. Noory hoped it was the former.

Soon Damascus stood in all his stark naked, demonic glory, while John, Evan, and Evan's mother turned away. Nick didn't seem to care one way or the other.

"Hmm. Nice abs," Catherine commented.

"True enough," Noory agreed. *Did demons work out? Did they need to?*

Damascus wiped the ashes of burned clothing from his arms and legs and walked over to a duffle bag, placed away from the danger zone. After seeing that, she wasn't sure anywhere was safe from Evan's inexperience.

Catherine interrupted her thoughts. "How are you doing without the serum?"

"It's been almost two weeks now. I think I'm out of the woods if I control my thoughts. You know how it is: you can't think about it too much or you grieve it like a person who's died. I couldn't have done it without Nick. I'm not sure I could have done it if Nick hadn't found the stash."

"I couldn't have done it without Lorien."

Noory didn't want to tell her Lorien had discussed it with her. She worried she might consider it a betrayal. She looked at her mother far away in thought.

Catherine said, "I almost killed Lorien. I told him to keep it from me. When he did, I fought him for it." She squeezed her eyes shut as if to banish the memory. "He never gave in. If you ever end up back there, you can trust him. *Don't* end up back there. We'll find a way to get Grace back." Noory watched her nod, the hallmark of a woman trying to convince herself. She knew better.

"Mom. It's not just about Grace. Janus showed me they'll go after my shelter. Damascus' wards can only protect it for just so long. Innocent people will get caught up in this. I've stayed too long already. They'll come for you to force me back. They'll—"

"I mean it, Noory. Let them kill me first."

"I can't do that."

"Yes, you can."

Noory knew there was no sense in arguing with her anymore. She looked back out the window, knowing what she had to do. Fire leapt from Damascus' hands as he showed him ways to bend and direct it. She became mesmerized by the fire and saw her own life as she knew it burning up too. She swallowed tears, knowing her time in the safety of this old farmhouse was coming to a close.

CHAPTER 52

The sun was setting outside the huge windows of Nick's penthouse. It reflected off the Atlanta skyline and bathed his dining room in a warm orange glow as Noory reached for the parmesan shaker. She was irritated that her hand still trembled, but the craving was nearly gone.

To his credit, Nick quickly looked away when she glanced up. He knew her well, and he was right; she didn't want him to acknowledge it. There were lots of things they weren't acknowledging right now. Those things hung in the air between them, an ignored grief that followed them from room to room. She couldn't take it anymore. "John killed another assassin this morning. None of the wards are holding."

"I know," Nick said. He sat his forkful of pasta down and stared at her across the table.

"He hasn't been to work this week. He's afraid they'll strike when he's not there."

"Please. Your mother is terrifying. She can take care of herself. Besides, they moved Evan and his mother to Damascus' house last week, so they're safe."

"Yes, but no matter how skilled my mother is, all it takes is one good shot. We both know it."

Silence permeated the room and made her want to jump out of her skin.

Nick said, "Once you go back in there, it could be years before you're . . ."

Noory felt her heart become a weight in her chest as she watched his eyes become glassy with tears.

When he spoke next it was so faint she could barely hear, ". . . in my arms again."

She turned her head so he couldn't see the pain on her face. She needed to be strong for him.

"Don't do this. Your mother said it herself. Lorien will take care of Grace, and they want what's in her head too badly to kill her."

"It isn't about Grace. They will kill my mother on principle and then start killing off anyone I love, including people involved in the shelter."

Nick nodded but said nothing. They looked into each other's eyes and finally acknowledged the grief, the truth.

She couldn't stay.

Chapter 53

Noory made it to the top floor, but nothing looked right. It appeared like a run of the mill boring old upscale downtown Atlanta office. The ornate runes and inlaid wood with spells worked into it were cloaked. It was all magical fuckery as Damascus would say. "Enough of this shit," she said under her breath. She surveyed the walls for the security camera. Finding it in a corner, she looked up at it and said, "All right. I'm here, jackasses. Drop the act and let me in. I'm offering my services in exchange for my mother's."

Like a falling mist the runes appeared on the walls. The inlaid wood crawled across the doors like snakes, and the lighting on the walls switched from well-appointed LEDs behind frosted glass to the yellow sliver of a captured ancient campfire behind an expensive modern sconce. The doors parted to allow her passage.

She walked down the hallway on her own. No welcoming party. There were no voices coming down the corridor. Second Sight certainly had no receptionist anyway. She'd expected to be tackled straight away. Surely there was some penalty for staying gone this long. Maybe they had done something to Grace. God, she wouldn't be able to live with herself. Her mind flashed through a dozen different scenarios.

Her dark ruminations were interrupted when she rounded the corner and felt a dart strike her on the thigh. She dropped almost immediately and felt arms like steel bands holding her down. She recognized Jericho above her. She couldn't move a muscle as a woman in blue scrubs appeared and knelt before her. Manda, she thought, the nurse who'd taken Grace. A syringe slipped between her lips and the serum ran down her throat. Manda dropped the syringe, held Noory's mouth shut, and massaged her throat to make her swallow. Tears ran down Noory's face.

All her hard work. All Nick's hard work, for nothing. Nothing mattered. She'd failed. This was her fate. She'd be beholding to them forever. She knew she couldn't go through withdrawals again. They knew it too. They'd won. Another needle in her arm, and she faded into the black.

A hard, cold slap stung Noory's face, then another. "Wake up!" a female voice commanded through the mush that had become her mind. She woke to find Janus standing above her, holding Grace by the hair of her head.

Noory sat up with her head throbbing even as she felt the effects of the serum in the background washing her cells with its strange mix of light and dark. It felt good and sinister all at once. Grief and ecstasy coursed through her veins.

"Pay attention. I don't have all day. Malachi wants you here for reasons I cannot fathom. I am sent to tell you that if you leave one more time, I have permission to turn my gaze to this little whore and she won't remember you or your little band of do gooders. A whole new start," she said as she turned to look at Grace with venom in her eyes. There was intense hatred there that Noory couldn't trace. While she had her gaze trained on Grace, Noory saw the eyes on the back of Janus' head. The eyes that had taken memories, lives, pasts, were demented, glowing, icy blue as what was left of once thick glossy black hair now hung in thin strings after Father Roy had burned half of it off when he'd destroyed the relic last year and more than a few demons had reached for it, Janus included. She turned her regular poison glare, which was bad enough on its own, back to Noory. "Are we clear?"

"Yeah," Noory managed to croak out.

With a final look of disgust, Janus shoved Grace at Noory and left their room.

Shame washed over Noory as she looked at Grace. "I'm so sorry. I thought I could get the serum out of my system and then come back here without the temptation to take it. I never intended to leave you here. You have to know that. As soon as I walked through the door, they shoved it back down my throat. All that work for nothing." Noory choked on her words, coughing and sputtering as despair got the best of her.

"I knew you'd be back and at the same time, hoped I was wrong." Grace walked over to the fridge and retrieved a bottle of water, opened it, and handed it to her.

"I'm so sorry. I made things worse than before."

"Not really. Janus already hated me for other reasons."

Noory tilted her head in confusion.

"Don't worry about it."

"I'm always worried about you."

"I know."

Noory put her arms around Grace and the two sat there for a moment of peace. "Is Lorien okay?" She whispered into her ear.

"Yes."

Noory felt relieved. At least there was that. She'd worried profusely that they would catch wind he was helping them.

"All right. I've got a boss to go talk to."

"What? You mean that big bad everybody is always whispering about? You can't go talk to that prick!"

"Sure, I can! If I'm going to be here, he can at least promise me my mother will be safe." Noory stood up and wobbled.

"My God! You're dizzy from all the freaking drugs. You were out for over three hours. Just wait a minute."

Noory took a long drink of her water and handed it back to Grace, then walked over to where she always suspected the security camera was located and started talking. "Hey! Weirdo that watches me and Grace sleep! I need to speak to Malachi, and I'm not going to shut up until someone takes me to him. Enough of this cloak and dagger bull-shit. If he's going to hold me prisoner here, then he ought to have the balls to talk to me to my face."

Another twenty minutes of Noory taking her frustrations out on a nameless, faceless person or creature monitoring a security camera from God knew where and Grace trying to talk her out of it resulted in someone coming to retrieve Noory, blindfolding her, and taking her to an escalator, removing the blindfold, and she opened her eyes to an office that was nothing like the rest of Second Sight. She stood in front of a heavy antique desk with carved legs ending in elaborate claw footed feet. The drapes behind the desk were heavy velvet in a dark green. On the walls hung pictures of the English countryside and men about the hunt on their well-bred horses and trained dogs about their feet. It was a stark contrast to her mother's sleek office of clear plexiglass with clean colors and lines.

Malachi himself was interesting. He was a stocky man though not quite portly. He looked to be in his forties. She was guessing perpetually so. The jacket he wore appeared to be concealing something in the back. Her guess was a set of wings. Though the jacket was clearly built to do so. She was looking for something out of place. That's also how she detected a just barely visible shimmer over his person. He had a glamour cast over him. She surmised this wasn't exactly his true form.

"So, you have my attention," he gestured to the chair in front of his desk. "Please, share your concerns."

Noory sat and tried to conceal the fact that she wanted to vault across the desk and claw his eyes out, but the truth was, a man or creature like this might contain more power than she could fathom. It would be unwise to challenge him until she knew what she was dealing with. "Well, I have many concerns. But I'm certain you won't let me walk out of here and take Grace with me, so my one request today, I'm here, I came back in my mother's place. A life for a life, right? I want you to stop hunting my mother. Please assure my mother's safety."

"Your mother was a trained assassin. We've invested time, energy, and resources in her."

"I've been hunting demons, drug lords, and I know these streets as well as anyone in the Atlanta office."

"She knows too many company secrets."

"So do I and a dozen untrustworthy demons that would just as soon kill you as look at you." Noory waved a dismissive hand. "Fear keeps all these bastards in line. My mother is smart enough to know what to keep to herself."

"Why would you do this? Go, be with Father Christmas." Malachi's eyes glowed an electric blue as he seemed to look a little too deeply into her eyes. She'd need to shield better around him. Clearly. "He needs you."

Yup. He read too well, but she wouldn't comment on her personal affairs to this . . . thing. "He'll be okay."

"Hmpf." He sneered. He had about as much confidence in that as she did right now, but on some level, as bad as she hated to admit it, maybe Nick needed to know he could be okay without her too.

"Fine. I like a little fresh blood now and then. You're younger, more innovative. Let's arrange the flowers differently. See what they look like. You'll have no contact with your family. They'll pay if I find out you've connected with them."

"You'll stop hunting my mother?"

"Yes. As long as she keeps her mouth shut."

Noory nodded sharply and fought the urge to vomit as bile rose in her throat and her heart hammered inside the cage of her chest. There was no going back. She wouldn't be able to see them again. Wouldn't be in Nick's arms again. She had just found her mother. She'd dreamed her whole life about what it would be like to have a mother to talk to, laugh with. Now she had her back, and she was forced to let her go. Just like that. Nick was right all along. The heavens were cruel. She would never walk into John's old farmhouse again. The little girl inside her wept for her father, curled up and bawled. How had her mother endured this horror? *Stop it! You can do this.*

Besides, she knew something this bastard in front of her didn't. Her family would tear a hole through heaven and Earth to get her back. You didn't have to despair when there were people who truly loved you.

She walked out of Malachi's office, down the hallway, and into her new life, carrying her family in her heart.

Chapter 54

Nick shimmered into the kitchen. "I can't find him," he said. He slowly sat down in one of the old farmhouse kitchen chairs. Without saying a word, John got up and left the room. He still held Nick responsible for Noory choosing to go back to Second Sight. Maybe now for not finding Roy, too? Probably, why not.

"I should go," Nick said.

"Sit," Catherine commanded.

Catherine retrieved the coffee pot and a cup and sat them in front of Nick, who mumbled, "Thanks."

"Do you think he might have decided to ascend after all?"

"I don't think so. I can usually feel that." Nick stared at the table, lost in thought. "I wish I knew. Maybe he's simply hiding himself from me because he knows I'll try to convince him to come back."

Catherine tilted her head and leveled a gaze at him.

"Oh, he's probably right."

She nodded with a sympathetic smile. "I suspect he's over there pounding on the doors of heaven." she said.

"Well, maybe he can get an answer out of the Almighty. Lord knows I never could." Nick picked up the coffeepot and poured himself a cup.

"And you can go back and look for him again. Maybe you'll have better luck later. Right now, let's think about what we *can* do. I have an ally inside Second Sight."

"Who?"

"He's actually a vampire believe it or not."

"Not."

"That wasn't really an option. Lorien is trapped there the same as Noory is, the same as I was. If we can remove the thing that binds him there, then they will have no more power over him, and he can help us from the inside once he has nothing to lose."

"How do you know you can trust him?"

"How do you know you can trust anyone? You spend time around them and watch their integrity. He has more than most humans I know, almost *any* human I know."

"What will we do?"

"We're going to wake a sleeping vampire."

"Lorien?"

"No. His sister. That's how they keep him there. They hold his sister in stasis at a remote location. When they want to keep him in line, they show her to him and remind him they hold the power. If that threat were removed, he'd be free to help us."

"And you think he will?"

"I do, but I think they will be on high alert for this. We're going to need backup, and John is being a stubborn ass about you at the moment. So, *I'm* asking you to guard the perimeter and make sure we pull this off."

"Whatever you need."

Catherine nodded and felt something small and warm bloom in her heart.

It felt a lot like hope.

Chapter 55

Nick's tires squealed as he took the turn far too fast. The luxury vehicle hugged the curb as it should. Damascus had called to tell him Evan was gone, and Maria was terrified. Worse, he'd been hinting that he could rescue Grace. He'd pointed out that since his gifts were genetic, he could likely get through Second Sight without his power being bound. But it wasn't true. Damascus' power was genetic, and he couldn't burn anyone while there. He'd driven instead of simply materializing, hoping he might spot Evan somewhere along the route there.

He knew Evan's intentions were good, but the only thing he would accomplish would be getting captured by Second Sight so they could exploit his gifts in the worst way possible. Nick slowed down when he saw Evan a block from the Truist building. He parked along the curb and got out. The sun was warm on his shoulders, and the May morning was heating up already. He ran to catch up, then fell in step beside Evan.

"Don't try to stop me," Evan said.

"You're a powerful magus, but Damascus and I were shut down the moment we walked through the door." Nick cringed at the amount of defeat he heard in his voice. He was talking quickly as they neared the building with no time to censor it or run it through a filter that was less despairing. "You will be too."

"You don't know that."

"Yes, I do."

Nick continued, "What are they going to say, 'Give this one a pass. He's clearly stronger than all of us. Let the girl go—Evan is here.'"

"Well, no. It's just . . . I have all this power. I have to at least try."

Nick knew they were getting closer. He didn't want to bodily tackle him. "Get in the car, Evan."

"I have to try." The entrance to the building loomed in front of them.

Nick grabbed Evan's arm. A couple of passersby in business casual clothing glanced his way. Nick nodded at them, and they continued on. He leaned over and spoke into Evan's ear, "You've got to listen to me. You have no idea what you're getting yourself into. You flung a little fire around with Damascus and now you think you're ready to take on a corporation of ancient monsters? That's pure arrogance, and it's going to get you killed."

"I can handle it. Besides, even if I do get caught, at least I'll be with Grace." He yanked his arm free and took off running.

Nick tackled him before he reached the building. As they fell, he slipped an arm in front of Evan's head to keep him from getting hurt. Unfortunately, his own elbow smacked painfully against the concrete. He took a breath to keep from yelling at the kid. "Stop this. Stay alive and keep your freedom, so you can look out for your mother. You're all she's got. Don't you think this is killing me, too? Noory is the love of my life. Don't you think I would have already saved them if it were possible?"

"I—"

"Damn it." Nick looked through the glass doors and saw two uniformed men heading their way. "Now security is on their way. Get up! They're going to arrest me and question you. Shit!"

Evan got to his feet, looking miserable. Nick pointed to the left. "Around the corner. We can slip away there. Move!"

He put his hand on Evan's shoulder, and they both disappeared and reappeared in the shadows of a parking deck one street up and then made their way to Nick's car. After they got in, the grief hung in the air.

Nick started the car, looked at the backup camera, pulled into the street, and then spoke softly, "One of the hardest things to accept about having this much power is that it doesn't solve everything, and you have to be patient, just like everyone else. It's a hard truth to come to."

"Maybe I could have . . ."

"If John and I, with almost four thousand years of experience between us, couldn't get in there to save her, then this problem is going to take some time and thought. The level of spelling on that building is going to take serious research. We just can't . . ." Nick stopped talking when he heard Evan sniff. He was a powerful being but still a little boy, and he was in tears.

Mentoring any child was tough, but this . . . this was going to take something extra, and it scared Nick . . . just a little.

CHAPTER 56

Catherine and John stood in the darkness of a nearly moonless night. In the backyard of a home in the upper middle-class neighborhood on the outskirts of Atlanta called Vinings was a charming, walkable, idyllic, community, but if anyone had guessed what Second Sight was hiding in the basement of one of these enviable slices of the American dream, they would have fled in terror.

In the next yard over, Nick and Damascus waited, quiet as death. Catherine pointed a palm-sized box at the security camera trained on the door and pushed a button, delivering a small electromagnetic pulse to disable the device. She also sprayed the hinges of the door so they wouldn't creak when she opened it, then she made quick work of the basement door lock.

She opened the door and then slipped inside, with John following close behind her. A guard slept in front of a console with two monitors before him. One was clearly medical and monitored vital signs. The other monitored the camera that had gone offline, but this guard had slept through it, and he would continue to sleep. Catherine smiled to herself. She pulled the plastic bag coated in ether from her pocket and held it to his mouth and nose. He barely resisted before sagging farther into the chair. She looked over the console and into the chamber with large glass windows and spotted what she came for. The container that held a sleeping woman.

John walked over to the entrance and tried the door handle. It was locked. "Now what?"

"Just keep rattling door handles and see if you can set off an alarm," she said.

John looked at her, and she gave him a quick smile.

Catherine tapped a PIN pad near the doorframe and typed in the password for most of the doors at Second Sight. She just hoped they hadn't changed the codes from when she'd left, or if they had, that they'd neglected to change this one since they didn't even know that she knew where Annabelle was. The door gave a soft click, and Catherine's shoulders relaxed from where she'd had them bunched up around her ears. They walked inside and approached the glass chamber.

John stood with Catherine looking into the clear coffin-like structure. The woman inside had thick, lustrous, dark hair, a flawless complexion, rosy lips, and long lashes. "Sleeping beauty," Catherine said softly, although the smart, black pantsuit she wore seemed a little out of step with that fairy tale.

"Pft. If you say so," John said.

Catherine knew John had a policy of avoiding this type of thing at all costs. He was a supernatural being too but saw himself as different since he came to be via the "Light Side," and vampirism was rumored to come from a dark curse. He'd tried to think of at least a dozen ways to avoid doing this, but Catherine knew this was the way to help her daughter. However roundabout it might be.

She'd done her research before coming here to wake her. Apparently, humans in this kind of stasis would require being slowly awakened over the course of a week. But from everything Catherine had seen and read, Annabelle wouldn't require that kind of "cooling off" period when coming out of stasis. Vamps could go from sleeping stasis to completely awake, with minor side effects. She'd found the schematics for the chamber years ago and memorized them. After a minute, the lid retracted, and Catherine motioned for John to step back while she did the same. She was there to help, but Annabelle wouldn't initially know that.

The vamp's eyes popped open, and she sprang into a crouch inside the box as she looked around. Catherine began speaking immediately. "My name is Catherine Abramson. I'm a friend of your brother, Lorien. I'm here to free you. I promised him I would. Second Sight has been holding you here for the last twenty years. We've come to take you out of here."

The woman just stared at Catherine.

"Lorien," the woman said the name with recognition.

"Yes. He's my friend. I promised him if I got free before him, I would get you out, but we must go before they realize you're free. Come on."

The woman nodded, placed one steadying hand on the side of the chamber, and climbed out with an unexpected grace for one that hadn't moved in so long. She turned to look at John with deep curiosity. "Ancient," she said simply.

"Yes," Catherine said.

Annabelle wobbled for the briefest moment before she brushed her hands across her clothing, cleared her throat, and spoke again. "I'm ready."

"Do you remember what Second Sight is?"

"I do," she said between gritted teeth. "Have they harmed my brother?"

Catherine wasn't sure how to answer that. Holding a person prisoner was harm, especially when he knew his sister was being held captive, but she didn't dare poke the angry vamp. "Other than holding him there for his expertise with you as collateral, no."

Annabelle looked around on her way out, testing the air, smelling, even opening her mouth as if tasting it as well. She gave a quick glance at the sleeping guard but seemed to understand it was best to leave him be. Once outside, the three of them started making their way back around the house where Damascus was waiting. John had grudgingly allowed him to come after Catherine had said his use of archaic spell knowledge would prove invaluable if they couldn't wake her. Catherine had also informed John that she didn't need his permission. She'd decided she actually liked Damascus and believed him capable of caring, and changing for that matter, despite John's apparent hatred of him.

"Stop," Damascus warned. "Someone's coming." He waved his hands for them to go back the way they came.

"Damn it," Catherine whispered. She knew things had gone a little too well. It was too late.

A guard emerged from the next yard over. There was just enough illumination coming from a back porch light to see that he held a gun. "Good to see you again, Catherine. We agreed to stop hunting you. Somehow, that daughter of yours actually got Malichi to agree to that. Can you imagine? I don't know what the hell she said to him, but he rolled over. Just like that." The man snapped his fingers. "That little bitch has the same kind of pull with him you did. The rest of us bust our asses for years and can't get even get a meeting with him, and she just waltzes in there like you used to and makes demands."

"Being held prisoner and kept from your family is not a privilege."

The man continued, "He's collected all manner of magical beings. So many have more power, more influence, more raw energy, and yet, when it comes to your line, he just . . . I've gone over it and over it again in my head. What the hell is it? Why are you so fucking special? I mean, I've had you. I just. Don't. Get it."

Catherine knew exactly who this was. It was the disgusting prick she had slept with when she was newly imprisoned at Second Sight and trying to comply to keep Noory safe and get enough information to keep her that way. She'd been afraid, vulnerable, mourning her daughter and John. He'd taken advantage of her. Then tried to do it again after she'd gone to see Noory last year. She'd thrown him across the Manhattan skyline from her penthouse balcony and thought him dead. He'd recovered from illnesses, broken bones, stabbings, gunshot wounds, and any other damn thing quicker than anyone should be able to, but everyone said he hadn't taken the serum. She thought she'd finally ended him.

"You wanna know what I think? I think Malachi knew the Messiah and wanted to collect him but couldn't, and it's been driving him insane ever since. The next best thing is owning his family, his descendants. Well, he's got one now and you are fair game. You're about to regret that stunt you pulled with me."

The sound of the gunshot rang out in the night, but Catherine barely registered it as a body went flying in front of her, taking the shot meant for her. Scarier still was the knowledge that the bullet would have been tainted with every spell meant to kill the unkillable. The bullets were hard to make and completely unaffordable to most, but Second Sight wouldn't have a guard here without it.

Damascus lay at her feet, bleeding.

A heartbeat later she saw Annabelle process what was happening, and she watched as the newly awakened vamp tore the gunman's head from his shoulders. Catherine couldn't say she was sorry for him. He may have come back from being thrown across Manhattan, but he wouldn't come back from this one. At her feet, she noticed John leaning over Damascus. She said a silent prayer that John's healing touch extended to demons. She wasn't sure whether it did, but she hoped with all her heart.

Annabelle turned and looked at them with blood splattered on the side of her face. Her eyes had gone black, her fangs were extended, and she looked hungry while she gazed back at the body as blood poured from the neck and she dropped the head with a sickening thud. Though Catherine had killed, she'd never seen this. Bile rocketed up her throat, and she swallowed hard. She wanted to look away but didn't dare take her eyes off Annabelle. "No," Catherine breathed. "Your brother wouldn't want this for you. Don't." She felt futility wash over her. She was trying to reason with a vamp that hadn't eaten in twenty years. Sure. Second Sight had kept nutrients flowing, but she'd not *tasted* it, and her kind was all about appetite.

Annabelle started to lean over. Her control was slipping. If she gave in, it could well result in "losing her" for a while. Detoxing a vampire was dangerous. They often needed help controlling their appetites initially, and whoever was helping them could be in grave danger.

"Annabelle. Please."

She looked up and the humanity Catherine had seen earlier could not be found. The vampire's tongue slid out and licked her upper lip. Then she was gone. A blur Catherine knew as Nicholas grabbed Annabelle and disappeared in a heartbeat. Whatever Nick was doing and wherever he was taking Annabelle, it was all for their good, whether

John thought so or not. She knew it in her bones. Just like her daughter did. She allowed a second of relief and hope to take hold, then turned her attention back to John and Damascus.

She knelt beside them and cupped the demon's high cheekbone. Blood trickled from the side of his mouth. "Crazy demon. Why would you do such a thing?" She'd managed to avoid tears for two decades. She'd become the rock she intended to be, but the sight of Damascus struggling to breathe, taking a bullet meant for her, made the tears fall. The irony of it slayed her and solidified her faith like nothing else could. She always did believe God was the most ironic of all beings. It would be fitting to orchestrate a demon saving her life. This was proof of faith, love, life.

She turned to look at John. Sweat poured from his face, dripped from his nose, as he pushed all his energy into trying to heal Damascus to no avail. John had never had to struggle with his gift. Even this wasn't rattling her like some distant part of her mind knew it should. She took John's hands off Damascus' wound. "It's okay, John."

John wiped his bloody hands on his pants and sat back. His voice shook as he spoke. "I'm sorry," he whispered.

A calm washed over Catherine as she leaned over and placed her cheek beside Damascus' and spoke into his ear. "Hear the word of the Lord and live."

At first, it sounded as if he were choking. Then he rolled halfway over and vomited blood onto the driveway and slowly sat up. He looked at her in awe.

He trembled, but otherwise seemed okay. "What did you do to me? I'm . . ." He opened and closed his mouth. "We better go. Others will be here soon, I would imagine." Whatever he'd wanted to say, he needed time; she realized she did too. She'd never healed anyone before and didn't know she was capable of it. Clearly John didn't either. The look he was giving her was half admiration, half fear. As long as the man had lived, as much as he had seen, he wasn't that great with pivots.

The three got to their feet and fled into the night.

CHAPTER 57

Nick watched Anna huddled in the corner of the cot with her knees up by her chest. Her shoes were abandoned on the floor below her. Perhaps the first time they'd been removed in twenty years. *How much upkeep did they do on a vampire in stasis?*

She was calmer now that Brother Thaddeus had given her the bag of O negative that he kept for just such an occasion. They got a rogue vampire now and then in their prison for the magically hard to manage. Thaddeus might have wanted to stake first and ask questions later, but the Abbot forbade it. The warrior monk now sat by his desk, appearing to be doing paperwork, but Nick knew better. The man knew every move any demon, vamp, changeling, elemental, or otherwise made in his prison. He'd allowed Nick in the cell with her after Nick had reminded him that, should Anna lunge at him, he could disappear in a breath, where an average human could not.

"How are you feeling? A little better?" Nick asked.

"Yes," thank you.

Nick had explained to her where she was as she frantically drank Thaddeus' offering. She had also come down from her vengeful rant about burning Second Sight to the ground for what they'd done to her. She was determined to rescue her brother, and he didn't blame her, but she had to cool down before she was let out of this cell, or she'd end up in a much fouler cage or right back in stasis and all their efforts tonight would be for naught. He thought he'd gotten through to her, but for now, she'd be better off here with Brother Thaddeus.

She turned her head to the side to look around her surroundings and he noticed dried blood on her face. He rose and walked the four feet to the stainless-steel sink by her cot, tore a paper towel from the roll sitting beside it and ran warm water over it. He approached her and started to hand her the wet towel before realizing she wouldn't know where to wipe and mirrors weren't allowed as they could be broken and used to make a shiv, and some demons made portals of them. "May I?" he asked quietly. "You have a little . . ." he gestured to the side of his face to show her where the blood was on her. She nodded.

He gently wiped the blood from her as his mind drifted back in time. Way back. It was 1847. A gas streetlamp illuminated Annabelle's glossy black hair in its elaborate updo as she leaned over a child, the child whose distress had brought him to Tyburn street in the heart of London. Blood stained the child's nightshirt and Annabelle's lace trimmed dress as well. She turned and looked at him and he knew instantly she was eternal and vampiric. He was on her in a flash and slamming her against the wall at the far end of the alley. He hated violence against women. Men could beat their wives senseless in most cities around the world and no judge would convict, but this, this was a creature. She was screaming, pleading. It broke through the haze of liquor, something about the look in her eye, the begging, the desperation. He'd seen it before.

"I'm a member of The Society. I didn't hurt him. I'm trying to help!"

The Society? "The Society of Free Vampires?" he said quietly.

"Yes. Please help the boy."

He realized what the familiar look was. He knew where he'd seen the look on her face, in his mirror. Not recently, though. She was an addict trying to live free. He was just . . . an addict at the moment. He hadn't had the courage to try and live free in a while. He released her and with a nod, he turned and sped to the young boy. Nick grabbed the boy, took him to the nearest doctor, but the child was already gone. Even John couldn't have acted fast enough.

Nick returned to the scene, backed up into the shadows, and stared at the spot where the boy had just been.

God enjoyed tormenting him.

That had to be it. Why else call him to such a scene? If God was all knowing, then he knew he wouldn't make it in time. "Sadist," he whispered and pulled the flask from his breast pocket.

"You?" a voice behind him said.

"The All damn Mighty."

"Hmm. I prefer the term, Warden. He's made me a prisoner here and likes to watch me live out my never-ending sentence."

Nick gave a wry laugh. "Apt description, my lady." He offered her the flask. She took it and tilted it up for the briefest second before handing it back. "Sorry about earlier," Nick said.

"No, I understand how it must have looked."

"My intentions have been misunderstood when I've been doing my job as well."

"I imagine they have, Father Christmas."

Nick laughed at the moniker. He wasn't surprised she knew of him. Many immortals did. "I'm no father."

"Better father than the plenty I've observed in my long existence. You save children, not slowly destroy them as many do."

They stood in the cool night air with the distant sound of horse's hooves on cobblestone and the occasional barking dog punctuating the night. The heat of the day would bring smog and baking sewage. For now, he smelled ouzo and the faint scent of lilacs coming from the woman beside him. She made him curious. She'd conquered a beast. He wondered for how long. He'd tried wrestling his own beast. The flask grew heavy in his hand. "You're a member of The Society. May I ask how long? It is none of my concern. I simply wonder if—"

She looked at the flask in his hand before answering. She made the connection and he felt naked for a moment. "Two years," she said with pride.

"Congratulations." He'd never made it that long. "How'd you do it?"

"The key is to find something worth fighting for. The ideal person you want to be."

Nick thought of John.

"I used to think it was because I wanted to be like my brother. He's kind and strong. There's a . . . I don't know how to describe it, a wisdom about him that I wanted. He's been a member of The Society for over a decade now. But then, I realized, I kept failing because I was trying to be like him, what I needed to do was to aspire to be like me, but I didn't know what that was, didn't value it, didn't love it. Once I figured that out, well, that's when it all worked. It wasn't easy, but it wasn't impossible anymore."

Nick shook his head and scoffed, then worried she would think he was scoffing at her.

"You don't see it, do you, Nicholas?"

He looked at her through liquored hazed eyes. "See what?"

"What I see," she said softly, reverently.

He swallowed hard but couldn't look away. She held out her hand to him. He took it and she walked him to her apartment. It was the first time in a long time that something had come along to break the cycle of grief, numb, grief. He woke before dawn in her bed. He crept silently away before she stirred, a coward.

He'd not seen her again until today. His heart had almost stopped beating when Catherine and John had walked out of the house with her, and he'd realized it was Anna. He had to force himself to move, to take action, before she devoured the man bleeding at her feet in that driveway.

"Thank you," she whispered as Nick wiped the last of the blood away.

"You're welcome." There was nothing between them now. No spark. He loved Noory. But he did want to help Anna. She'd seen something in him when he absolutely could not see it in himself, and she'd made him think it might be possible he was worth saving, but it wasn't until Noory that he'd actually believed it. He'd help her in any way he could. "Listen, I've got to go make sure my friends are okay, but I promise to come back and help you work all this out. We'll get you out of here, find you a place to stay." He threw the bloodied paper towel in the bin, crouched down in front of her, and placed a hand on her knee. "Everything will be okay."

She nodded and bit her lower lip. She looked so helpless and frail, despite the fact that she was truly a dangerous predator.

He shimmered out of the monastery and off to find his friends.

CHAPTER 58

Catherine took a chenille throw off Damascus' couch and placed it over his shoulders as he sipped a mug of warm tea. Damascus looked up at Catherine as if she were an angel.

John rolled his eyes. "Now why are you mothering him? He isn't hurt anymore."

Damascus made a face at John before speaking. "I still feel a little woozy."

"No, you don't," John mumbled under his breath.

Catherine heard John's mumbled reply but noticed it lacked the fight it had before Damascus had risked his life for her. John had moved into grudging admiration, or perhaps even actual acceptance, but John wasn't the type that would make an immediate about-face. He had to salvage some of his pride after how hard he'd fought against bringing the demon along.

"All right, you two." She let out a sigh. "He saved my life. He didn't have to."

Damascus shook his head and said, "I didn't have to," as he looked at John. The demon was nothing if not antagonistic. He was enjoying this entirely too much.

"I can't believe I didn't even see Nick arrive," John said.

"You were rather occupied. He was in and out in a flash. And thank God he was," Catherine said. "Annabelle was about to fall over the edge. Hard."

"But we didn't tell him about our plans," John said.

"Oh, I did," Catherine said immediately. Defiantly. Let John throw his fit with Nick if he wanted to. That was his problem, not hers. As much as she loved John, she wouldn't join him in resenting Nick.

"I also told him." Damascus nodded and smiled at John like a belligerent child.

She was certain John wanted to strangle Damascus, the demon he'd tried to keep alive half an hour ago. The sooner John learned no one was going to support him in ostracizing people he couldn't control, the better. She loved him with her entire heart and soul but wouldn't let him control her or her opinions.

"He probably took her to the monastery prison until she could get a handle on the bloodlust," Damascus said. "That's what I would've done."

"Yeah. I'm sure that's it," John said.

"Maybe Nick's old cell is still empty," Damascus said.

"How would you know anything about that?" John asked.

"Do you really think Amaros left a young, strong, immortal vessel like Nick and willingly jumped into a feeble shell of a man like Jonah all by himself? Now why would he do that? Who do you know with archaic knowledge enough to separate Nick from Amaros and contain it in another body so it wouldn't go find Noory because Nick was 'in breach of contract'?"

Catherine said, "We always wondered about that back at the office! That part never quite made sense to us."

Damascus did a little bow from where he sat in his chair.

"Did you and Nick plan that?"

"He didn't know. I couldn't tell him because then Amaros would have known."

"Does Nick know now?" Catherine asked.

"No, but speak of the handsome devil," Damascus said as Nick appeared. "Here he is now."

"Huh?" Nick said.

Damascus chuckled.

"Anna's at the monastery getting a handle on her bloodlust," Nick said.

The three of them nodded.

"I think she'll be okay. The incident was just a lot for her, having just woken up. I don't sense any ill intent in her."

"If she's like her brother . . ." Catherine said.

Nick nodded. "Yeah, I actually knew her briefly in the mid-1800s. She and her brother were members of The Society of Free Vampires. They were a group committed to abstaining. So, what now? Do we find a way to let Lorien know?"

Catherine laughed. "Oh, he'll know soon enough. A breach as serious as this will be all anyone at Second Sight can talk about."

"But how can we be sure he'll take it as a sign that he's free to betray them or that he even has you to thank for it?"

"Because I promised him if I ever made it out, I would free her."

"You promised to free a *vampire*?" John said. "This wasn't just to prompt Lorien to help Noory?"

"Oh, I would have done it anyway. Yes," Catherine said.

"This is simply delicious." Damascus leaned forward, closer to John and Catherine and looked between the two of them as he spoke. "What's going to happen now? Will steam shoot out of John's ears? Like in a cartoon?"

"We've got bigger problems," Nick cut in. "As good as I sense her spirit is, Annabelle wants to get into Second Sight and tear a path of vengeance through that place and then burn it to ash. If she ever gets free, I'm not sure we can stop her."

"Why in hell would we?" Damascus said.

"Because Noory and Grace are in there, and Annabelle is so angry that she might get herself caught again if she doesn't think this through," Nick said.

"We've all got to think this through," Catherine said. "If . . . when we get back in there, it has to work."

Suddenly, there was nothing left but silence and loss. No more plans for the moment. Just the absence of the person they all loved more than themselves.

Chapter 59

Nick appeared in front of the Savannah River on the far end of River Street near a now-deserted shipping yard where he wouldn't be seen by tourists. The water lapped against the old dock. The loneliness, the absolute absence of Noory tore a hole in his chest. "The patron saint of sailors can't navigate these waters," he whispered.

He remembered the first time he'd come here with Noory last year when they were looking for Grace. The sun was setting, and the saxophone street performer was playing "Moon River." She leaned over the railing, and the wind blew her hair back. The sight of her took his breath away. He was already in love . . . and terrified. He knew he'd have to do better if he were going to be with her. He'd have to kick his habit.

Now she was gone. Was there any point?

He felt the familiar weight against his chest and reached into his breast pocket. He took the bottle of ouzo out, opened it, and smelled the familiar notes of black licorice. He felt a little lightheaded before he even took a drink. He'd grown so accustomed to the association between the licorice taste and being inebriated. It was sunset this time as well. Only now, there was no beautiful sunset over the river, only a steel gray sky, threatening rain. He wanted to die again.

"Nicholas."

"Fuck." John was behind him. He didn't need this right now. "I haven't drunk any."

"Just holding it for a friend?"

"Nope. Holding it for me. Well, smelling of it at the moment." He put the cap back on it and turned around to see Catherine and Brother Thaddeus there as well. "How did you all get here?"

"Catherine knows more dark entities than I'm comfortable with just yet. One of them arranged transport for us. You'll have to take us back home, though."

Nick watched her roll her eyes at John and for a moment she looked so much like Noory it made his breath catch in his throat and tears sting his eyes before he could hide them from them. Damn it.

"I know," John said quietly so that only Nick could hear. "She looks way too much like Noory sometimes, doesn't she?"

Nick turned his head so that only John could see the tear escape his eye and run down his face. "Yes." His voice cracked on the word.

They both turned to face the water while the others stood a few yards away, allowing them some space. John said, "She isn't dead, Nick. She's just at Second Sight, and she's just fine. We'll get her back."

"I know."

"I can't tell you what to do. I'm not going to yell at you, and I think it's time our relationship changed, for good. But I really hope you don't start up with that again." John pointed at the ouzo in Nick's hand.

"How?" Nick swallowed, trying hard to keep it together. "How did you keep going, after losing Catherine? And you thought she was dead. I know Noory isn't, and it feels like it's ripping me apart."

"Yes, it does. That means it's real. I'm actually pleased to hear you love my daughter that much."

"So much I think it might kill me. I tried for years to end my existence, and this feels like it actually could."

John put his hand on Nick's back. "It only feels like it. It won't. I promise."

Nick looked up at the steel gray sky and saw a small break in the clouds. A shaft of light made its way through. He looked at the bottle of ouzo. It felt like an old, reliable friend. Panic raced through his veins when he thought about letting it go. He saw John reach his hand toward his head then stop. He guessed why. John likely realized he needed to do this on his own, no false calm, no healing touch, just Nick, doing the hard work, and he was right.

Nick's body broke out in a sweat as he flung the bottle into the river. When it was gone, John took his hand. It was the first time he'd done that, ever. There was no supernatural healing intention coming from John. There was the regular, human one, an everyday miracle, the kind they all had, and it was enough.

Catherine and Thaddeus stepped up to the railing, and Nick took them all home.

CHAPTER 60

Nick walked into the shelter of the Holy Innocents, took a deep breath, and looked around. Being there made him feel closer to Noory. Every time he thought of her, his chest hurt, but he knew she'd be happy that he cared enough to look after the shelter while she was gone. Besides, when he walked in here, he felt . . . joy, oddly. As depressing as it was on one level, to see these kids homeless for various heartbreaking reasons, on another level this was his chance to help without having to arrive at the moment of life or death, violence and chaos. He could offer something different, new. He could slow down and talk with them, make a meal for them, hand them a blanket or a jacket. This was different, and he was glad. He knew he would still get called away for his usual commission, but this somehow gave him a space to breathe. He whispered a prayer of thanks.

He walked into the kitchen, took out three cartons of eggs, a frying pan, bacon, and lit the burner. Time to start breakfast. Nick took a deep breath. It made it past the pain in his chest where he missed Noory constantly and to a place where he was glad to be alive, sober, and useful. Until she was back in his arms, this is what he would do for her . . . and him.

Chapter 61

Sometime during the night as Noory lay in bed, she drifted inside dark, troubling dreams. She walked down an Atlanta street, searching for Nick with an ache in her chest. Shadows loomed on the brick building before her and danced, twisting, turning into grotesque shapes, before disappearing again. Then orange eyes appeared first, blinking slowly before his body coalesced around that striking feature.

"Damascus?" Though it was yet another demon, she was relieved to see this one.

"Hey, girl. You okay?"

"No," Noory sobbed, knowing it was a dream, so it didn't matter if she let go.

He stepped forward and embraced her. She knew anguish rolled off her, sending waves of pain crashing into him. "I brought someone with me," he whispered in her ear.

Damascus stepped back so she could see. Nick gave her a smile.

"He isn't real."

"Girl, what did I tell you the first time we met?"

She thought back to their first meeting almost a year ago when she stood on the ledge of Robert Billings' office window, felt a presence behind her, and asked who it was. He had answered, "I am Damascus, ancient and powerful." The words echoed off the surrounding buildings, projected from her mind into the dream world. Damascus looked around as the words bounced as if in a canyon.

"Nice." He nodded in approval. "Although, I believe my voice is a little deeper. Then you ought to know, he's real, honey. I know astral projection isn't the same as flesh and blood but until you're back for good, *and you will be*, this might help."

He went on, "I'm going to go see what kind of freaky dreamscape you've created for me. Conjure something beautiful, will you?" Damascus winked and walked away.

Noory closed her eyes and thought of someone handsome, delicious, and half dressed, a gift for her friend. A moment later, she heard Damascus say, "Well, hello, gorgeous. Thanks, Noory!"

Nick stepped forward and reached for her. "You're going to be okay."

They wrapped their arms, their souls, around each other, and though it hurt to know her body was lying in bed alone, she knew he was right.

They walked along the Atlanta streets and then onto a beach made just for her and Nick. If they could be anywhere, why not there. They stood under the shade of softly swaying palms. It felt so real as intermittent dappled sunlight made its way through the fronds. She created a bench for them to sit on and laid her head on Nick's shoulder. She lazily ran a bare foot through the sand as she asked him about the shelter, and he told her about the peace he was finding in running it. It brought her joy to know it was in his hands. There was no jealousy or grief. She had the deepest sense of knowing this was part of a plan, a grander scheme. Was it because she was dreaming? Surely not. It felt right.

A dark shadow caught her eye slithering in from the left, then another from the right, sliding across the sand. "We're being infiltrated," she heard Damascus whisper behind them. "You both need to wake up."

Suddenly they weren't on the beach anymore. The three of them were in Holy Innocents. The shelter was on fire and people were screaming, trapped inside, while fire climbed the walls like a living thing. Janus stepped from the flames, unscathed and spoke. "There's nowhere to run, no reality, no dreamscape where I can't find you."

Noory woke from sheer terror and had no doubt the other two had done the same. She rolled over, pulled the covers tighter around her body, and willed the shaking to stop.

CHAPTER 62

At first, Damascus ignored the gasps of the saints as he walked the hallowed halls of purgatory. When he could take their pious glances no longer—curious, but too sanctimonious to admit that they were interested in the likes of him—he leaned over and startled the occasional pilgrim by extending his claws and yelling "Boo!" He laughed as their disembodied forms jumped. He decided he was teaching them a valuable lesson on their way to ascension. *You're welcome,* he thought.

He'd been searching on and off for weeks. He was doing it for Noory, at least that's what he told himself. Nick said he could sense when a soul had ascended, and Roy had not. So, Reverend Goody Two Shoes was still here somewhere, whining about not hearing God anymore, while his friends were neck deep in shit without him. *Selfish bastard.*

He'd finally gone to talk to the man's ex-boyfriend. Yeah, it was kind of low. He'd lied his ass off and gave him a lame story about his uncle having gone to seminary with Roy and what were his favorite haunts because he might want to mention it when he visited his uncle this fall. It was all too easy. It helped him figure out where the priest might hang out in the great beyond because purgatory was a shadow version of the real world, and Bob's your fucking uncle—there Roy sat, looking up at the Atlanta skyline from the vantage point of what one could see if they were sitting in Piedmont Park looking just over the trees at the skyline.

"Well, there you are, you self-righteous bastard. Your friends are going to hell in a handbasket and you're on the other side, pouting. Get your ass up and come help us."

Roy looked up and Damascus thought for the briefest of moments that the man was actually happy to see him. Something inside him fluttered. *What the hell?*

Roy said nothing, so Damascus continued. "Look, you're more powerful than any wizard, druid, demon, or immortal I've ever met. Use it. Help us! How could it be wrong to come back and help a descendant of the Holy Family of *your* God?"

"But you don't understand. He stopped talking to me. He cut me off."

"Well," Damascus threw his arms in the air, "he doesn't ever talk to me, and I'm just fine!"

He thought he detected a hint of a smile on Roy. "You're a demon."

"So?"

Roy turned back to gaze at the skyline. "You don't understand. His voice was like . . . it was like, magic, music, tasting the most beautiful music."

Damascus started to blurt out that what he was describing was an acid trip, not a conversation with God. If that's what he was looking for, he could get that from the right dealer and with less hassle and *certainly* less devotion. Instead, he bit his tongue and made his way over to where Roy was and sat down beside him. *Damn humans are making me so soft!* He thought of something kinder, gentler to say. "Maybe it's kind of like the serum Noory got hooked on. She said it washed every cell in her body with light. The hardest thing in the world to come off of."

Roy scoffed. "She was already filled with light."

"I agree, and yet, she never heard the voice of God directly."

"This is true. But I have reason to know that He is disappointed in me. I heard His voice, but I lost it because I did something that I knew I wasn't supposed to do."

"Oh, for God's sake. Maybe losing the voice was part of the plan. Maybe not saving your friends when you had the power to, just so you could keep the voice was selfish and would have damned you. You don't know."

"You bring a fresh perspective, my friend."

"Friend? I've never had a priest call me friend."

"I've never had a demon want to be my friend." Roy turned to face Damascus and plucked a line of energy in front of him and looked at him, around him.

"You're looking at my aura."

"Yes."

"And you look troubled."

"Not troubled. Just confused. I've never seen anything like it before."

"What are you talking about?"

"Well, it's streaked with something . . . I can't believe I'm saying this, but *holy*."

Damascus threw his head back and laughed. "I assure you, I'm all demon, baby."

"Oh, I've always had reason to believe that, and this holiness was not always in your aura. Something has happened. Something that isn't supposed to be possible. Priests can't bless demons. It's never been feasible, even if we wanted to."

Damascus quietly tapped his hands together to create a small ball of fire. "Yup, still works."

"It works, but a thin white glow hovers just above the flame."

"Oh, great! I'll be the laughingstock of demon society."

"Oh, please. You know you don't give a shit."

"Language, Father!"

"You are now the sacred and profane, but what could have caused this thing? I've never heard of any such."

"'Hear the word of the Lord and live,'" Damascus quoted softly as he let his flame flicker and go out.

"What?"

"It's what Catherine whispered into my ear when she healed me recently."

"She can heal?"

"Yes. I think it came as a surprise to her as well. I was dying. Got shot with a spelled bullet designed to kill an immortal. Only the rarest, most expensive, *designer* bullet can kill the likes of me," he said as he puffed out his chest. "Anyway, John couldn't heal me, so she gave it a shot."

"Huh, maybe that is how you picked this up in your aura, or maybe you've made yourself receptive somehow. Both, maybe."

"Well, whatever the case. My sacred and profane ass is here to bring you back. Come on."

"I have a different idea."

"I'm listening."

"For the first time since I stopped hearing Him, I'm at least feeling what I'd call Divine Inspiration. I think I might be close to . . . something. That inspiration is telling me that you should stay here, at least for a little bit."

"And when I want to go, I go."

"No one is holding you here. You aren't dead."

Damascus thought for a minute. He couldn't make the man leave with him, and he seemed hopeful for the first time in a long time. He was getting something: Divine Inspiration, whatever that was. Maybe he could get him to budge soon. "All right. I'll stay. Just for a little while."

Roy placed a hand on top of his companionably. Damascus looked down on it, half panicked, half filled with peace he couldn't quite process. Half profane, half sacred. It felt just about right.

EPILOGUE

Nick had consulted the text dozens of times by this point. He'd said the spell to protect himself and crossed himself once more just to for good measure. His head was absolutely dripping with holy water. He'd jumped in between the purgatory realm and this one more times than he could count, but he'd never opened a portal such as this. This one was guaranteed to break through the strongest of wards. It was also ancient, perhaps older than Second Sight, so could the writer of this spell have guessed about such power? He didn't know, but he had to try.

Damascus had told him not to do it in no uncertain terms. The spell was just too damn old and there was no one left alive to consult with about it which meant "Leave it the hell alone," he'd said to Nick with an extended claw for the fifth and final time before Nick agreed to drop it. Only, he couldn't. Not after that sadistic Janus demon had infiltrated Damascus' dream walk and threatened the shelter, all those children. Even Damascus had admitted he'd never had another demon infiltrate one of his dream walks that thoroughly. He was angry and bent on getting Noory back, but Janus could erase your entire past and redirect your future. Damascus felt they all needed to regroup, rethink, and take time to plan, but Nick had a fire in his veins.

He looked at the floor again to make sure the salt circle was unbroken. Nothing could jump in during transport. He knew he couldn't make Noory come with him now, not until her mother's fate was secured and she knew, beyond a doubt, that they wouldn't harm the shelter, but he needed to find a reliable way in and be ready the moment they had it all worked out. He closed his eyes and took a deep breath. Using Noory as an anchor point, he thought of the exact color of her hair, her eyes, even the way she smelled, and he recited the memorized spell. He felt himself become light, and then, as if he were in a pneumatic tube like the ones at the bank drive-thru, he slipped into the portal.

Fear crept up his spine, if his spine was even there while he was in the portal, as he sensed a presence in there with him. This one was strong, otherworldly, and determined. His mind scrambled to understand if it was a guardian of magic from Second Sight hair triggered to jump any magic doorways into the compound or some other dark thing. Surely not. This spell was old, archaic even . . . but they had people all over the world. Maybe even people from all over time.

He felt himself yanked out of the portal, and he slid across the floor with a heavy weight lying atop him. Salt scrubbed beneath his back. The entity began trying to pin him before he could even see who or what it was. He jabbed a fist into its side. It grunted. A man's voice. Nick sensed its humanity but something else mixed in, a buzz, an energy that spoke of ancient magic and smelled of trees, moss, and cold running water over ancient rocks. The being slammed a fist into his face. As it did, he caught a glimpse of the man behind it. Ignoring the pain, Nick grabbed the arm that hit him and drove the heel of his palm into the man's nose. Drops of blood flung across the floor and a couple hit his face. A buzz of magic came from each one.

Nick rolled to his side and onto his feet while simultaneously calling forth his knives. He stood in a crouch that almost mirrored the man across from him. But the green-eyed, auburn-haired man held no knives. Instead, blue sparks crackled from his fingers, almost a twin of the blue coming from Nick's holy daggers. Nick knew of this magic and now feared a little less, but only a little. This could still be a Second Sight sentinel, but he was no demon. However, his magic was as ancient as one. "Druid! Why are you hindering me?"

A smile spread across the druid's face, made grotesque by the blood dripping from his nose and coating his teeth. He spoke in a thick Irish accent as he appeared to study the daggers in Nick's hand. "Well, fuck me sideways, if it isn't Saint Nicholas himself. Would you kindly refrain from killin' me if I told you I've been good?"

He couldn't remember his name, if he'd ever even heard it, but after hearing him speak and seeing that half demented smile, he knew this to be the brother of Abraxas, a druid he'd had a history with. The resemblance was undeniable, and there weren't that many druids to start with. "Not sure I believe that, knowing your brother, Abraxas. How does that scary battle druid fare?" Abraxas had been so named for the Persian sun god when he was the sole survivor of a battlefield of thousands and walked off the field the next morning with the rising sun behind him appearing as a god. The Persian name stuck, though the druid himself was very much Irish.

Nick relaxed his stance but wouldn't dispense with his daggers until he found out what this man was up to. Neither did the other man put away his deadly magic. It still sparked from his fingers.

"What business would you be havin' with the prick savages at Second Sight, mate?"

"They have my girlfriend." He saw no reason to lie.

The man looked at him sideways. "Girlfriend?" The man made a tsking sound. "The Nicholas we know of is a man of the cloth. Did you hang up your frock, man? Celibacy a bit much for you?"

"Why, yes, if you must know, but I still fulfill my commission to protect the vulnerable."

The man narrowed his eyes. "And hunt down the guilty with a vengeance that even makes Abraxas shudder."

"Problem with that?"

"Not a bit," the man said.

"Why were you inside my portal?"

"I've been looking for a way into that shithole for the past month. I'm not proud to admit Santa Claus found a way in before a druid, mind you, but I'd hitch any ride to rain down hell on that place, even if it meant ridin' the devil's coattails with hell burnin' my arse."

"Why?" Nick asked.

The druid's face tightened, and he spoke through clinched, red-flecked teeth. "They killed my apprentice. He was just a kid. They wanted the cooperation of the druids, and when we didn't give it—" his voice fell to a mere whisper "—they killed him."

Nick sensed the truth in the man, flicked his wrists, and his daggers disappeared. "We have a common goal then."

"Aye, seems we do." The druid curled his fingers and opened them again, putting away his magic. "Name's Ruari."

"All right then, Ruari. Sit at my table, and I'll get you a rag for your nose." Nick walked into the kitchen, grabbed a dish towel, and wet it. "Here."

Ruari took the towel from Nick and spoke, "Perhaps between us we could burn their house down."

Druid magic was a force indeed, and an angle they'd not yet explored. There was a reason Second Sight wanted their cooperation in the first place. Nick sat down opposite Ruari and allowed his dark thoughts the sliver of light they'd been denied for a while now. "Perhaps we could."

He held out his arm and wondered if Ruari would still do the ancient "handshake"—actually a weapons check—that the modern handshake was derived from. He and Abraxas had done it when they'd worked together back in the day when his brother was helping him track a maniac that was preying on children in ancient Ireland. Sure enough, Ruari clasped Nick's forearm without missing a beat as the druid's ancient, wild magic mingled with his own.

"By the way," Ruari said, "my magic has been misfiring so bad lately it's about to blow my damn eyebrows off. Every time I try to use my scrying mirror to find out what the fuck is going on, the only thing I see is the image of some teenage boy." He laughed. "That can't be right. Did a friggin' magus roll into town or something?"

Nick smiled. "Well, you fell outta the portal just in time."

The Wayward Saviors Book 3 is Coming Soon!

To find out about upcoming books in this series and information about other series—including a free short story available only to my fans—go to:

kimconrey.com/newsletter

Author's Note

Please know that word of mouth and reviews are extremely important to an author and critical for a book to succeed. Please leave a rating or review whenever and wherever you can. We appreciate this more than you can imagine. Amazon, Goodreads, Barnes & Noble, and Bookbub are all fantastic places to leave a review.

I truly appreciate you!

About the Author

Kim Conrey is the recipient of the Georgia Author of the Year Award for Romance and the author of the Ares Ascending sci-fi romance series and the Wayward Saviors urban fantasy series. She also writes about living with clinical OCD. In addition, she serves as VP of Operations for the Atlanta Writers Club. You can also find her on the Wild Women Who Write Podcast. Her essays have been published in *The Bitter Southerner, Killer Nashville,* and others. She also writes a quarterly column in *Page Turner* (a publication of the Georgia Writers Museum). She marches in Atlanta's Dragon Con parade as a Box Hero Wonder Woman.

kimconrey.com